SILKEN SEDUCTION

Kate waited for him by the window, wearing one of the new silk shifts from her trousseau.

The slide of the silk against her skin made her feel beautiful. Made her wish Sean would hurry the business he had with the duke. Waiting heightened the tension that had been drawing tighter within her all day long.

She was nervous, but not sure why. She knew well enough what was to happen. She had listened to her married sisters whispering—not to mention the more interesting gossip that occurred downstairs in the kitchen among the servants.

She and Sean would do no more than any other married man and woman did when they began their marriage. Still, that it would happen tonight seemed almost unbelievable.

She moved restlessly, and caught the delicate scent of the rose petals that had been packed in with the new clothing for her trousseau. She couldn't doubt the truth of what was to be, though. Not dressed for seduction as she was . . .

BOOK YOUR PLACE ON OUR WEBSITE AND MAKE THE READING CONNECTION!

We've created a customized website just for our very special readers, where you can get the inside scoop on everything that's going on with Zebra, Pinnacle and Kensington books.

When you come online, you'll have the exciting opportunity to:

- View covers of upcoming books

- Read sample chapters

- Learn about our future publishing schedule (listed by publication month *and author*)

- Find out when your favorite authors will be visiting a city near you

- Search for and order backlist books from our online catalog

- Check out author bios and background information

- Send e-mail to your favorite authors

- Meet the Kensington staff online

- Join us in weekly chats with authors, readers and other guests

- Get writing guidelines

- AND MUCH MORE!

**Visit our website at
http://www.kensingtonbooks.com**

THE
TWELFTH
NIGHT BRIDE

Kelly
McClymer

ZEBRA BOOKS
KENSINGTON PUBLISHING CORP.
http://www.kensingtonbooks.com

ZEBRA BOOKS are published by

Kensington Publishing Corp.
850 Third Avenue
New York, NY 10022

All Kensington titles, imprints and distributed lines are available at special quantity discounts for bulk purchases for sales promotion, premiums, fund-raising, educational or institutional use.

Special book excerpts or customized printings can also be created to fit specific needs. For details, write or phone the office of the Kensington Special Sales Manager: Kensington Publishing Corp., 850 Third Avenue, New York, NY 10022. Attn. Special Sales Department. Phone: 1-800-221-2647.

Zebra and the Z logo Reg. U.S. Pat. & TM Off.

First Printing: October 2003
10 9 8 7 6 5 4 3 2 1

Printed in the United States of America

To Mom (the McCarthy) and Dad (the Duffy)—
thank you for being great examples as parents,
as well as human beings.

HISTORICAL NOTE

Just to keep the facts straight: Currently, there is a MacCarthy Mor, whose line traces down from the ancient Irish royalty, including the slippery-tongued fellow who kept Queen Elizabeth I exasperated by his lies and political maneuverings. He and his present-day relatives have nothing to do with this story.

Sean and his family—including the English title—come entirely from my imagining what might have happened had there ever been a McCarthy lucky enough (or unlucky, as the case may be) to win a true English title from an English monarch.

Chapter 1

December 1849

Climbing in windows was a good way for a man to get killed, Sean McCarthy thought as he scraped his shins on the stone of the windowsill and thumped to the hard floor. Fine luck for him, there was a tree with wide, inviting branches to make his invasion a bit simpler. And lucky, as well, that the woman in the darkly shadowed bed a few feet away slept with her window cracked open, even in winter.

For a moment he lay perfectly still, afraid the luck that had carried him this far might fail him, leaving him to face a screaming woman and her angry family. But when the blood ceased roaring in his ears, the sound of her breathing came to him—even and still. She hadn't heard him ease up the sash or thump onto her floor. Providence be blessed, she slept on. Dreaming of sugar plums and mistletoe, no doubt.

He stood slowly and carefully, unsure what an unwary shin or elbow might meet up with in the dark. Perhaps he should have done as Uncle Connor had suggested and put laudanum in the wassail he'd supplied her during the evening. She'd been smiling at him, telling her foolish tale of love and devotion proved, treating him like a hero, a man of consequence and honor. All the while, he'd been considering the best way to compromise her and be done with this plaguing courtship dance.

In the candle glow and the festivities of Christmas Eve, he'd been so sure of her love, of his skill, he hadn't felt the need to give her any more reason for a morning headache than necessary. But now, in the quiet of the night, the question begged to be answered. Did the girl love him enough to forgive him in the light of day?

He'd wager she did. Come to think of it, he was even now wagering everything that she would think him more bold than importunate. What would he do if the amused admiration that so frequently danced in her blue eyes turned to scorn? Regret twinged through him momentarily, but he shrugged it off with a silent rendition of a proverb: *Má tá moladh uait, faigh bás; má tá cáineadh uait, pós.* He surely didn't want praise enough to die for it, but he would risk her complaints willingly enough as the price of forcing the marriage. He'd be a fool to turn back this close to his goal, now wouldn't he?

If he were luckier than most McCarthy men, as his cousin Niall insisted he was, his sweet Katie wouldn't wake until morning. If luck abandoned him, she'd wake and be glad to see him—or not. Her heart was his to break or hold safe; he knew that well enough. But his actions were drastic, and a broken-hearted Kate awake and aware all too soon was not what he wished. No. A nice, uncomplicated discovery by the maid was what he was after.

He stood and shed his clothing, folding each

garment carefully and neatly on the silk-covered stool by her dressing table. He'd been in a few ladies' dressing rooms, but always before with their permission and by invitation. He felt oddly vulnerable removing his clothing, despite the darkness. An Irishman in an Englishwoman's bedroom, he'd always thought, should be in full armor, with a blade the size of Cuchulain's at his back. Unless that woman was his wife—or soon to be.

He debated leaving on his drawers, but opted for verisimilitude. A lover too impatient to wait for the wedding night would not be likely to be so careful. The scene would be better set with his clothes tossed recklessly around the room to shock the maid further, but they were his Sunday finest and already showing more signs of wear than they should for belonging to the Earl of Blarney. Sweet mother, how he hated that title.

He stood for a moment, freezing in the cold December night. She'd understood why he disliked the king's poor joke on his family. Blarney. Why not call him the Earl of Liars? Didn't enough of the English lords amuse themselves so? And now, fittingly, he was gifting his Katie with the name. It was Christmas Eve . . . no, it was past midnight and Christmas morning had come, though none of the inhabitants of the house were awake to greet it yet. They had all retired early, preparing to rise earlier than usual on Christmas Day so that the eager children would not have to wait to see what gifts Saint Nicholas had left for them.

Even the servants had been sent to their beds early, and Kate's coals had long gone cold. He stood for a moment, ignoring the chill air as he considered changing his mind, dressing, and slipping away—through the door, this time, though. He wouldn't risk his neck again this night.

Come on now, McCarthy, he chided himself. The girl is willing enough. He was annoyed at his own indecision. Why now? He hadn't been unsure until this moment, seeing her so still and vulnerable in her sleep. He sighed, quelling his sudden doubts. He was cold and he was only doing what was absolutely necessary. Under the covers with Kate would be a warm haven for him—unless his chilled skin caused her to wake.

Now or never, he told himself and slipped into the bed warmed by the woman he had been wooing for far too long. She roused and mumbled sleepily, her words inaudible. The heated scent of her reached him and he inhaled deeply, then froze, hoping in the dark and quiet she would fall back to sleep.

She lifted her head and he felt certain she was looking at him, though he lay perfectly still, not even daring to breathe. "Sean?"

Damn. He whispered as softly as his old nurse had done when he was a restless babe in need of sleep. "Of course, *mo mhuirnin*, didn't I tell you I'd see you safe in your dreams?"

"Mauverneen. I like when you call me that," she answered sleepily, settling her head back onto her pillow. He flinched when she reached a warm hand out to brush against his ribs. "You're cold," she complained.

"And would you be expecting a dream man to have the hot blood of true men now?" he asked with all reasonableness, ready to kiss her protestations silent if she realized she was not dreaming.

"It's my dream. I should be able to warm you if I choose . . . mauverneen," she murmured as she snuggled up against him.

Warm him up, she would indeed. Astonished by

how quickly she was succeeding at that dangerous task, Sean said only, "Fair enough. Your dream man will warm for you, my lady, so that you suffer no chill."

"Thank you." Kate sighed and settled back to sleep against his chest, clasping him as tightly and innocently as any virgin might clasp her pillow while dreaming of her lover. He began another sigh but halted it. Wasn't it the woman who should be sighing, to find her lover in her bed?

Contrary as always, his Katie slept as if she curled against him so every night. Though it promised an uncomfortable night, the sweet innocence of her body resting against his was better than a screaming virago—or a woman ready and willing for lovemaking. Either of which his Kate could easily become, he was certain, depending on how angry she would be that he had invaded her very bed and forced her hand to join his in marriage at last.

He settled back, content to hold her and consider what might happen come the morning. He'd been alive long enough to know that, no matter what he planned, circumstances might not go his way. He had been prepared for Kate to wake, and she almost had. But luck was with him. He hoped he could say the same in the dawn light, when discovery came to them both.

The duke—or Kate's brother, Valentine, more likely—might challenge him to a duel, of course. The risk was slight enough, however, given the history of the family. Kate had confided a few of the scandalous details of her sisters' courtships. This one, by comparison, would be almost traditional. Sean expected that they would simply arrange a quiet, hasty wedding. And they could hardly object on the grounds that he had not tried the most traditional methods of wooing first. After all, Kate had been on the verge of accepting his proposal for more than a month.

Her thick, unruly hair had managed to escape the confines of its braid and tickled his neck. He smoothed it back against her head with the lightest brush of his fingertips. Like a babe, asleep she seemed so guileless and sweet. But even at their first meeting when she was a child, she had not been afraid to go after what she wanted.

She had wanted, then, to ride Diablo. And he had let her, for a promise of marriage. It had only been a joke until he'd come to London looking for an heiress bride and she'd been there—in bad graces with the mamas because she'd had the sense to object forcefully to being mauled by an eager suitor.

He knew it wasn't only her dowry that had made him choose her. It was also her quick wit and her easy way with even the stiffest, sternest *cailleach*. Those qualities would be assets to him as he made his way through the political maze in London and took up his seat in the House of Lords. Yet her reluctance to believe him more than an importunate fortune hunter had been a challenge. She had set him to run in circles to prove himself to her. It was past time to call her hand. Hadn't he found the first wild rosebud of the summer for her—and scratched himself bloody tramping through a field of thorns to do so? And still she wished to play games with his future, to prove Lord Blarney's silver tongue spoke true.

Or perhaps she saw his blarney for what it was—a cover for a man who didn't wish to be in love, who just needed a well-dowered wife. She was a clever woman, his Kate. High spirited as well. He supposed, when all hell broke loose tomorrow morning, he'd be lucky if he didn't end up with the same bloodied nose that Fitzwilliam had gotten for stealing a kiss. That young dandy had been brash and unobservant enough to think he might take advantage of a Fenster miss, and had been properly dealt with, too, no matter what London gossips said.

But a bloodied nose would not be the worst of it. His reputation would suffer a blow. They would hold the fact that he was Irish against him, use it to explain his lack of patience, of discretion.

Lies, all. Hadn't he been patient? Even more patient than an English born and bred lord might have been, he wagered. He'd not complained when she met each and every proposal—from the time he rode up dressed in shining armor, to the quiet, heartfelt proposal in her greenhouse—with a gentle, "It's too soon. I have to be certain." He wished he knew how to ensure discretion, so that only the family would know. The duke had a reputation for being upright and honorable, but even that reputation could not stop those who lived for gossip from spreading it like wild seed among the bored aristocrats.

He hoped that this way, with only a household maid to discover them in the quiet of the countryside, the news would not spread to London more quickly than the ink on the marriage papers dried. Once they were married and he was seated in the House of Lords, any whiff of scandal would become old news. But he wondered if the gossip could be held back even for a week. The English *cailleach* had sharp tongues and their favorite words were bitter when they spoke of the young woman who had replaced them as society's lights.

Once his indiscretion was discovered, the matter would be completely out of his hands. A proper

Irish maid would, of course, have tiptoed away without making a fuss to find a pair of lovers anticipating their vows, so to speak. An English maid was an altogether different kind of creature. She'd probably start and mewl in alarm. But even if she didn't, she'd no doubt alert the household at once.

Kate turned her cheek so that her lips brushed his shoulder. Torture. Fair enough, he deserved it. He'd feel a bit more guilty if he wasn't following in the tradition it was whispered several of her sisters themselves had set—old gossip, old news, but not completely forgotten even now. But he didn't have time for the sport any longer. People starved while he played aristocratic games to win a lady's heart and hand. His people.

He could no longer wait for her to accept that he'd proved himself. Kate thought herself as clever as the warrior queen Maeve herself, but even Maeve had been defeated in the end by Cuchulain. Both were doomed to find out that a man's love for a woman is overshadowed from the start by his pride.

He'd tried to tell her that, when he'd told her the story of Maeve. But she had heard only the beginning of the tale and had seemed to dismiss the dark end to the story. No doubt the woman shared her sisters' penchant for turning the dark endings of fairy tales into happy-ever-afters. Hadn't she told him that he, an Irishman with a truly unfortunate title, could change the world? She had certainly taken to the story of Maeve with delight.

Sometimes he wished he hadn't told the tale to her. That he had found another way to woo her—perhaps even climbed into her bedroom window months ago. But that wisdom came from hindsight.

He remembered the gleam in her eyes as she listened to his stories, fascinated by the Irish myths and fairy stories, demanding to know more. He'd coveted her dowry. But her desire to know more about his people and their customs had beguiled him, he couldn't deny it. Almost as much as his need for the patronage and money that came with marrying her.

As if his troubled thoughts disturbed her sleep, she moved restlessly against him. "Hsst, all is well," he whispered, brushing his fingers lightly through her hair. She settled against him with a sigh. So he had only himself to blame for the fact that she had heard the story of Maeve and how she vowed to choose as her husband only the man who proved himself worthy of her.

The idea of an Irishwoman considering herself an equal to her husband—choosing her husband based on the traits she desired in a man—was an absurd one. Only Kate could think she might do the same. Perhaps there was a touch of the fey in her, after all, as his uncle claimed.

All of London had watched their unusual courtship with sly amusement. Some of the women had professed their approval of a man who would sweep his cloak onto the ground to protect the dainty slippers of his lady love. The men, however, whispered that it must be damned uncomfortable to carry a soiled cloak around afterward. He'd even heard that bets had been taken as to how long it would be before his valet left his employ. He'd gotten the worst of it, and not only because he was Irish. He thought of what she'd asked of him. To prove he was a man worthy of her. A man not just after her dowry, but herself in all her glory. A man willing to prove himself to win a woman for his wife.

The absence of meanness, jealousy and fear. He sighed. He had proved himself to her even now, by

this action. After all, who could doubt the absence
of fear in a man who'd dare to share his lady's bed
right under the duke's nose?

He wasn't so absent of jealousy, though, that he
didn't wish he was able to do more than lie beside
her, holding her as impotently as the ghost he had
pretended to be. The fate was only his just desserts.
She had not invited him to her bed. He knew well
enough that a woman gave and took more enjoyment when she was able to anticipate the night.

He supposed he had half hoped she might
awaken and welcome him, and she had—as a dream,
not as a flesh-and-blood man to make love to her.
Which was no doubt why she clutched at him and
slept against him in peace. Since such was his fate,
he gave himself up to it, enjoying the scent of her,
the sound of her breath, the feel of her body against
his. He felt a surge of impatience. When might he
feel it so again? When would he, at last, have her to
wife?

After tonight, he imagined they'd keep her well
away from him until whatever wedding the duchess
arranged for them. Lord willing, she'd be quick
about it. He'd be happy enough to head for Gretna
Green, if only the roads were not so treacherous
this time of year. But her family would more likely
ask for a few weeks.

He'd concede no more than a month. Her family was a close one, and he didn't wish to offend
the duke more than absolutely necessary. It occurred
to him, suddenly, that he was taking on more than
a wife, he was taking on a new family—and an English one at that. For a moment he wished he had
had the sense to find an orphaned heiress for a
wife. But, he admitted, he had wanted Kate.

He turned his head so that his lips pressed warm
against her temple and moved his hands—slowly,

gently, as a dream lover might do, so as not to wake her—against the curve of her hip and breast. A man could not be faulted for enjoying the little he was able, now could he?

He closed his eyes and breathed in her scent once more. *"Nollaig Shona,"* he whispered. But no, he was in England now. "Happy Christmas, Katie."

Kate woke abruptly from her very pleasant dream of lying entwined with Sean in a field of wildflowers to the sound of a loud clang. She sat up, shaking with the rough transition, her blood surging through her veins as if her life had been threatened.

Sarah, the maid, stood staring at her, the pan of coals lying at her feet.

"No harm done, Sarah. Just clean them up, and no one will know but the two of us." Kate tried to reassure the girl, but her voice was rough from sleep and tears sprang to Sarah's eyes.

For a moment she thought the girl would manage a trembling apology for the noise, but all that came from the girl's parted lips was a mewling whimper.

"Have you injured yourself?" Sarah was a nervous, trembly little thing, but surely a dropped pan of coals could not be the reason for such a reaction. Kate sighed. She would have to help the girl clean up the mess so that she would not be chastised on Christmas Day.

"Wait, I'll help you," she said, feeling for her dressing gown. To her surprise, Sarah's eyes widened and the girl turned and fled without warning.

"What's gotten into the girl?" Kate muttered to herself as she grasped the elusive dressing gown and pulled it toward her.

"I have no doubt the girl will be fine, as soon as she gets over the shock of seeing me in your bed."

For a moment the dreams that had warmed her
night seeped into the reality of the morning light,
and Kate thought that she had conjured Sean's
voice with the power of her imagination.

But he dispelled that possibility when he spoke
again. "I don't think she was prepared to see what
Father Christmas left for you."

She turned her head and saw him then. He lay
back among her pillows as if he belonged there.
He looked so right that she had to remind herself
he did not belong there. "Father Christmas leaves
his gifts under the tree," she answered, as she
reached out to lay her hand on his chest and regis-
tered the beat of a strong heart under her palm.
He was, without doubt, no ghost.

She glanced at the door, thinking to halt disaster before it could begin. Sarah had fled, not stop-
ping even long enough to clean up the coals,
which lay scattered on the carpet. It was not the
spilled coals which had upset her.

She turned back to the man in her bed, regis-
tering his half pleased, half apologetic smile and
the gleam in his alert green eyes before she realized she wore only her nightgown. She sank back
beneath the covers and closed her eyes, even as
she said a small prayer that she was still dreaming.
But the feel of him—unexpectedly large and warm
and very real—sent a jolt of panic through her.
She sat up again, prepared to escape at any cost.
To call Sarah back, to stop this insanity.

The warm hands she thought she had imagined
gripped her more tightly, and he said softly in her
ear, "Poor thing was startled enough. You wouldn't
want to frighten her to death with a scream, now
would you?"

"You've no qualms about frightening me to
death," she answered, her heart racing. What was

he doing here? Even as her mind formed the question, she realized the absurdity. What reason did any man ever have for climbing into a woman's bed?

"You've a stouter heart that that, Katie. Haven't you proved time and time again that you've Maeve's own courage?"

For a moment, pleased despite her shock, she relaxed against his chest, back into the same position she had been in during her "dream." And then she tensed, a sensation of lightheadedness engulfing her despite the fact that she was prone. He wore nothing. Nothing. She twisted away from him, drawing the bedclothes up around her, which had the unfortunate consequence of revealing even more of him.

The naked man in her bed laughed as if he were doing nothing more or less unusual than he did every day. "Surely you wouldn't chide me for wanting to be the first to wish you a Happy Christmas? Anyway, a considerate husband should see his wife has a good fright every now and again to keep her sharp."

Husband. For a moment the word sounded so comfortable, so right, that she wondered if a marriage ceremony had simply slipped her mind. But no. Definitely not. "You're not my husband yet, or have you forgotten?"

"Surely you would not be so ungracious as to refuse my Christmas gift to you? Have you never heard the saying *Níl leigheas ar an ngrá ach pósadh*? There is no cure for love other than marriage. Katie, don't condemn yourself to a long, lingering illness by refusing me." He grinned unashamedly. "Even if you were to do so, nothing is likely to stop a wedding now."

It dawned on her that he had done this deliberately, intending to hurry her into accepting his proposal, and fury rose like a whirlwind inside her. "No?" She wouldn't stand for this. She would—

He cocked a brow at her and sat up, exposing a broad expanse of chest, covered by nothing but an indecent amount of finely curling dark hair. "Do you see the duke allowing me to run away?"

"The duke need not know—" She stopped herself. Of course Sarah would tell him. If the maid did not, if discretion—or timidity—held her tongue, she would at the very least tell Miranda, since the duchess was mistress of the household. Miranda, as the eldest of the Fenster sisters, had taken her responsibilities seriously since their parents died when Kate was just a baby. She would not hesitate a moment when Sarah brought her news of this indiscretion.

Miranda would, at the very least, inform their brother, Valentine. Kate felt the fine net of the trap Sean had sprung on her tightening until her choices were limited. "If I refuse—"

He kissed her, to stop her words. A light kiss, not threatening, despite their odd situation. "Will you? After all I've done to prove myself to you?"

Damn the man, he had been patient with her little games. At least, she thought he had been. "No. I suppose you've proved yourself fearless enough— to the point of foolhardy recklessness, some might say." She would have preferred that he had been patient a little longer, though.

He didn't seem surprised at her words, although she realized, when he let out a breath, that he had been holding it in, waiting for her answer. "I am Irish, am I not? What else should I be if not foolhardy, reckless and willing to take a shorter, more unorthodox path to marriage?"

Despite herself, she laughed, feeling the anger

drain away into a belly-tightening swirl of awareness. So. They were to be married. And he was here, in her bed as she had dreamed so many restless nights. She ran her palms up over his arms to the smoothly muscled shoulders and rested for a moment against his neck, feeling the rapid beat of his pulse, enjoying his look of alarm at her sudden change of mood. "Why didn't you wake me?"

He didn't pull away. Nor did he kiss her again, as she half wished he would. "You were such an angel, sleeping peacefully."

"There was no use to make a waste of this night." She tightened her grip on his neck so that he could not pull away and leaned up to kiss him. "After all, everyone will assume we've taken matters into our own hands, so to speak."

To her chagrin, he pulled away and patted her cheek lightly, as if she were a child. "I would never have anyone think badly of you, if I could help it. Would you like me to tell them the truth?"

She realized he was being deliberately disingenuous, so she turned her head until she could kiss his fingertips. "They'd never believe you."

"Then the only answer is for us to be married as quickly as possible so I can call out anyone who dares say a word against you."

"You sound almost eager to risk a bullet to your heart, my lord."

"Not until after our wedding day, my love—I have your reputation to repair by giving you my name, after all."

"But to slip into my bed, sleep beside me all night, without a kiss . . ." She drew her forefinger lightly along his palm, over the wrist of the hand that rested at her waist. "I wouldn't have expected you to let such a potentially . . . fruitful moment go unexplored."

His fingers tightened for a moment on her hip and she thought he might draw her to him and kiss her. Instead he pushed her away and withdrew his hand. "We have all our married lives to bite into that apple."

She wanted to believe he was simply being a gentleman, but a quiet voice in the back of her mind whispered that he might have done all this to win her dowry more than her person. She took his hand in hers and pressed it against her heart. "We have now. Perhaps you might consider this your last test—the one that will win me?"

There was a satisfying catch in his breath. "I've no objection, I assure you. But I'll not shortchange you the first time I take you, so tell me now—are you certain that you want the duchess to see me in my full glory when she bursts through the door?"

Chapter 2

Kate suppressed an unladylike oath and leaped from the bed. "Where are your clothes, you awful man?" The chill of the unheated air struck her like a slap, little mitigated by the dressing gown she threw over her chemise. At least it quickly subdued the heat that had coiled inside her while she tried to seduce her soon-to-be husband. She wasn't certain whether she was more embarrassed or disappointed.

"Surely not awful, just impatient, Katie love. Haven't you kept me on a string long enough?" There was not an ounce of regret or shame in the man, she realized with a mixture of chagrin and amusement.

"Where are your clothes?" she asked again, seeing the neat pile even as she spoke.

He stretched lazily, lionlike, and took on an expression of mock hurt. "In a hurry to have me gone, now that you don't need me to please you?"

Please her. Her imagination took flight, and the heat began coiling inside her again. But, regretfully, there was no time. "As you say, my sister might prefer you to be dressed when she enters the room—

perhaps it would even be better if you were entirely absent." She lifted the neat pile of worn wool that held his familiar scent. He had taken the time to fold them carefully, but one frayed cuff had been ripped and a twig clung to it. "Did you climb in the window?"

His green eyes twinkled with pride. "You should have seen me."

She went to the window and looked down the sheer granite wall at the ground below. Looked across at the tree growing there—at least two feet from the window. "You could have been killed!"

He shrugged, but his lips curled up in a smile of pleased bravado. "How else could I prove to my doubting sweetheart that she ought to judge me fearless?"

She tossed his clothes at him, annoyed. Soon enough he could buy himself new with her dowry; she wouldn't give him the satisfaction of treating them carefully after he'd climbed through her window last night.

And hadn't even woken her.

She knew she should be furious with him. Most definitely she should refuse to marry him. Simon would not insist they marry if she truly objected.

But Miranda knew well enough that Kate fully intended to accept her importunate Irish suitor—after a little more torture, of course. Worse, she could hardly fault the green-eyed devil for circumventing her torments—she'd have done the same to him if the situation had been reversed.

She shook her head at him, trying not to smile. "A fine Christmas present you've given Simon and Miranda, Sean McCarthy. Miranda has been working herself frantic to see that the children had a happy Christmas. When she learns of this, I doubt she'll take pleasure in the smiles and giggles of the children—even if there are any."

"Do you think the mites will care a jot for what has happened here?" He crossed his arms as he dismissed her charge, daring her to argue. "Children have an infinite capacity for enjoyment, despite the foolish preoccupations of their elders."

"Much like you, my lord." She shook her head, marveling at his lack of remorse. "You should be ashamed of yourself."

"On Christmas morning? Would you give me coal in my stocking, then?" He stood, presenting himself to her as casually as if they had been married for fifty years, rather than not at all.

"Not coal—you'd only use it to warm your toes." She certainly didn't feel the same comfort, though she would be damned if she'd turn her eyes away. He'd be her husband soon enough—Simon and Valentine would both see to that as quickly as they could.

"That I would. You know me well enough. Tell me, are you displeased with me? Or with yourself for being bested?"

She turned her back on him, unwilling to dress in front of him, no matter his own casual attitude. "Don't be so smug, or I may refuse you yet."

He laughed softly. "Yourself, then. Well, if it's any help, you must tell yourself that you'd no chance of besting an Irish devil who has kissed the Blarney stone as a lad and a man—not to mention taken his title from it—seeing as you're only a poor English lass yourself."

She allowed herself to laugh with him. No man would have gone to such trouble just for a dowry. He wanted her as well, and it was high time she allowed herself to believe that. "We'll see what happens after I kiss the Stone myself."

There was a small silence before he said softly, "There are times I wonder what devil made me tell you the stories of the Stone—or of Maeve."

"Everyone knows the tale of the Blarney Stone, Sean." She turned to see him frowning at her and smiled at his discomfort. "And don't tell me I would be the first lady to kiss it."

His frown slipped into a grimace of surrender. "If I let you do such a dangerous thing, you must agree to hang over the precipice only if you have my hands to hold you safe."

His heartfelt concern reassured her somewhat. "You'll have hold of my feet, Sean McCarthy. And you won't let me fall."

He laughed, but for a moment she thought she saw a dark shadow cloud the clear green of his eyes. In a moment, he was fully dressed. He opened the door a crack and peered out. The gesture was somewhat out of place, considering he had intended for them to be found.

Mockingly, she whispered, "Shouldn't you use the window, my brave hero?"

"Wouldn't want to break my neck before the wedding, now would I?" His grin brought out that dimple that had made her fall in love with him when she was seven years old. As if he knew she'd be annoyed at him for having the last word, he closed the door behind him and was gone before she could reply. Damn him.

She began to wash and dress, even before Hattie, her lady's maid, came into the room, eyes downcast and face pale. After a sweeping glance of terror about the room, she asked Kate which dress she would like to wear, still without looking at her mistress.

"The scarlet one, of course, to commemorate the day," Kate said sharply.

Hattie turned crimson. "The day?"

"Of course," Kate replied as innocently as she could manage. "It is Christmas Day, is it not?"

"Of course, my lady. Scarlet would be very festive." Thankfully, Hattie, who was a sensible girl, seemed to get over her nervousness with the reminder that it was Christmas Day. She dressed Kate's hair without incident and was helping her into her gown when there was a scratching at her door.

Sean's prediction about how soon the consequences of the maid's discovery would come down upon them was more than correct. Sarah entered, eyes downcast, most likely so that she'd not catch a glimpse of the Irish devil who'd compromised a lady of the house. She seemed to feel she had received a reprieve when she saw that only Kate and Hattie were in the room.

Kate's stomach knotted as she watched Sarah work up the courage to deliver her message. It wasn't a good sign that Miranda hadn't come herself.

Sarah's voice quavered when she informed Kate that her brother Valentine, her sister Miranda, and the duke wished to see her in the duchess's parlor as soon as she was able to dress herself. Which was quite quickly, since Hattie wasted not a moment making her presentable.

She felt as if she were going to her own hanging as she walked down the wide staircase and past the impassive footmen. Byron, the youngest and newest, had a flush on his cheeks, but he did not move his head, nor meet her eyes as he sometimes did. Her heart sank. She'd known him since he was a scrawny stable boy of six.

She wondered, for a brief moment, if anyone would listen to her protest that she hadn't even known Sean was there until the maid woke her up. Most likely not, just as she'd told Sean. It wasn't as if the family didn't have a tradition of unusual circumstances that required hasty weddings.

She squared her shoulders. She had survived the "talk" after she'd disgraced herself at a rout and everyone had agreed she'd never find a man willing to marry such a hellion. She'd survive this. Though it wouldn't be as easy. At least she'd been prepared to be a disgrace in society and remain the spinster sister forever.

And then Sean had come. No longer on Diablo, but having grown even more handsome than he'd been at seventeen—when she, a mere child, had blithely promised to marry him if he let her ride his magnificent stallion.

She supposed it was the way he had presumed upon that childish promise at first that had made her worry he wanted her only for her dowry. After all, most of her suitors fell away from her coterie because of the unfortunate incident during her first season.

Her "difficult nature" had not beaten away all her suitors, of course. There were always those willing to put up with a spirited woman in order to take possession of her dowry. But she had not been fooled by the easy flattery or seemingly easygoing natures of those men. Their desire to please her would evaporate into indifference or cruelty once the vows were exchanged and she was just another acquisition to be shelved.

Sean had stood out from the crowd, in her eyes, but his motives were just as suspect to her—especially when he made his claim to a prior understanding. She'd known him at once, despite the fact that the careless, almost arrogant, confidence of the boy had matured into a more sophisticated assurance.

At their first meeting she'd been amused and alarmed by the fact that he had instantly tried to hold her to the promise she'd made as a child. She'd assumed he was mocking her at first, using the silver tongue the Lord of Blarney was half derided, half envied for. She had only gradually realized that he was seriously wooing her.

She'd expected that her challenge for him to prove himself worthy of her would send him in pursuit of an easier, more docile heiress. But it hadn't. His compliments had seemed sincere even as they struck at her heart. It wasn't just that he easily met her challenges, but that he seemed interested as he stood beside her, patiently listening to her explanation of the latest grafting technique, or her dream of creating new and beautiful rose varieties. Still, she'd known that a man might be handsome and charming and still quite an unsuitable catch for a husband.

She'd wanted to believe he was sincere, despite his damnably easy charm. The attraction she felt toward him was even stronger than the attraction she'd felt for his horse when she was just a child. That was saying quite a bit, although she had been careful to confide such an unflattering observation only to her dearest friend, Betsey, who could be trusted to understand.

It was Betsey who had suggested that she only needed to set him some impossible task, as Hercules had been set, to prove his sincerity to her. The idea had taken root and bloomed when she heard the story of Maeve from Sean's uncle. She'd known what to do even before she'd heard the end of the tale. Besides, Maeve had been the cause of her own undoing, and Kate would not be so foolish. No, the Irish tale of a woman who wanted a husband who would be her equal had quickly decided Kate. She would ask Sean to prove himself suitable before she'd agree to the marriage.

Perhaps she shouldn't have baited him for quite so long. But it had been enjoyable—until now, she thought, as she entered the duchess's parlor and came face-to-face with the three who had served as her parents since she was a child and her mother and father had died in a carriage accident.

Their faces were stern and—a difference from her last disgrace—full of pity. She'd seen them impatient, frustrated, furious and saddened before, but not this. Not pitying. The gravity of what she had done sank in deeply for a moment, before she roused herself to remember that she was wholly innocent, except for the one understandable lapse once the damage appeared to be done.

It was the pity, not the flanking of stern gazes which made her smile and say, "I suppose you have heard that I upheld the family tradition and you want to make certain that I will do the right thing and marry the poor man."

Valentine stood, a flush on his face, and she felt a moment of sympathy for her brother. "I would ask if you must be so flippant, Kate, but I already know the answer. So I will content myself with asking if you have any objection to being married on Twelfth Night?"

Poor Valentine. He would so have preferred to have married her off in a more usual, respectable way. She shouldn't have baited him, any more than she had continued to do to Sean. Men had very little patience with such things; she knew that well enough.

She considered objecting, but a quelling look from her sister decided her against it. Miranda had been through enough. Christmas morning had been a favorite of hers forever, and Kate refused to let this foolishness ruin it. Despite events, this Christmas would be the same perfect holiday that it had been since she could remember.

Even when they had been nearly penniless, Miranda had found a way to make the holiday special for her younger sisters—especially Kate, who had been much too young to understand how dire their circumstances truly were. If she argued against the marriage, she'd be presenting her sister with a very unwelcome dilemma as a gift.

"Twelfth Night?" she repeated, in a delaying tactic. She couldn't quite bring herself to accept that her decisions had been taken from her and that she would be a married woman in less than a fortnight. Oddly, there was a small part of her that wished the wedding would occur today—under the tree. Silly woman, no wonder Sean had become impatient with her.

She heard the soft click of the door closing behind her, and the question was answered before she could bring herself to do so. "Twelfth Night is acceptable to me." After all, January 6, the feast of Twelfth Night—and official end—of the twelve days of Christmas was fitting for her wedding day. The end of Christmas cheer, when visiting family spent the last day of fevered celebration together before they would be parted, sometimes for an entire year. The end of her courtship dance, when she and Sean must break from their families and move into society as a couple.

She turned. Sean stood in the doorway, looking appropriately apologetic—as he had not in her room. Perhaps, she thought a bit snappishly, it was an expression he did not find natural unless he was fully dressed.

* * *

Sean could see that she was feeling the strain of the consequences that were heaping upon her unwilling head. While he felt sympathy, he did not wish to show any weakness in front of her family, whose unfriendly faces had not changed, despite his conciliatory agreement. He needed the duke's influence, or his seat in Parliament would be no more than a coach seat in a railroad car.

She narrowed her eyes at him in irritation. "Please don't presume to speak for me until *after* the wedding, my lord."

He smiled, as if she had tossed words of love at him, rather than scorn. "I was speaking only for myself and my willingness, *mo chroi*. I well know that you are able to speak for yourself."

The duchess's stern expression lightened for a moment as she fought a smile, and he relaxed a fraction. If she was not unforgiving, the duke would come around sooner or later. "Yes, Kate. We all await your answer. Will Twelfth Night suit you?"

When Kate remained stubbornly silent, the duchess added gently, "Everyone will still be here to help celebrate the happy occasion that way."

Sean detected a note of hope in her voice and felt a sudden spurt of sympathy for the duchess. He'd met most of Kate's sisters, with the exception of Rosaline, who'd run away to America a few months earlier. He'd thought his own sister a handful—what would his life have been like if he had had five such sisters to raise?

At least, he appeased his own guilt, she'd have some respite from the folly of headstrong young girls for a good long time since her niece was a baby and would not be able to carry on the tradition for at least another eighteen or so years. He thought of his little sister and felt a sharp pang of recognition. When would he be able to relinquish his worry for her?

Valentine, suffering from the same hope as the duchess, no doubt, grew impatient with Kate's hesitation. He sighed loudly and then asked sharply, "Well? Would you prefer a ride to Gretna Green instead?"

Like a trapped animal, Kate's gaze shifted from face to face before she snapped back a denial that was as sharp as a fox's bite. "Of course not, Valentine, although you might find Sean willing enough—if only the roads were passable."

"They are not." Sean smiled into her eyes, as though he did not realize how angry she was. "But even if they were, I would prefer to seal my vows here, among family." He allowed his gaze to slip from the duke to Kate's brother to express his sincerity as he added, "I would not want anyone to doubt my desire to cherish my bride."

Her scowl indicated that his words had not quite reached to her heart to charm away her bad mood. He was pleased to see a slight rise in color flushing up her neck, though. As if he had not spoken, she said, "As for myself, I am certain Twelfth Night will serve as well as any other day as a wedding day."

"That is a wise decision, even if you don't realize it at the moment." Miranda, the duchess, again. Her eyes held sharp sympathy and a hint of weariness.

The duke added, "Very true. I will announce the happy news at dinner. I trust you will conduct yourself as if you were overjoyed at the news, so that the children's pleasure in the day will not be diminished."

"Rest assured, I shall smile brighter than the sun itself," Kate said sharply.

She turned, not waiting for them to dismiss her. Her eyes were bright with tears, so she did not slow before she ran full into Sean. He put his arms around her for a moment, despite the frowns of her family. He wished he could ease things more for her, but that was not possible in the circumstances.

"Before you go, Kate, I think you owe your sister an apology." The duke, of course. Proper as always. Too proper to realize how hurtful his words were to Kate, who stiffened and pulled away from Sean's embrace.

She turned, her smile much too bright to be authentic, and walked a few steps toward where her family sat lined up like a small, inflexible, jury. "I should, I suppose." She gave a deep curtsy to the duke, and another, even deeper, to Sean. "I am ever so sorry the maid came into my room at such an unfortunate time."

Fortunately, Sean managed to suppress the shocked laughter that threatened to erupt at her defiant apology. She didn't stay to listen to the exasperated murmurs of chastisement that followed her frustrated broadside, but simply turned and strode away.

Sean wondered if she would walk into him once more, and prepared to catch her if she did. This time, though, she walked with careful dignity around the man she had just arranged to marry, without once looking him in the eye.

She was more than angry, she was frightened and hurt. Sean wondered how badly he had miscalculated. Would she be resigned to the marriage by Twelfth Night, or not?

He felt the need to defend her, since he was the one who had put her in this situation in the first place. "I assure you that all blame for this unfortunate circumstance rests upon my head. I would not see Kate lose the trust of her family when she is blameless."

Valentine drew in a sharp breath, half laugh, half cough. "That is an interesting concept. Kate. Blameless." He shuddered. "I hope you are simply taking her part out of loyalty and don't believe that, because she'll be your responsibility very soon now and such naivete could prove disastrous."

Well, he had expected harsh words for himself, but had not anticipated that her family would be angry at Kate—of course, if she hadn't baited them, circumstances might have been different. "Your sister may be a bit impulsive and prone to arranging things her way, my lord, but she will be an asset by my side."

The duke nodded. "I'm relieved to hear you know that."

"I do indeed. She will be a jewel in my scabbard when I take on your government, so to speak." He smiled to take the bite from his words—and to remind them that he had tried the conventional method of obtaining a bride first. "I would never have offered for her if I thought we would not do well by each other, I assure you."

Kate's brother and the duke exchanged a speaking glance before the duke nodded once again and said stiffly, "And I trust you will understand if we agree to sign the final settlement papers after the ceremony on Twelfth Night."

Sean felt the sting of the duke's unbending words, though he knew they were deserved. "Perfectly," he lied, careful to hide his chagrin. "That would have been my suggestion, as well."

"Excellent." The duke rose, taking his wife's hand to help her to her feet. "Then let us enjoy the rest of this day as it is meant to be enjoyed— with family."

Family. Sean thought of his sister, Bridget, and wished fiercely that he was home at the abbey.

There was where *his* family was. At the very least he wished he had not listened to his uncle and had brought her here. He had been swayed by his uncle's fears that seeing his somewhat undisciplined young sister Bridget might give Kate's family a reason to reject him.

Sean, taking Kerstone's words to heart, though perhaps not as he meant them, hurried to let his uncle know what had transpired.

"Excellent." Connor McCarthy was more than pleased. "I am not fond of this land and I will be glad to be gone from it soon. Too bad you could not convince the girl to run off to Scotland with you."

Too bad indeed, since he was now forced to endure a family Christmas without his sister—and without the customs their small family had come to treasure. "If I had done so, I suspect the duke might have delayed the signing of the papers even longer. Haven't you told me yourself that I need the funds from Kate's dowry with as little delay as I can manage?"

Connor frowned. His color, which had begun to lighten after his initial anger, began to grow red again. "What delay is that?"

"There was some distress over the circumstances, naturally," he said, bracing for his uncle's full-blown ire. "It was agreed—by all of us—that we wait until after the ceremony to sign the papers and transfer the dowry."

"Damned Sassenach." His uncle did not hide his feelings, despite the servants who moved about the house. "He'd never have suggested such a thing if you weren't Irish by birth. The money matters should be settled before the wedding, just as they'd do for one of their own."

"I don't believe the duke was concerned with

my heritage as much as my character." Sean had felt the sting of the words and wondered for a moment if the duke's action truly was a reflection of his birth, but somehow he didn't think so.

"What else would make him insult you so grievously?" Connor would not give up his grudge easily.

Sean tried to reason with him, though he doubted there was any hope of Connor understanding anyone's viewpoint but his own. "I think it is only the fact that Kate was on the verge of accepting me for months that has softened his heart enough that he will not delay our marriage even longer. After all, Uncle, it is not an easy thing to forgive—a man climbing into a young woman's bedroom."

His uncle contemplated what he had told him for a moment, frowning, and then nodded. "Even so, it is an insult. You could refuse—you're in the position of power."

"Power?" Sean failed to see how being as poor as a church mouse and caught in a woman's bedroom gave him power.

Connor grinned and rubbed his hands together. "If you don't marry her, she'll be ruined." He seemed to find the idea satisfying somehow, considering how his smile grew as he spoke. "Never find a husband."

His uncle's ruthless streak sometimes shocked Sean. But it was that very ruthlessness which had allowed Connor to convert a monarch's gratitude into a title for Sean's father—an Irishman, at that.

Though Sean's father had allowed his brother to maneuver him into an earldom, he had not wanted to further the rebellion, as Connor did, but to make a diplomatic effort to right things in his own country. Despite his elevation, Sean's father had not wanted to encourage his son to be as cold and calculating as Connor. He had told him so more than once before his death.

Almost as if he were there, Sean heard his father's words—"A man who takes violence and hatred into his heart has already lost the battle and, unless he changes, will lose the war." It was so often a question of judgment for Sean whether to take his uncle's advice.

He thought of his sister Bridget, still a child at twelve. Of what he might do to anyone who would hold her ruination over his head so cavalierly. His decision seemed clear, in that light. "Fair enough, Uncle. We both know I am going to marry her. And what need is there to quibble over a few hours more or less before the papers are signed?"

"At least this will all be over soon and I can be off home, away from these fools. Christmas in England is nothing like at home. They've no heart, only pomp."

"Please, for my sake, pretend to enjoy the day." Sean had promised not to ruin the holiday for the children of the house, even though he had most certainly ruined it for Kate. No doubt she'd have infinitely preferred that he sneak into her room for another reason entirely—and sneak out again before anyone was the wiser.

Would she be able to keep up the appearance that she was a willing participant to their upcoming nuptials once the duke had announced the happy news of their engagement? If not, he'd have to find a way to ease her mind. He needed her on his side, if he intended to accomplish his political goals. Ruefully, he acknowledged that his home life would be infinitely easier with a willing wife, as well.

Chapter 3

The dawning of Christmas Day had been Kate's favorite morning of the year for as long as she could remember. Even before the duke came into their lives, to marry Miranda and change their financial status for the better, she had loved the excitement of the day. The sight of the infant who appeared in the small crèche during the night, the plum pudding baked from a special family recipe over two hundred years old, all held special significance for her.

In those days, they had not had the tree, of course. That was a custom added just recently. Kate had heartily approved the first year when she had hurried down the stairs to see the gifts which might have been left in the night and saw the first, magnificently transformed spruce glittering with candles and crystal ornaments. Miranda had ordered the crystal to be handmade in the shape of characters from her favorite fairy tales and had spoken not a word to her sisters about the surprise.

This morning, however, the sight of the tree only made Kate want to cry. Marriage meant leaving one's family. Leaving the home she had come to love. She sighed, reminding herself that she and Sean would be in London. Though, on her dowry, they would not have a lavish life style, they would be more than comfortable if they were not so frivolous as to order hand-blown glass ornaments for their tree next Christmas.

"Aunt Kate, do you see Rapunzel? I cannot find her this year." Three-year-old Margause was a serious child, very much like her scholar parents, Hero and Arthur. There was a tremble to her lips as she asked her question.

"She's up here," Kate reassured her, pointing to Margause's favorite ornament.

"Good." Shyly, she added, "May I kiss her?" The ritual was one that had begun last year when Margause was two. Kate smiled as she lifted the ornament carefully from the tree and lowered it. Margause kept her hands carefully behind her back as she leaned in to kiss Rapunzel's crystal head.

"Thank you, Aunt Kate." Margause beamed now, her traditional Christmas task complete, freeing her to enjoy herself again with her cousins— Valentine's rowdy boys, Edward and Henry, and Juliet's mischievous son Will.

As she watched Valentine's wife, Emily, cradle her sleeping daughter Anne in her arms, it struck Kate, with a moment of wonder, that within a year or two, she might have a child of her own sharing the joy of Christmas with the family. If only she could shake her unease at the way things had gone. . . .

She could barely bring herself to look at Sean, who was much better at hiding his feelings than she, apparently. His smile seemed genuine as he heard the children exclaim at the sight of the lighted tree, at the opening of each gift. He spoke easily to her sisters and brother. The one thing he did not do, whether for her own comfort or his she could not say, was to approach her—or even glance her way.

Though she avoided the mistletoe hanging in the doorways, Kate was otherwise careful not to let the children see that she was not as joyful as usual on Christmas morning. She hugged each child after they had unwrapped the gifts she had given them—roses she had created and named after them.

Only Betsey sensed her unhappiness, but even her best friend thought the feeling stemmed from a more prosaic source than it truly did. "They'll appreciate such a present more when they're a bit older—old enough to gift a favored young woman with a few dozen, I'll wager."

"Do you think?" Kate smiled, trying to imagine the energetic young boys who had given her dutiful thanks and kissed her cheek just before dropping her roses onto the nearest convenient table growing into young men—suitors as importunate as Sean, no doubt.

"I have no doubt of it." Betsey helped Margause, who had kissed her rose gently and was now struggling to put it behind her ear.

Kate was grateful she had had the wisdom to strip the thorns from the stem. She wished she could strip the thorns from her upcoming marriage so easily. She wanted to cry at the thought that she might never see her greenhouses again, despite the fact that Simon had promised they would be hers no matter where she lived. She wasn't a fool. Roses needed a watchful eye and constant attention, even when they weren't yet in bloom. As the London wife of a political figure, she would have little time to travel to the greenhouses. At best, she could supervise someone else's work.

She comforted herself with the knowledge that

Ceddie, a young stable boy she had stolen from the stables to help her in the greenhouses, was ready to take over. She would tell Simon so, too. The boy was talented, and if anyone would be a good guardian of Kate's work, he would be.

She had always known this day would come, but somehow, this morning, it seemed so heartbreakingly close. She sighed. There would, of course, be compensations for her loss. Children. Sean. She shivered as heat rose through her to sweep away her chill and she glanced at him surreptitiously. He had been in her bed that very morning. Her fingertips still remembered the shock of his warm and muscled chest. The beat of his heart. Warm and strong and so very sure that marriage was right for them.

As she watched, a puppy with a red bow tied carelessly around its neck toddled over and sat on Sean's foot. He bent to pet the pup with careless grace. She wished she could be as certain as he was. Could let go of the last of her reserve and believe they were meant to be, as he had professed. But without her dowry, Sean would never have been able to consider marrying her, and the sum would never allow her to live in the lavish comfort that Simon allowed her so indulgently.

She glanced more openly toward her future husband, who was laughing now with Valentine's oldest son over the antics of the puppy. One question quivered through her, stopped her from embracing the future with him. Would he have wanted her without the dowry?

As if he knew what she thought, he glanced at her for the first time that morning and gave her a wink before turning his attention back to the puppy, which was intent upon chewing off the toe

of his boot. He seemed so happy. So comfortable.
So sure of himself. He sampled from the bowls of
nuts and oranges freely, and his appetite was not
impaired in the least when they all went in to
Christmas dinner. He heaped his plate as dishes of
turkey and roast vegetables were paraded by, despite the fact that Simon's announcement loomed
at the end of the meal.

Kate herself only picked at her food, pretending
to eat so that her sisters might not notice that she
was upset. Betsey, however, noticed immediately.
"Kate, are you ill?"

"No."

"I've never seen you turn down plum cake."

"I'm not hungry."

"Don't you want to know if you've been lucky
enough to get a gold piece?"

She glanced at Sean quickly, then back to her
plate. "I don't think my wish would come true,
even if I did." She pushed her plate toward her
friend. "Here, you may have it, if it is there."

Betsey turned to glance where Kate had. A merry
smile brought out her dimple. "Are you ready to
accept his offer, then?" Not for the first time, Kate
wished her friend did not know her quite so well.

"No," she answered, just as Simon stood to make
his traditional Christmas toasts. The first of which,
of course, would seal her fate forever.

"I have great news, very fitting for this day."
Simon glanced at Sean, then at Kate. "Kate has, at
last, accepted Lord Blarney's request to be his wife."

He allowed a moment for the natural congratulations that announcement elicited. Kate forced
herself to smile, and wished she could feel the joy
that her sisters seemed to feel for her.

Juliet could not resist teasing her, "I didn't believe

you would ever concede the battle to him, Kate. You seemed to be enjoying your wooing much too much to give in to marriage."

The duke added quickly, as if to take attention away from Kate's sudden pallor, "She has not only accepted him, Juliet, she has agreed to be married on Twelfth Night."

"Twelfth Night?" Juliet's look grew speculative.

There was a tiny hesitation in the smiles and congratulatory murmurs. Betsey's eyes widened, and her mouth opened on a question, but closed without asking it after a sharp look at Kate's expression.

Emily, Valentine's wife, did not seem surprised, but no doubt her calm demeanor was due only to the fact that Valentine had told her what had transpired earlier. He told his wife everything.

Fortunately, Emily was not one to judge, and her smile was wide and genuine, aimed directly at Kate, as if to reassure her that all would be well. Betsey squirmed in her seat in shock and Kate, afraid her friend might explode from curiosity, managed a gesture that conveyed she would tell all as soon as they were retired and in private.

There was some comfort in her family's support, though. They obviously liked and admired Sean and did not feel that the match was unlikely to be successful. Much of that had to do with their opinion of Sean, she knew, because her family uniformly worried that Kate herself would bring wrack and ruin upon all she touched.

Perhaps she should trust her heart at last, instead of listening to the warning her head gave her about men who needed to marry for money. Perhaps.

She retired as early as she possibly could and was not at all surprised to hear the secret knock that let her know Betsey had followed.

She opened her door wide, near to tears. She hadn't been prepared for things to move this quickly. Betsey would understand.

"What will I do without you?" Betsey's thin, strong arms embraced her, and Kate felt the tears that had been threatening all day push behind her eyes.

"I hardly know what I will do."

Betsey released her and stepped back, the blue eyes relentless as they searched her expression. "Are the rumors true, then?"

Kate blinked away the urge to cry and turned her head away as she smiled. "How should I know? Since I am the subject of the foolish things, I have heard not one whisper."

"Of course not. I didn't hear a thing until I went down into the kitchens." Betsey's voice was low, a habit they had acquired when they were the youngest girls and Kate's sisters had been fond of listening in and reporting to Miranda any transgressions that might be revealed by their unguarded conversation. "They're saying Sarah found him here, in your bed."

"True enough, I'm afraid."

"How did—" She cast about, as if searching for the polite way to ask the unthinkable.

"He climbed through the window." She thought again of the tree, the danger, and shook her head at his daring.

Betsey asked, hesitantly, "He climbed through your window—"

She nodded.

Betsey's ivory skin pinkened with sudden outrage. "If he hurt you, I will not let you be forced into a marriage—"

"No. He did not hurt me. He didn't even wake me. He only climbed in my window and into my bed." This morning seemed so far away, so unreal. Except that she could feel the heat of him against her skin if she closed her eyes.

"He didn't—disrobe?"

"And folded his clothes neatly right here." Kate smoothed her hand over the seat of her dressing table chair. "Before climbing into my bed. Without waking me." She looked at her friend. "Do you think Battingston, if given the chance, would climb into your bed without a stitch and then not wake you?"

Although her cheeks pinkened even further, Betsey ignored her reference to Battingston, the young lord who'd been making eyes at Betsy since the day the headstrong young girl, at twelve, had told him he was no better than her, even if she was only a governess's daughter. "He took off all his clothing, then folded his garments before getting into your bed? And he didn't wake you?" She pressed her lips together, and her blue eyes narrowed thoughtfully. "Perhaps you shouldn't marry him."

"Don't be silly. There's no good reason to refuse. I've only been tormenting him because I'm afraid."

"You? Afraid?" Betsey smiled in disbelief.

"Terrified, actually. I know it is the way of things. Nevertheless, I don't relish the idea of being a man's possession, with no legal rights of my own."

Betsey asked quietly, "Then why have you even contemplated marrying the man?"

Kate shrugged. "I have to marry. I can't live with Valentine and Emily, or Simon and Miranda, my whole life."

"I wondered if you might feel the same way I did, but I was afraid to ask," Betsey said softly.

"You have no need to feel like a burden. You know how the duke adores you, and you are helpful around here. There is no one better at spying out those rare herbs, unless it might be your mother.

You will always be welcome here. I don't think the same could be said for me."

Betsey's voice was warm with sympathy, even though her words stung. "If you behaved with a little more decorum—"

"Even so. I'd be like that unfortunate Lady Penelope who lives with Battingston and his family—one room and only let out to walk the gardens or share a meal with the family."

Betsey stiffened. "Lord Battingston cares for his sister a great deal."

Kate remembered the last time Battingston and his family had called. He had indeed been solicitous of his sister—much as he might have been for any burden in his care, relative or not. "True, just as Valentine cares for me. But still, men do not seem to know what to do with a woman who'd rather fence than float around a ballroom—although I do love the waltz."

"I think you are simply frightened of the change," Betsey said with sudden surety.

Kate wasn't fond of change, but she didn't believe that was the heart of her worry. "If it were only that simple."

Betsey, however, was certain. Her certainty rode over Kate like a horse bearing for home and a bucket of warm mash. "Nonsense. You have never been one to welcome such a sudden change—especially one not of your own choosing."

Kate felt a desperate need to change the subject before Betsey's certainty had her heading for a wedding across the border just to rid her of all doubt. "Are you telling me that you would elope with Battingston if he asked?"

She'd hit a vulnerable spot with her friend, and she regretted it as soon as she saw the color drain from Betsey's face. "Battingston has a duty to his family, and I am only a governess's daughter. Do stop speaking of him as if he is a beau of mine."

"He loves you, everyone can see that. If he only dared to face his mother's wrath, you would be married by now."

But Betsey only laughed, a trifle wearily. "You are truly incorrigible, you know."

Incorrigible. And hopefully marrying a man who would love and respect her—as well as not attempt to change her. "Let's hope Sean knows it, too, shall we?"

Betsey had no sympathy for the man, obviously, as she answered tartly, "He deserves only what he gets, coming into your bed like that, shameful man." A wicked glint sparked in her blue eyes. "Perhaps if he'd had the sense to wake you, you wouldn't be so full of doubts now."

Would she have? Kate wondered. "Do you think he loves me?"

"He acts as if he does, Kate, but does anyone truly know another's heart?" Betsey had a faraway look on her face, and Kate suspected she thought more of Battingston than she did of Sean. "If you are truly not certain, perhaps you should explain the unusual circumstances to Miranda. Surely she would not force the marriage then? Or have you already explained to her?"

Kate frowned. "I wasn't in an explaining mood when I saw them—they had already tried and convicted me anyway. Besides, everyone knows I've led him a dance with the intention of accepting him eventually."

With a sudden frown, Betsey added, "I suppose that's to Lord Blarney's credit then, that he found a way to force your game to end without actually taking advantage of your person."

Kate was surprised at the conservative viewpoint

from her partner in childhood crimes. "He wouldn't have done anything last night he won't do on our wedding night."

Betsey shook her head. "Still, it seems gentlemanly to me that he waited—just in case he was struck down by a carriage or some horrible disease before you could be married. You won't have to worry a moment that you might be left with an illegitimate child."

Kate was surprised how much the thought of a disaster preventing her rapidly approaching wedding distressed her—unlikely as it was. "I suppose you're right, but I find it difficult to imagine the blasted man ever succumbing to something so mundane as a carriage accident."

"Good." Her friend grinned, all dark thoughts banished for the moment. "Then perhaps you're not doing something you're going to regret."

"How could I?" Kate asked wryly. "If any man has surely proved his love and devotion, it must be Sean McCarthy. He could have broken his neck climbing in that window."

Betsey laughed. "Then keep that thought in your mind whenever you have doubts in the little time you have left before the wedding."

"What? That he's not likely to die before Twelfth Night?"

"No." Betsey's smile dimmed. "That he loves you enough to risk a broken neck to marry you."

Roses. Sean thought of roses whenever he looked at her. His bride. Mid-January was not the time for such delicate blooms—unless one had the Duke of Kerstone for a brother-in-law and he was willing to indulge your passion for roses with a well-staffed hothouse.

He chided himself for the churlish thought—no doubt he was just jealous that she had a green thumb when he did not. He'd studied crops that could rival the potato, but so far, all his attempts to make his lands productive had failed miserably. While she, with the backing of her wealthy brother-in-law, had created a rose-filled fairyland in both her greenhouse and her sister's gardens.

Not, of course, that Kate didn't deserve such largess—her roses had taken prizes as far away as London. But they hadn't fed anyone. And they never would, now that the brief marriage ceremony was over and the guards had departed the small chapel.

"You've done it, my lad." His uncle's words hit Sean at the same moment as the man's meaty fist pounded on his back.

"I have, at that," he admitted, with a touch of relish. He wished he didn't feel the twinge of guilt, but he had no regrets about the marriage itself.

His uncle said, a bit too loudly, "With that fat dowry and a duke in the family, we'll soon see the castle in our possession, rebuilt, and the crowning glory to proclaim our rightful place restored."

Sean shook his head, not wanting to disappoint the man who had raised him, along with his younger sister Bridget, when his mother and father both died. Kate's dowry would do little to bring about that impossible dream. "At least those at the abbey will eat well for the rest of the winter."

"The harvest will go well this year, I can feel it in my bones."

The harvest hadn't gone well in years, no matter his uncle's optimistic bones. If it hadn't been for the famine, which had cut down his people like the most fickle of English kings, he wouldn't be here now. "I've been studying the latest techniques in planting, and this time I feel certain I will get it right." So many were depending upon him.

"I don't know if you can trust the things you've studied here—a place where they'll cut an entire tree down for their foolish decorations. Only a Sassenach would be so lavishly wasteful when for the rest of the world a few sprigs of holly and ivy do fine."

"I trust what I've learned, and I'm eager to show the Horticultural Society's papers to Paddy and begin making some of the necessary changes." He looked at the large tree, brightly lit candles and colorful bows of ribbon. "Besides, Uncle, I believe the Christmas tree custom is German in origin."

Uncle shuddered. "No doubt they'll all be speaking German soon, the way that Prince Albert is tainting perfectly good Christian customs."

Sean forbore to mention that Germans were as Christian as the English—perhaps even more than the wild Irish themselves. His uncle would never agree.

"Have you signed the papers yet?" Connor asked.

Sean tried to mute his own bitter annoyance at the further delay. "Not yet."

Connor, ever ready to find fault, scowled. "Don't trust your word, do they?"

Sean wished he could feel a righteous anger. But he could only think of Bridget and whether he would have handled the same situation any differently if his sister had been in Kate's place. He didn't think so. "I'll sign the papers before the night is through—we both know it, so there's no need to worry ourselves."

"In their good time." Connor was not to be appeased so easily, not even with the truth.

"Do you blame them?" Sean shook his head. "If any man were to climb in Bridget's window, I'd be more inclined to hand him his head than I would her dowry." Not, of course, that she had had one, before now.

Connor grimaced at the unwelcome change of subject. As usual, he had harsh words of criticism to offer. "Then you'd best lock the girl up."

It was an old argument, and Sean answered wearily, "She's only twelve."

"Twelve," Connor agreed, with a sigh that indicated his heart was not in the argument any more than Sean's was. "But unnatural pretty."

"True." There was a delicate beauty to Bridget, and her big green eyes had a way of commanding attention without demanding it. He had been very young when his mother died, but he remembered her best when he looked at his sister, who was so very like her.

"And wild at that." Connor seemed to be warming up to the argument, his voice sharpening.

But sorrow and regret softened Sean's answer. "She hasn't had a mother's gentling hand."

"A girl as fey as that one needs more than a mother to gentle her. She needs a father to lock her up in a tower so she can't wander where she will, talking to the animals and the enemies."

Enemies. Wasn't that what he was here to change? "She hopes to bring a truce with the boy. They are only friends." Jamie Jeffreys was not yet old enough to be the enemy his father, the English landowner, was.

Connor snorted in disgust. "He's thirteen, now, lad. You've got to separate them."

True enough, he supposed. "Once the papers are signed and the funds mine, I'll send for her. I don't suppose that Kate will mind. She has enough sisters of her own."

"Best you come back home."

"I have work to do here." Sean looked around the room full of powerful men, all of whom he needed to impress. He smiled when he saw Kate, laughing with the wife of one of those men. "Besides, my wife deserves better than a leaky roof and broken chimneys."

"Leave her here. Once you've signed the papers. Give up the impossible idea of changing minds that are set in stone. Unless you did all that tomfoolery because you do love her."

Sean sighed. Perhaps he should do as his uncle suggested. After all, he had never changed Connor's diamond-hard beliefs in all his years of arguing. "You would have me leave before I begin? Abandon my wife?"

"She'll cry at first, to be sure—especially as you were foolish enough to let her think she was more than a dowry to you."

He sighed. No, he could not change Connor's mind. He would simply have to hope that those in Parliament were not quite so stubborn as his uncle. "She is more than a dowry to me, Uncle. She is my wife, and she will be the mother to my children—if we're not separated by a width of sea. Or did you not think of that?"

"I suppose you must have a son."

The old argument was familiar, but wearying. "And I know I can do more in Parliament, with the duke's backing, than I can at home."

His uncle shook his head. "When you see I'm right, what will you do with the lass then? Or your children? Leave them here for the English duke to raise?"

Children. Kate's family would embrace them eagerly. Would they be more English than Irish then? Sean wished again he had set his sights on an orphan heiress. "Do you doubt me? You've always said I have a golden tongue—surely you don't think I won't woo Parliament with it?"

"You do have a golden tongue, lad, but those lords don't have ears, just grasping, hungry mouths. They'll eat you up if you let them, you'll see."

"Didn't the king give my father an earldom for saving his life—and him an Irishman through and through, even if he was raised in France?"

"Gave him the title of Blarney, didn't he? Lifted him with one hand and slapped him with the other." But his uncle was not to be appeased; his voice grew louder, attracting attention from the closer guests. "And he wouldn't have done it if I hadn't kissed the Stone myself and managed to convince him the land I'd purchased, and that ramshackle abbey, would be entailed to the earldom. They didn't give us the castle, now did they, though it is ours by rights."

"Jeffreys might disagree, considering his family has held title there for two centuries."

"He wouldn't have refused to sell it to the king. But did the king ask? No. He knew I'd pay for it. The money wouldn't have to come from his pocket. But he wouldn't. And he named your father Earl of Blarney—without the castle and half a jibe at me."

It was true enough. Blarney was a name that carried with it a hint of trickery and cunning, and Sean had seen the resultant blink of uncertainty as to whether he was serious when he gave it. But that would change. He would change it. In London. With Kate by his side.

Sean scanned the crowd to catch a glimpse of his new wife. "I didn't say it would be easy, Uncle, just that I would do it. Have some faith in me."

Kate glanced up at him from across the room

and smiled. Her eyes caught his and held him, for a moment, mesmerized. He wanted to turn away, but remembered the part he played—at least for the rest of the evening—the love-struck bridegroom.

"Let's save this talk for later, not my wedding day, Uncle." He forced an answering smile and moved toward her, just in time to hear a young miss sigh and say, "What a romantic story!"

Kate laughed, but her cheeks were flushed and her eyes held secret amusement as she glanced up at him. "A fairy tale come true, Miranda would say."

He smiled at his bride of three hours. "Trust the duchess to share the Irish fancy for the *sidhe*—that was how I knew I'd found my bride." That and the ten thousand pounds the duke had put up for her dowry.

"The *Tuatha Da Danan* have nothing to fear from me. I know the value of the land—be it English or Irish." She smiled at him. She'd let go of her fear and anger at last. He wanted to crawl into a devil's hole and hide deep in the earth with the fairy folk.

"They would indeed adore your way with growing things, as I do." Three months ago she had been certain he was only after her dowry, but now she looked at him as if he could hand her the stars.

Her disappointment was inevitable, but he was determined to play the gallant for as long as he could—after all, he had forced her into the marriage sooner than she wished. He didn't need to open her eyes to the truth of married life right away.

As if she could read his mind, she said, "Respect, as well, I hope. I have ideas that your estate manager should hear."

"I don't doubt it," he answered. Estate manager? Did Paddy O'Dean count? Sean suppressed a smile and stretched his lips into a smile that hid his heavy heart. Would this intolerable day never end?

Chapter 4

Kate sensed the distance that had come between them in the scant hours since they said their vows. Sean had been careful to keep to the other side of the room, though he had glanced at her often enough that her own worried eyes had caught his more than once.

Now, standing next to her, smiling widely enough to show his dimple, she felt the tension thrumming through him. He didn't want to be here. She realized, with a start, that it was now her responsibility to ease the way for him with the people in this room, to whom Lord Blarney was simply a somewhat infamous name.

She tried to suppress her own doubts and confusion. She knew she had a tendency sometimes to make assumptions because she wished they were true, rather than because the facts suggested they were true. That was one reason she had insisted Sean prove himself to her before she agreed to marry him. Now it was time for her to prove herself.

She pointed discreetly to a duke sitting in a cor-

ner nursing a lemon water. "He would be a good
man to meet. Shall I introduce you?"

He smiled—approval, she thought. "If you think
he's sympathetic to an Irishman, surely."

"If he is not, you will soon change his mind."
There was a warmth in her belly, lit by the gleam in
his green eyes. "Am I a satisfactory wife, then?" she
teased.

"Surely you can't expect me to say with any certainty until after tonight?" he replied, brushing her
arm lightly with one finger as they hurried across
the room.

It was all she could do not to stop stock still in
the middle of the crowded room, paralyzed by the
thought that she was his now, in all ways. Just as he
was hers. She must have faltered, though, because
he swept her to the side of the room and glanced
down into her eyes worriedly.

"Did I frighten you?" His expression was shadowed. Doubt?

"No." She felt herself flush crimson as he stared
down at her. "I'm not frightened."

He grinned. "I take it you've decided to forgive
me."

She hadn't spoken more than three words to
him since Christmas day, so it seemed understandable that he might ask. "I have. Especially since I
intend to be awake tonight when you come to
bed," she added boldly.

"Then by all means let us do our duty here, so
that we can retire all the sooner." His eyes shifted
to the duke she had promised to introduce him to,
an eager look in his eye.

Part of her wished he had decided to sweep her
upstairs and forget the stuffy duke. She didn't like
to think she was more eager than he. She would
not doubt his love. She would not. She had made

him prove it, and she was no naive girl to be taken in by a handsome pair of green eyes and a roguish grin.

No. He had proven himself to be a serious suitor, not one simply after her dowry, but after a partner, an equal. So why did she have a chill down her spine when she looked at him now? If she had made a mistake, it would be the biggest in her life. For there was no going back now; they were well and truly married.

She left him with the duke, happily debating the custom of trees in the house at Christmas—a tradition the duke found abominable and apparently blamed on the queen's husband. Her sisters were clustered in one corner, and Kate hurried there, wondering when she would see them again, after she and Sean had set up house in London.

Juliet smiled. "I think the story of your courtship should be added to the myths and fairy tales of Ireland herself—it certainly is the most romantic tale in our family."

Kate raised an eyebrow at her sister's teasing. "More romantic than yours—Juliet and Romeo?"

"Our story is hardly worth mentioning. A balcony. A moon. Ho-hum. While yours . . . a silver-tongued earl accepting challenges to prove his love for his lady . . . what romantic would not sigh over it."

Kate vowed she would not let Juliet's teasing bother her, even as she replied sharply, "Why? Because he won me? Or because I let him?"

"Because, from that childhood agreement you made—and the ride on Diablo that could have broken your neck—he knew you were no tame miss to follow his lead." Juliet glanced at her husband, who was across the room, no doubt talking dull business he found fascinating, and her gaze softened. "It's not every man who'll take on a challenge like you."

"I was perfectly capable of riding Diablo—there was no danger I'd have broken my neck."

"Your words prove my point. You don't realize, even now, that a young girl should not have been allowed to ride such a spirited stallion. Think of Margause on the back of a stallion."

Her niece, at three, already showed signs of being a poor horsewoman, but Kate didn't think now was the time to make such a remark. "She is much younger than I was, but perhaps you have a point. Still, you cannot deny that I have grown wiser since then."

Juliet laughed musically. "Your reputation would suggest otherwise."

Kate might have been annoyed at the teasing on another day. But now the familiar banter warmed her, for who could say when she would see Juliet next? "I plead innocent—Lord Fitzwilliam deserved the bloodied nose I gave him for not adhering to the rules of a gentleman."

"We are supposed to keep ourselves above such interactions, Kate, not fight our own battles. But I suppose there is no worry for you now. You have your very own earl to protect you."

"I only require that he show me the respect and affection my own older sisters receive from their husbands." She enjoyed Juliet's faint frown at the 'older' adjective. "I have done a fine job of protecting myself all these years, and I certainly intend to continue, husband or no."

Kate was well skilled at swordplay and she was no mean shot—she had a set of pistols of her own. She had shown them to Sean once, and he had been shocked for only a moment or two before he complimented her on keeping them clean. One reason she had favored him.

Juliet, however, was bored, and wished to make things a little more exciting, as was her wont. "I suspect you'll have something to say about that, won't you, my lord?"

Kate saw that Sean had returned and now stood beside her. She wondered if he had overheard her assertion. "Indeed. Because my bride showed the perspicacity of Maeve herself by asking for the absence of meanness, jealousy and fear from her bridegroom, I hope I have proved that I would lay down my life for the lady. I expect she will be happy to tend to her roses, now that she's gotten the husband-acquiring business over with."

Lord Dinsworth, who had been eagerly listening in, no doubt so that he could accurately report the conversation at his club, chimed in. "Soon enough, if I'm any judge of these things, you'll be keeping her busy raising your heirs and those pistols of hers will gather dust."

"I'll never let them gather dust, my lord," Kate replied. "I have to keep them in good condition to pass them on to my daughter."

Dinsworth didn't seem to hear her reply, whether intentionally or because he had been going deaf for years. He turned to Sean and said heartily, "Kerstone says that you will take your seat in Parliament this year."

"Yes, I will."

"Good thing for you, not to have to go back to Ireland right now with all the nastiness."

Sean answered dryly. "Yes, it would be uncomfortable to see all those hungry, unhappy people."

Sensing that he had been a bit thick, Dinsworth added, "Though I'm sure it will turn out all right

in the end. Just a bit more hard work and less dev-
iltry should get the country right soon enough for
you to safely visit now and again. But London, lad,
that's where you belong if you want to help those
poor souls. No one will blame you for wanting a bit
of civilization. Leprechauns and all that, eh?"

Sean's unhappiness at last broke through his
false cheer and he said sharply, "I have accepted
that I must forego civilization in order to serve my
country, sir. I have my land, my home and my people to see to. After all, I can't leave them in the
hands of the *leigth bhrogan* forever, now can I?"

Dinsworth's smile disappeared, and he looked
as uncomfortable as a fish lifted from the water, his
lips flapping and his jowls shaking as he glanced to
see if the duke had overheard the exchange. "Of
course, of course. Meant no offense, my boy."

Sean's ready smile was back, but his eyes reflected
anger, not joy. "I have taken no offense, sir. I assure you, I could see no reason to do so."

Kate could see the bristling frustration that threatened to turn a pleasant conversation into an unpleasant one and she stepped in, taking Sean's arm
in hers. "My niece and nephews made me promise
that you would come up to wish them good night,
since they are too young to take part in the festivities."

He softened at once, although she felt an under-
current of nervous energy still running through
him as she led him up the stairs. "One day you will
make them understand that Ireland is not a country of poor papist oafs, but today is not that day."

"No. I suppose today I should concentrate on
making you happy." There was a wickedly joyful
light in his eyes that touched her heart and set it
aflame.

Before she could say a word, however, Sean's uncle approached. His face was gray, from shock or illness she could not tell.

"What has gone wrong?" Sean asked with a fatalistic certainty that set a chill upon the heat that had been creeping up her spine.

Connor stared at him for a moment as if he had not understood Sean's words. And then the older man blinked and frowned. "Let us not discuss grave matters here." Without another word, Connor turned abruptly and strode away—obviously intending that Sean follow.

Sean turned to Kate and squeezed her hand. "Let me see what has rattled my uncle and then we can go upstairs."

His smile was warm, if a bit distracted. Kate felt like a wife, truly, for the first time. "Of course. Should I come?"

He took her hand and kissed her fingers lightly. "No, this is family business. I'll return to you as soon as it is done."

Family business. Kate watched, hurt, as he ushered his uncle away. Did he not consider his own wife family? She'd heard enough from his uncle to know that there was little love for anything English at the abbey. Sean himself had never come out to say as much, except for a few oaths muttered under his breath whenever she set him to a new task to prove his love. What tasks must she perform before he considered her family?

Sean was aware of her quick, questioning glances, but still, he felt he could congratulate himself quietly. His bride was smiling more, and he had the sense she was adjusting well to the idea of being his wife at last. Hadn't she even managed to step in and smooth over his disagreement with that pompous fool Dinsworth, just as a good political wife should?

Things were looking up, he thought, as he followed his uncle to the library. Worried that Connor had been provoked into an unwise statement—he hoped not a duel, not on his wedding night—Sean faced his uncle. Just then he noticed the messenger—a boy no more than fourteen and Irish by his mop of wild red hair. Even the child looked sick with fear.

Connor, his expression as dark as a thundercloud, said, "There's trouble at home, lad. Bad trouble. Bridget went missing for two days."

"Missing?" He thought of fragile Bridget and fleetingly wished he had heeded the advice of others to lock her up in the abbey tower before her wild ways got her into trouble. He started to rush from the room. "We'll have to go find her."

"She's been found." Connor's bleak tone was not reassuring.

"Where?" He had the sick feeling that he was going to hear that Bridget had been found floating drowned in a nearby pond and resisted the childish urge to clap his hands over his ears.

Connor was so angry that foam flecked his lips and his eyes blazed. "Seems Jeffreys has had her taken up for attempted murder."

At first he only understood that his sister was alive. And then the meaning of what his uncle had said crashed through him. "Murder?" Sean exploded with cold fear and rage, fed by the patronizing comments of the English peers who had attended his wedding but still seemed to feel he was beneath them. Taken up for murder? Bridget? "Who would she try to murder? She's gentle as a kitten."

"The boy, of course." Connor's contempt was palpable. "I told you to separate them."

The boy. Jamie. They'd never get the old man to see reason if his son was pressing charges against Bridget. "It must be a mistake. I'll talk to him. I'll clear it up. Bridget would never do this."

He turned to the boy who had brought the message. "When will the ship be ready to sail?"

The boy's voice cracked as he stumbled over his tongue to say, "Captain said to hurry, winds are favorable now and no telling about tomorrow this time of year."

"I'll be ready before dawn," Sean said, pacing to the window to survey the darkness beyond.

"Be sure to sign the papers before you go," his uncle cautioned.

He'd forgotten for a moment that it was his wedding day. His wedding night. Suddenly, the dowry he had worked so hard to attain mattered very little to him. "Time enough when I return."

Connor grasped him firmly. "You're dealing with Jeffreys, lad. Sign the papers first—and say nothing to your bride or her family until you do, if you know what's good for you."

"Say nothing?" he asked blankly.

"They might not think kindly on having a murdering Irish girl in their family."

He shook off his uncle's grasp. "She is no murderer. She is twelve years old, for God's sake."

He might have ignored the old man's words if he'd spoken angrily. But Connor's voice was soft with true fear. "She's Irish—that's all they need. You know that well enough."

Sean rejected the idea hotly, then reconsidered. If it took funds to get Bridget released, he would not want to beg the duke. Connor was right. He would say nothing until the papers were signed. But they must be signed soon.

He returned to find they had already gone in to supper in his absence. He found his bride anxiously looking for him and forced himself to smile at her as he approached.

"Is anything amiss?" she asked.

"Just family business," he reassured her, suppressing his urge to confess his fear for his sister to her. "Nothing you need worry about today of all days." After the papers were signed he would tell her. He didn't suppose she would be pleased to learn her bridegroom was leaving her on her wedding night. But it couldn't be helped.

Kate would simply have to understand. She had a family—surely she would? Surely they would not, none of them, think Bridget didn't deserve rescuing because she was Irish. Because she was accused of attempted murder. He shook his head to rid himself of the unwelcome thought. It didn't matter what they thought. Bridget was his sister.

He sighed with relief when, at the end of supper, the duchess came for her, the duke for him. Kate glanced once at him with a smile. "I believe it is time to retire." There was a shy anticipation reflected in her eyes.

"Go and let yourself be made even more beautiful, then, while I settle matters with Kerstone."

She said, with a bold smile, "I promise you, no matter how long you delay, my lord, I will be awake this time."

The heat of the desire that flared between them took his breath away for a moment. "I will hold you to your word, then," he answered, knowing that it would not matter if she stayed awake all night long. He would not be coming to her bed tonight. The regret which sliced through him was sharp. But Bridget needed him.

The duke, as if sensing Sean's eagerness and mistaking it for the eagerness of a bridegroom for his bride, said apologetically, "There are a few papers to sign, now that the ceremony is accomplished. Unless you wish to wait until tomorrow."

Sean laughed as if he had nothing more serious than his wedding night on his mind. "Best do it now; tomorrow I may not be able."

The duke nodded, his mouth quirked in a small smile, taking the words as Sean had meant him to—an implication that he might be worn out from fulfilling his duties to his bride.

He felt guilty for misleading the duke. For a moment he considered appealing to the man to help him ensure his sister's release. But Kerstone was English to the core. He couldn't trust him on this matter. He had learned early the truth of the saying, "It is no secret if it is known by three people."

He read each document and signed with a flourish. When the documents were sealed with the duke's seal and safely in his possession, he bowed formally. He liked the duke as much as was possible in the situation. He had seen to his sister-in-law very generously. And he obviously adored his wife, despite the fact that they had been married well over a decade and she had not yet produced an heir.

He knew that they all hoped for a son for the duchess—although the duke had often said he would not mind a houseful of daughters, and England would not suffer for one less duke. On that sentiment, they both agreed.

With the formalities at last concluded, Sean bowed and said quickly, "I have word that I must travel tonight, so I shall take my leave."

Kerstone showed his puzzlement with a slight lift of his brow. "I believe Miranda was under the impression that you and Kate would stay with us, at least through the holiday, before taking up residence in your town house. I'm not sure Miranda has the staff in place yet."

"I'm afraid my plans have changed suddenly." Sean could not bring himself to be unkind to this man who had shown him such kinship. Nor could he trust him with the truth.

There was a slight shift in the duke's expression, a chilly reserve that had not been there before. "Changed?"

What explanation would satisfy him? "I'm needed urgently at home and I must go."

"Home?" The duke frowned, puzzled. "Ireland?"

"Yes." Sean thought of elaborate lies that might make his leaving seem less callous. But he did not give them.

To his surprise, the duke did not question him further. "I will have Miranda prepare Kate for travel."

"No need. I believe it would be better for her to stay here with you for now." He did not want to drag Kate into these matters. They were delicate, and though she might mean well, she could also make things worse.

The duke made no attempt to mask his shock at that unexpected statement. "On your wedding night—"

"Regrettably, yes." Impatient, Sean suddenly thought of a way to avoid the torture of having to explain matters to Kate. "I would appreciate it if you might have your wife inform my wife of my departure?"

The flash of Kerstone temper came out then, at last. The imperious English sense of superiority. "I most certainly will not. If you do not at least do her the courtesy of telling her yourself, I will see that those papers are burned in the grate."

Sean shrugged, as if the duke's words did not make him want to throttle the man. He told himself that it would be a true test of his political abilities to reassure Kate before he took his leave, to pretend that he did not burn with fury because his sister's life rested in the hands of his enemy. Another Englishman, one they'd most likely all be more sympathetic to.

But a man's true mettle showed when the battle was most terrible. All Kate could give him was a bloody nose or a blackened eye. Even she would not likely thrust a blade into his heart for hurrying home to take care of his sister. He needed her good will—and that of the duke—when he returned to take up his seat in Parliament.

She waited for him by the window, wearing one of the new silk shifts that Miranda had had made for her trousseau.

The slide of the silk against her skin made her feel beautiful. Made her wish Sean would hurry the business he had with the duke. Waiting heightened the tension that had been drawing tighter within her all day long.

She was nervous, but not sure why. She knew well enough what was to happen. She had listened to her married sisters whispering—not to mention the more interesting gossip that occurred downstairs in the kitchen among the servants.

She and Sean would do no more than any other married man and woman did when they began their marriage. Still, that it would happen tonight seemed almost unbelievable.

She moved restlessly, and caught the delicate scent of the rose petals that had been packed in with the new clothing for her trousseau. She couldn't doubt the truth of what was to be, though. Not dressed for seduction as she was.

Not in this bedroom, bigger than hers, decorated in a Spartan masculine style. She had spent her life in rooms decorated for females—single females for the most part. Young females at that. The heaviness of the furnishings made the evening seem the most serious of her entire life.

Yet again she found herself wishing Sean would finish his business and come up to join her. She felt alone here in this unfamiliar room, waiting for her husband—almost as if her family were somewhere far away. Which was absurd.

She was not alone. A pull of the rope by the bed would bring a servant immediately. Her sisters and their husbands were, if not still downstairs dancing, then in their rooms preparing for bed or in the nursery tucking in tired children for the third or fourth time this evening.

Miranda had been here not long ago, to help her dress, to congratulate her once more.

Her eldest sister had squeezed her hand and kissed her cheek. There had been tears in her eyes when she gazed at the youngest of her sisters, the one she had raised like a mother for so many years.

Kate supposed she'd have offered reassurance on the events to come this evening—if Miranda had known that Sean had done nothing more than kiss her the night he came to her bed. However, Kate had kept that slightly embarrassing fact to herself, and Miranda had not spoken to her about such things.

The sound of the door latch lifting sent her heart into a skittering response. She turned toward the window, suddenly afraid to see his face. The night was dark and shadowed outside, but the candle glow inside the room—from the dozen candles that had been lit to add yet another bit of romance for the newlyweds—caused his entry to reflect in the window glass.

He came in quietly, as if he thought she might be asleep despite her promise earlier in the evening. He glanced at the bed with a puzzled frown.

"I was afraid I'd break my promise if I waited there," she said softly. "Besides, after last time, I couldn't be sure you wouldn't climb in through the window again."

He smiled at her as he shut the door behind him. "I prefer doors, for the most part, if that sets your mind at ease for the future."

She waited for him to cross the room to her, but he stood with his back against the door as if he weren't certain what to do. She didn't like to think what it boded for the night if he was as uncertain as she.

She turned to face him. "I wonder if the maids will dare enter this room before noon tomorrow," she said, smoothing the silk of her gown. Was he waiting for her to give him the signal that he could approach? Perhaps she should have confessed to Miranda that she had no idea what a bride should do with her new husband once they were alone together.

There was a puzzling hesitation in him, though she saw the warming of his attention when she shifted so that the silk slid against her curves. She felt a moment of weightlessness as his eyes kindled at the sight of his bride dressed to please a husband, her hair brushed to a shining fall.

"So, am I worth all the trouble you had to go through to get me?" She wanted to hear an unequivocal yes. So the way his forehead wrinkled and his mouth tightened ruefully made her stomach twist unpleasantly.

His words confirmed her worst fears. "I've spoken to the duke. I'm afraid I've had some fearful news from home. I'm to leave tonight for Ireland."

Chapter 5

Kate braced herself against the windowsill as the confusing haze of anticipation drained away so quickly that her knees threatened to buckle. Leaving. Tonight. "It is our wedding night."

For a moment she dared hope she had misunderstood, but his brows were drawn together in a serious frown that told her she had not—nor was he teasing her.

"I am devastated to have to postpone it, Katie, but I've no choice in the matter." There was no hitch of indecision in his voice. Regret perhaps, but no doubt that he would indeed leave her to sleep alone tonight.

She struggled to understand, searching his expression for a sign that the dread creeping up her spine was uncalled for. She was a wife now, it was her job to understand, to make things easier for her husband. But she could not seem to get past the simple fact that he was willing to leave her on their wedding night. "Why?"

He moved beside her to gaze out the window

into the moonlit darkness. "There is trouble that needs attending to at home."

The tension she could feel thrumming through him was stronger by tenfold than it had been earlier this evening. His uncle's news must have been bad indeed. "What trouble?"

He turned to her and smiled, but his eyes were dark jade and serious. "Nothing you need worry about."

He was dismissing her again. Was this to be the pattern of her marriage in the future? Not without a fight, she thought. "Of course I must, if it takes my bridegroom away from me on my wedding night."

He brushed her cheek with his palm, and she leaned into the warm strength of his hand. "Do you not know without asking that I'll be back as soon as I can?"

"Surely you could stay the night?" She brushed her thumb against the inside of his wrist restlessly. "What business cannot wait until morning?"

The space between them seemed charged with a potent force, like magnetism. For a moment, she felt him sway toward her almost imperceptibly. "Surely I wish this devilish business could wait, Katie."

"What is so urgent, then?"

He gazed down at her almost sightlessly, as if it were not she he gazed at, but something, someone, much farther away. "My sister is . . . ill. . . ."

She felt the pull of his force diminish as her senses cleared abruptly. His sister? She had not even known he had a sister. And then, with a chill of dread, she found herself questioning whether or not he told her the truth. "You did not mention a sister before now."

"No?" His gaze came back to focus on hers, and he frowned as if thinking back through what he had and hadn't told her during their courtship. She wondered how much there might be untold, if he had not mentioned a matter so critical as a sister back in Ireland.

"Well, I have one—only one," he said, as if he had read her thoughts. "And she is ill and needs me."

She could feel the distance between them as if he were already in Ireland and wondered how to bridge it. How to bring him closer to her. To make the magnetic pull of a moment ago return. She put aside her dismay that he had not spoken of his sister before the marriage. It didn't matter; they were married and his sister was now hers. "What is her name?"

She shivered as the distance between them widened even as he spoke. "Bridget." He seemed a thousand miles away, rather than close enough to kiss.

If she hadn't known better, she would have believed he didn't want to tell her his sister's name. Was there some problem with the girl? Was she simple? She couldn't ask that, however, without sending him even further from her, if such was possible.

Uncertain, yet desperate, Kate put her hand on his arm, tighter than might have been wise, although she knew she had no hope to keep him against his will. "How old is she, your sister?"

Again, he hesitated before speaking and his answer was almost a whisper. "Twelve."

"So young." Kate could imagine just how frantic she would be if one of her sisters was ill and far away. "Do you trust her governess to see to her well enough until you arrive home?"

His mouth twisted into a grimace and his words were bitter. "I sacked her governess."

The girl was without a governess? No wonder he

was a slow simmer of restlessness and impatience beneath his apparent calm. She bit back the more obvious question—why? "When did you do that?"

He looked away, and she could see he was holding something back from her. "Some time ago."

She wondered if it had been a matter of finances and felt a twinge of guilt. While she was making him dance to her tune, had his sister been forced to go without a governess? Would he blame her for the illness? "Then of course you must fetch her at once."

He seemed neither pleased nor displeased by her words, almost as if he hadn't heard her, though he nodded his head in response.

Kate felt as if he were slipping away from her as she watched. The dread in her belly coalesced into a more solid form—she was afraid that if he left he might never come back. There was only one answer. "I'll pack quickly and come with you." She moved toward the bell rope to summon the maid.

Sean felt pulled in two directions, forcefully enough to split him down the middle. Come with him? Impossible "No." He intercepted her and pulled her into a rough embrace.

"I must. You are my husband now. You need me—"

He pressed a light kiss to her lips. "I need you here." Another kiss. He could feel her unyielding lips begin to soften. "I need to know you're safe here, among your family."

"I'd rather be with you than safe. Especially if your sister is in need of a good nurse." Kate was warm and rose scented in his arms; the silk of her gown slipped through his fingers easily. But no matter that her breathing came slightly faster and a blush sat high upon her cheeks, she was determined to have her way. "The poor thing doesn't even have a governess, Sean. You need a woman with you for the child's sake."

Holding her so closely, his mind grew muddled and unfocused, so it took him a moment to think up a rational objection to her accompanying him to Ireland. An explanation that would not expose his lie. "There has been another breakout of typhus at the abbey. It is not safe for you."

She was about to protest again, so he bent and kissed her more thoroughly than he had before. After all, he wanted to and he knew well enough from the expression that had been on her face when she first turned toward him that she had hoped he would. Her lips were soft and warm and welcoming. For a moment he was lost to the sensation that he had longed for all day. All the days since he had known her.

But such human frailties as lust must wait. With effort, he pulled away, afraid he would forget Bridget entirely in another few moments. He embellished his lie, determined to convince her quickly so that he could leave temptation behind. "What kind of husband would I be, to risk you falling ill just as I have finally managed to win you?"

His words brought a shadow to her eyes, but she stifled the protest that she had been about to make and said only, "You must bring her here as soon as she is strong enough to travel—I will see to her education and care now."

Her heart was gentle and for a moment he hoped that he would indeed bring his sister here, to be welcomed into this family. If Jeffreys hadn't bound her over for hanging by now.

She frowned at him. "I wish you had told me

about her in the first place. We would have invited her for the holidays and perhaps she wouldn't have fallen ill."

He rubbed her cheek gently with his finger. "You are generous, as always, but I thought it best for Bridget to remain in Ireland until I had settled upon a bride, married her and set up a household suitable for a child."

She turned her cheek against his palm and sighed. "She must have been so lonely."

"She was at home, Kate. Bachelor's quarters are no place for a twelve-year-old girl." He thought of Bridget, who loved to wander the hills, in a prison cell. London wouldn't be much better for her, he realized, but at least she would be alive.

"Can't you stay for the night?" She clung to him tightly for a moment, but then, as if ashamed of her selfish request, she released her hold. "What am I to do without you?"

For a moment he considered whether it would be better to consummate the marriage now, no matter how hastily. He owed her more, though, considering the way he had rushed her to the altar. "A wedding bed needs more than haste and worry, does it not?"

She nodded, but without conviction.

He sighed. "Our wedding night will be all the sweeter for the waiting, *mo chroi.*" The thought of Bridget clapped in a filthy jail cell had galvanized him, though, cutting through the sensual haze of being alone with his bride. He pushed her gently away from him and bent to kiss her forehead as he lightly ran his hands along the silk-clad curve of her waist and hips. There was no time for anything more, he acknowledged grudgingly. "Prepare for Bridget's arrival." He would not allow himself to believe that he would return without his sister.

She stepped away from him, as if to break the spell that had enveloped them both. Worry for his "ill" sister clouded her expression. "Very well. I will ask R.J.'s sister what can be done for those suffering typhus—she is studying to be a doctor. That way, when you return, you will not have to doubt that I am prepared."

"You are an angel." She looked like an angel, as well, he thought as he left her there, again by the window. The white silk fell about her with an almost unearthly glow from the scented candles blazing around the room.

As he closed the door, Sean put the image of her away from his thoughts with a sigh and sought out his uncle. Bridget could not afford for him to be distracted now. All his focus must be on winning her release.

He found Connor pacing in the library, with his bag packed and sitting beside him. "All is set," he told his uncle.

Resignation settled on Sean's shoulders like a mantle and he realized he had been hoping for a reprieve—only momentary—in which he could properly celebrate his wedding night. "Then let us waste no more time here."

Ever pragmatic, Connor asked, "Have you signed the papers?"

Thinking that the sudden wealth in his coffers would make for a cold bedfellow tonight, Sean nodded. "Indeed I have. The funds are in my control."

Connor grunted his satisfaction. "Jeffreys will have to take you seriously, now that you have the duke's backing. He does so love the titled English, even if he has no respect for a family that ruled in Ireland for centuries before—"

Sean made a harsh sound, half to acknowledge

the bite of the winter air as they left the duke's home and half to interrupt his uncle's diatribe. "If he is wise, Jeffreys will have released her before we arrive."

Connor stilled, and then glanced at him with sharp assessment. "And if he has not?"

Knowing the answer would please his uncle, considering how long it had been withheld—how long Sean had held out for peaceful counsel rather than blood and open warfare—he said firmly, "Then God help him."

Connor grinned, a blood-glint in his eye. "That's the way I like to hear you speak. It's hard words like those that will see Bridget free."

Sean wasn't so certain that any words—or bloodshed itself—would right things for his sister. What had she done? And what would he have to do to make things right? To bring his sister home safely?

The journey home passed in a blur of frigid wind and overly warm hearths. Sean didn't even stop at the abbey before confronting his sister's captor. Fortunately, his uncle argued only a few minutes before he agreed to ride on ahead and warn the abbey of their coming. Sean wanted to face Jeffreys alone. Connor had almost seemed to admire that sentiment.

"Congratulations on winning a wealthy bride, McCarthy." Jeffreys was surprisingly amenable to him when he interrupted the man's dinner. He did not call him Blarney, of course, as the name still rankled Jeffreys after almost four decades. "I'm sorry to pull you away from the festivities." He glanced behind Sean, as if expecting to see Kate. "Did your lovely bride not come with you?"

Sean had no intention of making a pretense of

civility with this man. "Have you hung her already?" he asked bluntly.

"Where is that vaunted silver tongue, McCarthy? Have you left it with your bride in England? Or did they strip it from you as a bride price?"

Sean did not answer with words, only a glare that promised bloodshed if he was not answered.

Jeffreys sighed and answered as if Sean should have known without asking. "Of course I haven't had her hanged." The sanctimonious man smoothed his mustache before he added nervously, "I was within my legal rights—"

Sean had no interest in the questionable legalities of Bridget's situation. "Where is she?"

"Not so fast." Jeffreys held up a hand, then indicated a chair with a wave of his hand. "Sit and discuss the matter with me."

Sit? While Bridget's life hung in the balance? Was the man mad? "I want to see her."

Jeffreys frowned. "You will, as soon as you and I come to terms."

Terms? What lunacy had possessed the man? "There are no terms; she is a twelve-year-old child."

Jeffreys shook his head. "She tried to push Jamie over a cliff."

"What did he try to do to her?" The question had been a stumble in the dark, but Sean's gut clenched when Jeffreys's gaze skittered toward the biscuits arranged on the platter by his right side.

The man blustered, "He did nothing but rescue our property from her possession."

Had Bridget stolen something? It didn't seem in her nature. But perhaps he had been away so long that he no longer knew her nature. "Your property?"

Jeffreys smoothed his fingers down the glossy tails of his mustache before answering. "It seems your sister has discovered an illuminated manuscript hidden within the castle walls."

A book? Sean cared nothing for a book. But, he realized, Jeffreys did. And like his ancestors before him, he didn't want a McCarthy laying claim to anything at Blarney Castle. So perhaps this was the concession Jeffreys wanted from him before he released Bridget. Sean tried to judge how important the book was to Jeffreys. "No doubt hidden during the time a McCarthy lived there."

The man straightened in his chair with an alacrity that suggested he would have much rather launched himself at Sean for a good scuffle to settle the matter. "The castle is ours, and has been for two centuries. The manuscript is ours."

"So you wish me to drop any claim to an old book in exchange for your not pressing these ridiculous charges against Bridget?" He was tempted to refuse. But he wanted to see Bridget first. He was uneasy that Jeffreys had refused his request to speak to his sister.

"You have no claim to anything upon the castle grounds—whereas several of my men saw your sister struggling with Jamie on the cliff and are eager to testify so." There was a shadow in the other man's eyes. Almost as if he did not relish the idea. Odd, considering how prickly he had been to Sean's family since the king had granted them the title.

Sean's father had said that the Jeffreyses were simply afraid the king might take it upon himself to give back the castle. When Connor had said he should, Sean's father had merely laughed. "What need have we of a ruined castle? Let us build new and be glad no Englishman will ever have his boot on our necks again."

The money had been thin, though. Connor had spent almost all they'd had for the land and the gifts he'd used to curry favor with the king and convince him to reward Sean's father with a title.

Despite the grand plans of his uncle, the abbey had yet to be made entirely comfortable, and some said it was not even truly habitable, though Sean thought of it as home.

Impatient that his sister would be made vulnerable for Jeffreys's greed for possessions, Sean stood. "Blast your greedy English heart—two hundred years on Irish soil hasn't made you an Irishman, or you'd know that book belongs to me and mine."

Before the man could protest, he added, "I will make no claim for the book if you release my sister to me without pressing your ridiculous charges of murder—for a twelve-year-old child. Is it agreed?"

Jeffreys pressed his lips together, unhappy to be rushed. "I must have your solemn word."

"Would you take it?" Sean asked with a snarl of displeasure.

Jeffreys hesitated only a moment before dipping his head in assent. "If you give me your word, I will hold you to it, rest assured."

"I give you my sworn word, on my mother's grave, if you need. Now release my sister."

But Jeffreys was not yet satisfied. "It is agreed, owing to my good will and my son's pleas on your sister's behalf, that I will give you one more chance to rein in the girl. She is wild. Jamie could have died—and I assure you, if he had, there would be no saving her."

Thank God, the man was not determined to see her dead. His heart eased, though his blood boiled as he said mildly, "Perhaps, given that the boy has turned thirteen and has grown bigger and stronger than Bridget, you might remind him not to wrestle a lady."

Jeffreys' color grew high. "My son was protect-

ing himself from a madwoman, not a lady, I assure
you. Perhaps if you were home more, rather than
pursuing your useless course to win the hearts of
those in London, you would know that."

The blow had struck too accurately, and Sean
reined in his temper just barely. "Where is she?"

Jeffreys rose and rang for a servant. "I shall have
her sent to your carriage."

So. He was to be dismissed, was he? "I have no
carriage, Jeffreys. I will wait no more than a minute
for her. If you are playing some game . . ."

"I play no game. I will see she has a mount."

"Do not bother, she can ride with me." Sean
turned his back and strode away before he gave in
to the temptation to murder the man. He had barely
reached his horse when he saw two cloaked figures
approaching, one of Jeffreys's carriages following
a slight distance behind them.

One figure pushed back her hood and he recognized the stolid features of one of Jeffreys's
maidservants. The other, he knew by the graceful
movement, was his sister.

Glancing at the carriage and the nervous driver,
his blood boiled more furiously as he realized that
Jeffreys had been prepared to have his maidservant flee with Bridget should Sean have tried to
free her with violence. But he forced his emotions
into tight rein. His father's favorite proverb ran
through his mind: *"Is fear rith maith na drochshea-
samh."* This was truly a bad stand, and his sister
needed him to get her to safety. He had no time
for anger as he examined her, searching for any
signs that she had been afraid for her life—or that
she had been harmed. He had not forgotten
Jeffreys's discomfort earlier.

Jeffreys's voice carried in the crisp winter night.

"As promised. Your sister, alive." At a gesture from Jeffreys, the maid pulled at Bridget's hood, revealing her face. Sean was shocked by her appearance. Bridget was neat and clean, virtually expressionless, and her hair hung smooth and plaited where normally there would be wild strands escaping and a wide smile or a tight frown on her face. She did not look at him, but followed the maidservant, who led her to his side and then scurried back behind Jeffreys, eyes downcast.

Sean had not missed the momentary fear in the maidservant's eyes as she glanced at him before turning away, and dread curled in his belly as he asked, "Are you well, Bridget?"

Her green eyes focused steadily on his. "I am." But there was no fire in her, none of the usual lilt to her words. Her voice was as unnaturally smooth and tame as her hair.

"Then let us return home." He contented himself with holding out his hand to her, knowing that she would not welcome the crushing urge to hug her tight to him that pressed at his chest. His sister did not like to be touched, confined, held captive. Damn Jeffreys.

To his surprise, she came into the half embrace of his upraised arm and buried her head in the wool of his coat. "I'm sorry, Sean."

"No need for that, *mo cridhe.*" He enfolded her fragile frame in a full embrace, but she stiffened and pulled away, lifting her hand to brush away an uncharacteristic tear from her pale cheek.

Sean saw the bruises on her wrists as she moved, purple finger marks that spoke of brutality on her pale flesh. Fury filled him as he turned back to Jeffreys. "What have you done to her?"

The other man's eyes narrowed and his words

were sharp, but he took a step back from Sean and Bridget. "My men were a bit rough perhaps, when they intervened to save Jamie."

Jeffreys didn't look him squarely in the eye, and Sean grew cold inside. What had they done to her? She was just a child, just a little girl . . . "A bit rough?"

Jeffreys said, with a chilling hint of apology that was worse than any attack he might have launched, "Under the circumstances, McCarthy, you're fortunate they didn't leave her for dead—they witnessed what certainly appeared to be her attempt to murder my son."

He understood, now, why Jeffreys had not allowed his son to be present at the meeting. "You said the boy made a plea on her behalf. Why would your men—"

"They saw the attack, McCarthy." Jeffreys's voice was firm, although his gaze refused to alight on Bridget, despite the fact that she stood at Sean's side. "Boys will lie gallantly at times. He was not to be believed and they knew it."

Sean looked down at his sister's pale face and gently took her hand, lifting it, exposing the bruises that went all the way up as far as he could see under her sleeve. "Where are they?" He would kill them. No one put hands on his sister.

And then he was struck by another suspicion. "Bridget, did Jamie do this to you?" The boy had been the same size as Bridget last time Sean had seen him, but that had been nearly a year ago.

"I told you what happened, McCarthy." Jeffreys said angrily.

Bridget said nothing, just shook her head almost imperceptibly.

"Jamie did not do this to you?" Again, she shook her head.

"I told you what happened." Jeffreys sounded impatient, but there was an undertone of guilt there, too. "I've already disciplined them."

Disciplined them? Sean could guess the indifference in such a punishment. "What did you do? Take away their biscuits?" English justice had always been lacking, always been biased against those who'd been here for more than a few centuries and didn't relish bowing to any English king or queen. "Or did you beat them as badly as they've beaten her?"

Jeffreys bristled in indignation. "I've done what needed to be done."

"Where are they?" Sean was amazed at how calm he sounded. Inside, his guts were churning with fury.

"They are far away. I'm not fool enough to leave them around here to suffer an 'accident'."

The maid's expression flickered and it seemed for a moment she would disagree with her employer, but then she lapsed into silent misery, staring in fascinated horror at Bridget, who stood unmoving and stiff beside Sean.

Sean knew that he was moments away from true murder himself, unlike his sister. "I want the names of those cowardly—"

Jeffreys tugged sharply at a pistol at his waist. "I am at the end of my patience with you. If you didn't let the girl run around like a wild animal, she would not have gotten herself into this mess."

Sean heard the sound of boots in the hallway. "Your son—"

Jeffreys interrupted coldly. "You have one minute to leave with your sister before I change my mind and see that your sister pays the full price for her folly—and she will, I promise you."

Sean's finely honed sense of self-preservation told him he should save this battle for another day.

But Bridget, hurt, was more than he could bear.
"She—"

Jeffreys interrupted brusquely. "Either this matter rests, here and now, or I will bring charges of
attempted murder against your sister, as I should
have done in the first place. If it weren't for her
tender age—"

"Her *tender* age didn't stop your men from beating her as if she were a man hard bitten by life."

Against his will, Jeffreys glanced at Bridget and
then quickly glanced away. "She's alive. And perhaps
she's learned a lesson. Take her back to England
with you. Let those who know how to bring nations
to their knees try to civilize the wild creature you've
let her become."

Sean put his arm around her shoulder, as if to
protect her from the harsh words, but she gasped
and flinched away. London was the last place he
would take her now. "Why should I force her to
live in a land entirely populated by those who don't
believe she's worthy of justice—isn't it bad enough
that there are too many of you over here?"

As he stared, feeling helpless with rage, he wondered what further damage was hidden by the
cloak. He wanted to kill someone. Anyone. Jeffreys
would make a good start.

The man he wanted so badly to kill stared at
him impassively. "Well, your time is nearly up. Should
I take her into custody again?"

"Remind your son, for me Jeffreys. *Fillean meal
ar an meallaire.*" Evil returns to the evil doer. He
felt little satisfaction at Jeffreys's slight flinch. Sean
lifted the slight burden of his sister into his arms
and sat her in the saddle. He did not look behind
him once as he swung himself behind her and rode
away. Damn the English. All of them.

Connor met him at the door, his eyes darkening

with the same fierce anger reflected in Sean's gaze as they stared down at Bridget, who lay limp and unresponsive in his arms. Two serving maids, who had served as rough governesses since the last had gone flouncing off, took her into their care, clucking and moaning softly into her neck as they led her docilely away.

"Shall we kill him, then?" Connor asked.

"Not unless we wish to see Bridget hang for the crime of attempted murder," Sean answered bleakly. "You can't take her back to England with you now."

"Just as well I'm not going back, then, isn't it?"

Connor couldn't muster a grin, his anger still strong in his blood. But he nodded, a glint of approval in his eye. "About time you knew where you belonged." A glimmer of worried practicality surfaced. "What will you tell—"

"Have no fear, Uncle. I'll not kill the golden goose. I'll only leave her on a string—a long string that stretches across the sea."

He rummaged through his desk for paper and took a deep breath to clear his head and relax the tight muscles in his hand—a hand that longed to hold a weapon more satisfying than a pistol or rapier. A broadsword would be more fitting for the iron grip of his fingers right now. Instead he settled for a pen. The words came surprisingly easily to him.

My Dearest Wife,

I fear I have been delayed. My sister's illness is worse than can be told with mere words. It is well you did not accompany me, or I would have to worry for your safety, too.

Know that I dream only of you, and that I will return to you as soon as my duty here is acquitted.

May you always have these blessings—A soft breeze when summer comes—A warm fireside in winter— And always the warm, soft smile of a friend.
Dream of me until I shall be with you again.

He signed with a flourish and blotted the lies dry before he had time to change his mind. Or even to regret the destiny he now embraced.

Chapter 6

December 1854

Kate slapped the man who had just kissed her. "You presume too much, Mr. McCarthy." She regretted her action as soon as she saw the white handprint standing out starkly on his cheek.

Niall McCarthy laughed and plucked a berry from the mistletoe above their heads. "Your husband has asked me to watch over his bride until he can return for her. Surely he would want you well kissed under the mistletoe, even if he is not here to do the job?"

Kate moved away from the greenery she had not seen in time to avoid. "Your humor leaves much to be desired, as does your kiss. I thought you would not come this year. Christmas is but three days away."

"So serious," he chided her. "This is not the season for frowns and sighs. Haven't I been a faithful watchdog, keeping you company while my cousin cannot?"

The unrepentant man pulled a letter, tied with a

ribbon and sealed with Sean's maroon wax, from his breast pocket. "Delivering his letters so that you know he is still alive? Delivering yours so that he might not return to a stranger after all this time?"

"I thought so, but now I doubt it." Kate held out her hand. "What is his excuse this time? He is afraid to sail the seas in winter? He has lost his soul to the devil?"

"I think you chide the wrong person. I am not my cousin. What have I done to cause you to doubt me, but deliver his husbandly missives?" He held tight to the letter as he put his hand to his heart and affected a distressed expression, but she was not fooled. Niall McCarthy was not a lighthearted man at the moment.

Kate sighed and wiggled the fingers of her out-stretched hand. "Perhaps I'd have more faith in you had you delivered my husband to me, instead of his letters."

"You cannot blame Niall for your husband's absence." Miranda stirred by the fire, where she sat cradling her sleeping son, Sinclair. The toddler looked almost angelic in his mother's arms, though awake he had the force of a mighty windstorm. Four-year-old Gillian sat at her mother's feet, drawing. The child had inherited her artistic ability—and her intensity—from her Aunt Helena.

"There, see? Even the duchess knows that I am innocent." Niall placed the letter in her hand with a bow and a flourish.

Kate closed her fingers. Thin. One sheet. He had not had much to say in reply to her last correspondence. Obviously he was not to celebrate Christmas with her in England, as she had requested. The only question that remained was whether his answer to her alternative was positive or negative.

Would he allow her to come to Ireland? Or would he refuse her again, with some ill-reasoned excuse?

"Are you going to open the letter or try to read it through the folds?" Miranda asked quietly, so that she did not wake her son. Gillian looked up abstractedly from her drawing paper, found nothing of interest in the faces of the adults around her, and went back to her work.

Kate loved the children, but seeing how they had grown only reinforced the years of her life that had slipped by, sometimes so easily that she did not notice until Christmas, when yet another year of her marriage had passed.

"I've written him, as you suggested, and I'm afraid to see what he's replied."

"What did you ask?" Niall had moved to stand by the fire, and his expression was more wary than Kate liked. Had Sean told his cousin her request? No, better to say her demand.

She held her breath as she broke the seal and unfolded the paper.

> *Ni dhéanfadh an saol capall ráis d'asal.*
> *It is for the best, Kate. All the world could not make a racing horse from a donkey. I should have known it long ago.*
> *Yours, one last time,*

He had signed it with his usual scrawling flourish. But what did it mean? Was she the donkey, or was he? Why could the dratted man never speak straightforwardly to her? He professed love and devotion in pretty phrases that, in the end, were no solace in her lonely bed, no matter how carefully she stored them, or how many times she read them to herself by candlelight.

She looked at Niall's carefully averted profile

and the words to ask fled her as her throat closed in fear.

Her struggle to breathe, to find the words to ask what she most feared to hear, ceased when Simon came into the room in as undignified a manner as she had ever seen. His glance first went to Miranda, who sighed a moment, as if he had conveyed all in that one quick glance. And then he looked at Kate.

At first she thought his banked fury was aimed at her. But then he turned his gaze upon Niall, and Kate was astonished the man did not turn to ash at once, such was the heat of the duke's glare. "What is the meaning of this?" He held up a thick sheaf of papers.

Niall replied defensively, "I only carry the letters, my lord, I do not read them."

"Did your cousin not tell you what you carried?"

"His business is none of mine," Niall said stiffly.

Simon snorted. "This certainly is. He intends to sue you for alienating his wife's affections."

"That's absurd." Niall rubbed his cheek absently. "The lady has never treated me more fondly than any cousin should be treated."

"Apparently your cousin does not agree." Simon moved forward into the room and then stopped, as if not certain he should go to his wife or his sister-in-law, or deal with the man who stood by the fire. "He has informed me he intends to divorce Kate. Because of you."

There was no sound for a moment, such was the shock at his announcement. As he stood uncertainly in the center of the room, Gillian dropped her pad and pen and ran to him. The child was unaware of the distress of the adults and only wished to greet her father. She held up her arms to him. "Papa, I missed you today."

With a troubled look, Simon pulled her into his

arms and kissed her cheek gently. "I missed you too, sweetness. Have you been a good girl for your mother?"

"I did not believe the Irish allowed divorce." It was all she could think to say. Simon looked at her sympathetically over his daughter's head. "Your marriage is English made, subject to our laws, not those of Ireland."

Divorce. The word echoed in her mind. Kate had been surrounded by happily married couples—even her sister Rosaline, who had sworn not to marry, was happily wed to a wagon train master, of all people. Only Kate had no husband to share her bed. How could he divorce her, when he had never been a true husband? "Whyever would he divorce me?"

Simon set his daughter onto her feet and whispered in her ear. He did not speak until the girl had skipped off to complete whatever errand he had sent her to accomplish. "Whyever does any man divorce his wife? Sean claims that his cousin has stolen your affections from him. He wishes to set you free so that you may be together."

"That is sheer nonsense. I've no more affection for Niall than I do for one of Gillian's kittens." Nonsense. Of course it was. Just as her silly belief that his letters promising to come for her soon were truthful. She spoke the truth even as she realized it herself. "He wants to be rid of me."

Miranda spoke soothingly. "Perhaps he has heard some foolish rumor—"

She interrupted her sister's attempts to calm the voices in the room. "There is no perhaps. Even if he has heard a rumor, he has no call to believe it without speaking to me. I've waited long enough. I know what I must do, and I intend to do it at once." Five years. Waiting for Sean to explain why he did not send for her. Why he sent occasional letters asking for her patience, claiming that one more item must be taken care of before he could rejoin her.

Niall McCarthy, Simon and Miranda all stared at her apprehensively. "What do you mean?" Miranda asked, the sharpness of her tone waking Sinclair.

Kate spoke decisively, though her heart beat at twice its normal rate. "I am going to the abbey."

The duke shook his head and straightened forbiddingly. "I don't think that's wise."

Kate had no intention of being dissuaded. "You've said that before, Simon, but this time I have no choice."

"I'll come with you, then. We can both explain it to him. No doubt he will see reason." Niall did not sound at all enthusiastic at the idea.

"Don't be absurd. If you were to accompany me, Sean would have all the evidence he needs for his divorce, Niall. No. This is something I must do for myself." She turned to Miranda, who cradled Sinclair against her as if Kate had sworn to take the baby with her. "I should have done it years ago. I would have." But she, fearless Kate, had been too afraid to see the truth. Had been more willing than the most gullible child to believe her sister's certainty that Sean would one day send for her.

"I won't allow it." Simon said.

She felt the choking fear leave her as she made her decision. "I'm going—and this time no one will stop me. Especially not any of you."

She ignored the spate of argument her announcement provoked, turned on her heel and left the room. Betsey would understand. Betsey would help.

Unfortunately, when she found her friend, kneading the life out of a round of dough in the kitchen, Betsey's first words were, "You'll regret it, Kate."

Kate asked softly of her best friend, "More than I regret not going years ago, when I realized my husband would not come back for me? Would not send for me? When I realized everything was lies and still let his letters draw a veil of fantasy over me because I so very much feared the truth?"

Betsey smacked the dough with a particularly hard slap and tossed it to rise in the pan without answering Kate's question.

"Betsey?"

Without glancing into Kate's eyes, Betsey wiped her hands on her apron before removing it. Her voice was sharp as she said, "You've been hiding from the truth for years. Why stop now?"

The bitterness stopped Kate's breath.

"The letters . . ." She held up the thin sheet that held Sean's odd message.

"Lies. Just like Battingston's promises to me."

Battingston? Belatedly, Kate realized that Betsey had been crying. Her eyes were red-rimmed and there were faint tear tracks down her cheeks. "What has he done?"

"He has married the Chesterville heiress—the news is everywhere."

"He didn't." The engagement had been of such long standing that Kate had begun to think Battingston would finally get the courage to break it.

"Of course he did. He explained to me—as he asked me to be his mistress."

His mistress? The cad. "You didn't."

Betsey put her hands on her hips and stared at Kate in challenge. "Why not?"

Had she? No. Not Betsey. "You couldn't."

"Why can't I? I am no one of consequence. If I had been one of your sisters rather than your governess's daughter, he would have ignored convention and his family's wishes and married me."

"You are not just a governess's daughter. Simon . . ."

Betsey dismissed her words with a sharp wave of her hand. "He would let me stay on suffrage forever, he is that good a man. But I don't want to be in a world where I am not good enough and never can be."

"You are my friend. Do you doubt it?"

"No." Betsey's pent-up fury burned to a quiet sorrow. "You have always been my friend, just as I have been yours. And your family has been good to my mother and me, but I cannot stay here a moment longer."

Kate sensed that Betsey was not in the mood to be convinced that her broken heart would heal. "Then you must let Simon help find you a place."

"A place." Betsey laughed unhappily. "I do not wish to be a governess. I wish to have something of my own. A house. A family."

A husband. Betsey wanted a husband. "Battingston is not every man. I will find you a husband a thousand times better than that coward."

"Find me, a governess's daughter, a husband?" Tears brimmed in Betsey's blue eyes, but her voice was harsh with anger. "You cannot even find your own."

Kate answered sharply, "I hardly think that's fair."

"You're right, of course. I'm not being fair." Betsey brushed away her tears and nodded. "You might as well know. I'm leaving for America."

America? Surely she was joking? "Running away? Like Ros?"

Betsey shook her head. "Not quite. I am not running from a marriage, I am running toward one."

"What?"

"I have accepted a proposal of marriage from a

very eager gentleman who tends a lighthouse in Maine."

Kate thought perhaps she was trapped in a very unpleasant dream—first the news that her husband wished to divorce her, and now this. "Maine? Where is Maine?"

"Miles above Boston and far from civilized, I am happy to say. Which is why men such as my intended Mr. Laverdiere, who has two young children in need of a mother, must advertise far and wide for hardy brides."

Could it be true? But yes, she could see in Betsey's unwavering gaze that it was. "You must be mad, to marry a stranger."

"No more than you."

Any protest died on her lips. A stranger. Yes. What else could one call a husband who had not set eyes on his bride since his wedding day five years before? "Why didn't you tell me?"

"You would have talked me out of it—and I cannot afford to be dissuaded. Not this time."

"What will I do without you?"

"Straighten out that husband of yours, as you first intended to do when I selfishly put my burden on your shoulders."

"Don't be silly. We are friends. There is no burden we cannot share. Not even the betrayal of the men we love." Kate hugged her friend. "I'd thought myself so clever, having him prove himself."

"Men can only prove themselves ignoble—never noble."

Kate might have argued if she didn't agree so thoroughly with the sentiment. Because of one rotten viscount, her best friend was heading to America. And because of another, Kate herself would miss her family's Christmas celebration for the rough winter journey to Ireland.

"Do not go to Maine. Go to Ireland with me and I promise to find you a husband much better than this Mr. Laverdiere, the Maine lighthouse keeper." She and Betsey had been inseparable companions since Miranda married the duke. And now they would live on different continents.

"I will not spend another moment as a charity case in the duke's home, Kate. I will be married and have a home of my own—and I'll thank you to say not one more word on the subject or I shall have to challenge you to a duel—and I might not blunt my tip."

"Do you hate me so much then? For isn't that what I've done—let Simon take care of me instead of forcing my husband to tell me the truth?"

"He is your sister's husband. It is not the same." But Kate saw that Betsey did not believe that. Not completely.

"It is. And you are right. If Sean will not have me, then I should be on my own. Have my own household and my pride to keep me warm at night. Not false charity."

"You could not . . ."

"I would not have expected you to argue with me, considering why you flee to America."

"I am not fleeing—there is every reason for me to go. I am not the sister of a duchess."

"No. But that does not mean the man you loved had to abandon you for the daughter of an earl."

"I am the daughter of a governess, Kate. I was not suitable for him."

"Suitable. I hate that word."

"So do I. Perhaps I shall never hear it again once I am in America."

"I shall miss you."

"No you will not—you will be too busy trying to make your stubborn husband see sense. How can he possibly believe that you would cuckold him with Niall?"

"Do you think I can change Sean's mind, once I am in Ireland? Once he must look me in the eye and see that I have not betrayed him?"

Betsey laughed, and her expression lightened. "If you can't, then no one can."

Kate hugged her tightly again, knowing that she must let her friend go, though she could hardly bear the pain of the thought. "And I hope you find the place of your own that you are in need of with this American lighthouse keeper."

"I'm not asking for much," Betsey said softly, a far away look in her eye. "Just a home to keep neat, a small patch of ground to garden, and a family that is mine to claim."

A family. Yes. That was what Kate wanted, too. And it was high time she went to claim her due from her husband.

The duke called her into his study right in the middle of a grafting session. Not wanting to put off making it clear that he would not change her mind, for fear that she would lose courage, Kate left Ceddie to finish up and stripped off her gloves with uncharacteristic carelessness.

Niall McCarthy, with a thundercloud expression, perched on a chair as if he were prepared to leap up and defend himself if she attacked him. She supposed he had hoped to enlist the duke in preventing her trip to Ireland. Foolish man. He should know enough about Fenster women by now to know that even a duke couldn't stop her from doing what she thought was right.

The duke's expression was forbidding when he said with grave disapproval, "McCarthy tells me you have not given up your foolish plan to go to Ireland to confront your husband."

Gathering all her courage, Kate challenged him with a question. "How else am I to change my husband's heart and mind? How else might I turn him away from this foolish idea of divorce?"

"The charge is absurd." There was a hesitation, a question, in his voice. To his credit, he did not ask, but she still felt the sting of betrayal.

If he doubted, even for a moment, what would those in the rest of London think? Had the blasted man she'd married foolishly five years ago no idea what his suit would do to her? She would not allow it. "It is absolutely a lie, and he knows I can prove it."

"Prove it?" That assertion seemed to surprise him. Some of his stern certainty fled, to be replaced by puzzlement.

Niall cleared his throat gently. "Such allegations as my cousin makes are hard to prove, my lady, but the making is all that is needed. Though you and I may protest all we wish, neither's there any way to prove such a thing false."

"You are correct, in the most part, Mr. McCarthy." Gossip was usually that way; Kate had to admit he was right. However, in the hours in the greenhouse since she had talked to Betsey, she had had time to contemplate the matter quite thoroughly. She thought she had come up with a solution that would satisfy them all. Including Sean. She nodded, feeling slightly faint as she perched on the edge of revealing her most private secrets. "Fortunately, I have no need to rely on my word. I can prove my innocence."

"How?" Neither man seemed to take her meaning; both appeared puzzled, though Simon had had the sense not to speak his question aloud.

Kate wanted to scream at his obtuse refusal to understand her meaning without explication. "There is only one way."

Simon's frown deepenend for a moment and then cleared with a shocked exhalation. "But—"

"He left too quickly to finish things between us," she said bitterly. He'd wanted to, she was almost sure of that. But he hadn't. And that omission would cost him the divorce. She'd see to that. "He should have taken the opportunity to do more than hasten the marriage—he should have sealed his devil's bargain."

"If this is true—" At her angry inhalation, Simon softened his tone. "Of course it is true, Kate. I do not doubt you for a moment. But surely you see this does not change anything."

"Of course it does. I must prove—"

"And if he does not wish to know the truth?"

"He will know it nonetheless."

"Think, Kate." Simon leaned forward, urgently. "It may not be wise for you to travel to Ireland. You will be vulnerable to him there. Even if he is suing for divorce, until it is granted he is still your husband."

Vulnerable to Sean? Could she be any more vulnerable to him than she was now? She brushed aside the sense of his statement. "Once he knows the truth, he will not continue with the divorce."

"Kate—"

"I can't believe it until I see it in his eyes. Hear it from his lips. You can't understand—"

"I can." He sighed and began to ink his pen. "How much will you need for your travels?"

"Surely you will not allow her to pursue this foolishness, your grace?" Niall protested.

Kate cut him a quick look that silenced him with a blush. "I can pay for them out of my funds."

Simon looked at her, as if he was reluctant to tell her more bad news. But, at last, he said gently, "Until the divorce suit is settled, the funds are frozen."

"What?"

"They are your husband's, by right of marriage."

Of course they were. Fury burned through her at the unfairness. She was his wife until he managed to free himself from her. Until then, all she owned was his to command.

Niall McCarthy objected, "Surely, your grace, you will not allow her to go unaccompanied?"

"She will have a maid."

"I will—"

The duke raised his eyebrow and silenced the man. "I hardly think that would be appropriate, considering the circumstances."

"I cannot condone this—"

"The charges are not true, and he owes her an explanation. As he's said often enough, 'Fair's fair.' Is it not?"

Niall scowled. He did not insist on accompanying her again, though.

There was something she needed to know. "Niall? Did you know what he intended?"

"Of course not," he protested.

She did not believe him, but that was not important at the moment. "Then you must go ahead of me to tell Sean that we are not lovers. That I am a faithful wife. That I am coming to him, to prove it beyond all doubt."

She saw that he did not wish to oblige her. But there was little choice, and at last he stood and made a slight bow to her. "I'll take your words of innocence with me when I leave tomorrow, my lady."

"Tomorrow?" She could never be ready that quickly. He must know he would have almost a week's head start. But she would not show fear. "Very well. Please assure him that I will be following in your footsteps in very short order, Mr. McCarthy."

He frowned at her unhappily. "Surely you would not wish to miss Christmas with your family, my lady?"

She smiled with false brightness, though it made her cheeks ache. "Of course not. I intend to celebrate the season with my husband—he is my family, after all."

Simon said sharply, "You'll not likely make the journey by Christmas, Kate. Perhaps you ought to wait—"

"I'll be there by Twelfth Night, surely? And we shall celebrate the end of the season as well as the anniversary of our marriage."

The men looked at her unhappily. But she was a Fenster woman. They knew better than to try to talk her out of her determination to face her husband and assure him his charges were unfounded.

Chapter 7

Sean looked up from his paperwork and frowned at the man who had burst into his study unannounced. "I didn't expect to see you here, Niall. Did the duke banish you from his sight?"

Niall shook his head, an unsettling light in his eye. "Not so much banished, as sent to deliver a message." His gaze caught Sean's and communicated trouble.

A sudden fear struck Sean, but he hid his weakness from his cousin, allowing himself to ask only casually, "There's nothing wrong with Kate, is there?"

Niall, not fooled by his cousin's attempt at an indifferent tone, merely grinned at him as he settled into a chair with reckless care for the mended leg, which groaned under his weight. "You'll see for yourself soon enough, Cousin."

Connor shifted in his chair, and the fragile furnishing groaned under his weight as he frowned at his son. "You've not brought her with you, have you? She's best away from here, especially tonight."

"I've not brought her. Although I offered, seeing as she feels I am somewhat to blame for your loss of faith in her."

Sean didn't like the pleasure on his cousin's face. He didn't like that his cousin had seen Kate not that long ago. Or that he had given his cousin license to do what he could not. But that was unimportant. He had only done what was necessary. He waited just long enough to strip the impatience out of his question before he asked, "What do you mean?"

Niall smoothed his sideburns in a nervous gesture that worried Sean even more, despite his cousin's rather amused expression. "She'll be here in under a week if the weather is with her."

Here? He suppressed the urge to kick out at the chair and splinter it to bits under his cousin. "Will she have her pistols with her?"

Niall laughed. "Her sword, no doubt. She'll want to see your blood run free, as angry as she is."

"You should have found a way to travel with her." He did not want to say more than that, with his uncle present, but that would have been extra evidence to add credibility to his suit.

"I'd have feared for my life." Niall looked almost sincere.

"Do you truly believe she'll bring a weapon?" He'd not thought of her as so bloodthirsty. He'd been gone so long, he'd thought the divorce might have brought a bit of relief to her.

He sighed. How foolish of him to allow distance to persuade him she would take his blow without retaliation.

Niall shook his head, his expression more rueful than amused, now that he had made his point. "Just her tongue, I suppose, though it is a sharp enough weapon, as I know all too well of late."

"That it is." Especially when she was hurt or angry. "I take it she is incensed about the—" He broke off for a moment with a glance at his uncle. He had not told Connor about the divorce. He knew his uncle wouldn't approve, but he was determined to free himself—and Kate—from the disastrous mistake they had made in marrying. "The latest letter I sent?" He had simply told his uncle that he was informing Kate that he would not return to London, ever.

For a moment Niall's grin made him worry that his cousin would not be as discreet, but all he said was, "I would say so."

"Could you not persuade her that I was a jackass and better things await her elsewhere, as I instructed?"

"I couldn't persuade her snow is cold and white at this very moment, I'm afraid. She thinks me to blame for this 'misunderstanding,' as she calls it."

"If you had handled her properly, as I asked . . ." Sean didn't finish his sentence. He had asked Niall to seduce Kate, to give him irrefutable grounds for the divorce, and the images that accompanied his words were too unpleasant.

"Fair enough." Niall laughed. "I've done a poor job at turning the lady's thoughts from joining you. Your wife was not susceptible to my charms, despite my earnest efforts." He glanced at his father, and added cautiously, "And she's coming to prove herself to you."

Prove herself? Niall was being cautious because of his father, but Sean wondered what Kate thought she might prove to him. He could not ask, not with his uncle in the room. He vowed to ask later.

"Now that she's taken matters into her own hands, perhaps you can use her to get additional funds from the duke?" His uncle seemed interested in the conversation at last.

Sean lifted his hand to silence this train of argument. "Uncle, I have told you I will do no such thing. If we need money, we will get it some other way."

"You didn't bring her here, providence did. Who are we to frown on providence?"

Niall said, semi-piously, "Even providence could not bring the duke's favor upon us at this moment, Father. Sean's abandoned bride has understood her fate and has come to change it, with the duke's blessing."

"The duke's blessing?" Sean could not bring himself to believe that. Perhaps the man had decided he had no other choice but to give his blessing?

Niall said solemnly, "And though I was not permitted to escort her, the duke made it clear in no uncertain terms that I must ensure her safety while she is dealing with her errant husband."

"Does he think I will harm her?"

Niall shrugged. "Who am I to say what the duke thinks. He charged me to bring her back again safely when you—as he is certain you will do—fail her in person, rather than in absentia this time."

Sean bit back an angry retort. The duke's charge was only the truth, after all.

His uncle spoke, a dangerously thoughtful expression on his face. "Still, providence has dropped her in our laps, and the duke would not dare harm Sean while he holds his wife here. . . ."

Sean made a sound of protest, but his uncle ignored him and continued, " . . . as is his legal right, even if she has come against his wishes and his will."

He stood up, intent upon cutting off the discussion as soon as possible. "I didn't bring her here. But I'll be the one sending her home—and right away."

Niall did not seem to take the hint. "If you can convince her."

He glanced at Niall, wishing his cousin was speaking anything but the truth. "What words will soothe her pricks and send her home?"

"Simple ones, I should think, Cousin." Niall grinned. "Either that you intend to head straight to London and take up the life you abandoned five years ago—or that you've died and gone straight to Hades with no chance of pardon from St. Peter."

For a brief moment Sean considered pretending to have died, but he abandoned the absurd idea almost immediately. She would demand proof—and a dead man could not be divorced. "Her timing is not the best. She cannot stay—she might inadvertently discover what we're doing and who knows what she'd do then."

"Perhaps she would admire you. She did want you to display an absence of fear, didn't she?" Niall's cheek twitched, but otherwise he showed no expression of his annoyance. "And your recent activities are so very mad, they could only be performed by a man without fear."

An absence of fear. He had done so many foolish things to prove himself to her. And now . . . "That was five years ago. I doubt any display of courage I could show would appease her now." Belatedly, Sean remembered how resentful his cousin had been at being relegated to England to keep Kate distracted while Sean got to play an Irish version of Robin Hood and help even the score between the Irish and the English just a little.

Surprisingly, Niall smiled and said flatly, "She wouldn't turn you in to the Crown."

He supposed his bride wouldn't be pleased at the jealous surge that shook him. His cousin spoke with such certainty about the wife Sean himself had not seen for too many years. "She may very well, if she doesn't like what we're doing." Despite Niall's certainty, it was a risk Sean was not willing to take.

"No doubt you could use your persuasive skills to convince her that you are a hero. After all, your letters used to put a glow in her eyes for days."

Sean felt a tug at his heart to hear that confidence. "She's not likely to understand—not given her life of privilege or her English heritage."

Niall shrugged, unwilling to argue the matter, as usual. "Perhaps she'd speak to the duke on your behalf, as Father suggested?"

"Excellent suggestion, lad," said Connor.

"No, Uncle." Sean had made up his mind. "She will come. I will soothe her pride, if I can. But she will know that I will divorce her, and then she will go home resigned to the fact I am needed here more than I am in London."

Connor frowned. "Foolish action, that, making an enemy of the duke."

"I have no need for the alliances of English dukes or the House of Lords, either. I've chosen the other path. I thought you were pleased by my choice."

"I can understand why you might want to rid yourself of a useless wife." His uncle shook his head and sighed. "But to cut yourself off from a ready source of funds . . ."

"She is not a useless wife." Sean wondered what his uncle would advise if he knew what riches had accumulated from Kate's cultivation of roses. He could guess—so he said nothing of it. "She was a wife for the man I wanted to become, not for the man I have decided to be."

"The duke is already alienated," Niall said firmly. "He has already begun looking into how to protect his wife's youngest sister from the harm to her reputation."

Sean hoped Niall did not know of Kate's nursery business; he would tell his father and then Sean would never hear the end of it until he'd left his wife destitute. He sighed.

Kate. Here. For a brief, cowardly moment he wished for urgent business in another part of the county. He could handle her—but he was afraid she'd leave with a bruised and battered heart, unless he could think of some gentle way to ease her pride and still continue with his plans.

It didn't help that he had a fierce desire to see her again. He'd thought he'd put her behind him. Signing the papers to begin the divorce suit had caused him only a few faint twinges. But now, knowing that she was on her way and would soon be on his doorstep, his heart raced and he was warm all over.

All for a woman he had decided to divorce. A woman he hadn't seen in five years. A woman he hadn't even bedded on his wedding night. He sighed. Perhaps that was the problem, then. The possibility of seeing her awakened, the thought of business he had left long unfinished and thought himself content to do without.

He held Niall back for a private word, after his uncle had left the room to see that the horses were saddled for their latest foray into the countryside. "Are you certain she will come?"

Niall smiled. "Only the burning of all ships ever made would keep her from our shore, Cousin. She is convinced she can change your mind with her sweet words."

"Damn." Sweet words? Kate? Somehow he doubted it. "What shall I do, then? She cannot stay here."

"Don't worry, Sean. Your wife thinks of you as that charming rogue who swept her off her feet so long ago. No doubt if you show her the man you have become, she will beg to be divorced from you and plead with me to take her home, damn the damage to her reputation. Perhaps then she might even favor me with her affections, as you had hoped."

Sean buried the anger that threatened to erupt. "You sound as though you'd like to be her savior."

"Why shouldn't I? She's a beautiful, spirited woman who's been faithful for far too long to a man who wishes she'd fall off the face of the earth."

"I wish her no harm."

"And she wishes you none, cousin. She merely wants to correct this misunderstanding between you."

"You did not read her last letter, then, if you think she does not wish me harm. She demanded I arrive for Christmas. Demanded. Or she would move herself across the sea to be with me."

"Perhaps she might fit here, Sean. Have you thought of that?"

"You can't be serious. An Englishwoman? Here? Do you want to hang?"

"She'd brighten the place until then, at least," Niall replied flippantly.

"Have I more cause to press this suit than I thought?" Sean asked with sudden unpleasant suspicion.

But his cousin was in no mood to indulge him. He shrugged. "I'll let your bride answer that question, Sean. She should be here soon enough."

* * *

After disembarking from her ship, Kate found herself reevaluating the wisdom of her decision to travel alone, with only a maid, who was more than a little afraid of the Irish "divvils."

"I'm afraid for my life, my lady—and yours too," Sarah said with a quavering voice as they looked about for a carriage.

"We are stout enough at heart, Sarah, we shall be fine. But here—take this to give you courage." Kate gave her a little dagger to ease her mind, hoping that some helpful lad did not find it stuck between his ribs for no better reason than the maid's faint heart and suspicious mind.

She hired a carriage from the friendliest driver she could find—which wasn't saying much. They were all fairly taciturn once they found out where she wanted to go. But a few extra coins got her acquiescence if not exuberance. Sarah, she noticed, kept the knife clasped in her fist until they were well away from the docks.

As she stared at the rude huts dotting the landscape on the rackety ride, she began to wonder in horror whether Sean had an estate, or just another windowless cottage, as so many here lived in. He was an earl—surely he had a more sturdy abode.

A sudden memory of his frayed collar and cuffs assailed her. Of him, proud and pleased with himself the morning he had climbed in her window. He had never made it a secret that her dowry would be welcome, but she began to suspect that his need had gone beyond desperate and into the realm of dire.

Everyone knew one part of the story—how his ancestor had lost their holdings in Ireland and how his father had gained a title by saving Prince George's life when he foiled a secret plot abroad.

There had been some mention of lands, but she thought that those had been purchased by Sean's father. Or was it his uncle?

The castle and the extensive lands that his ancestor had lost in Elizabeth's day had gone to a private family nearly two hundred years ago and were not the Crown's to gift any longer.

She had often held that fact up to him—citing his own father's honorable effort which had earned the reward the monarch had bestowed upon him. He had argued that not everyone could save a future king's life, but they might still deserve to own a horse and be educated.

She had scoffed that those laws had been repealed, but here, she understood more clearly what he had meant when he argued that lifting the laws didn't always right the wrongs that had accumulated under them.

Sarah seemed to be as fascinated as she, even though the maid was clearly frightened and appalled by what she saw as she peeked out the windows of the moving carriage. "My lady—how does that man expect such a poor horse to pull a cart so heavy? Perhaps we should stop and advise him to get a better horse?"

"I suppose that is all he can afford," Kate said as charitably as she could, though she was certain the poor horse was about to collapse under its load. She supposed that the man she saw, leading a cart hitched to the broken-down nag and with hunger in his eyes, might have a hard time finding a way to improve his business with a horse that needed to rest every few miles.

"I heard tell the Irish were lazy, but I didn't believe it before now. That Aoife we had at the duke's house was a hard worker, and cheerful, too. Here, it seems no one's working hard at all."

Kate understood her prejudice, but looked beyond the slow-moving workers to see the want in the prematurely aging faces. "I suppose we'd all work more slowly and with less enthusiasm if we hadn't had a good meal in our stomachs in some time."

Hunger was apparent everywhere in the thin faces and angry eyes. She found herself hushing Sarah whenever they were near people who would turn to look askance at them, as if their voices marked them as devils.

"Hard work is the only way to fill your belly," Sarah said adamantly. "My ma taught me that when I was little and I never forgot it."

Hard work might have helped these people get back what they had lost throughout the years. But, as she drove by the small, neat parcels of land that could hardly support a crop to pay the landlord, never mind feed the occupants, the thought occurred to her—work doing what?

Should all these people leave their land to work in England? Or perhaps just a few able-bodied sons? She knew of more than one second son in England who'd had to go out and make his own way far from home.

Was it so very unfair to have to leave your family if you wanted to better yourself? And what would happen to them when you left? Certainly there would be one less mouth to feed, but also one less pair of shoulders to carry the burden of everyday life.

Why had Sean never spoken of this personal misery? Their discussion had always remained in the realm of the philosophical, never descended into the reality of hunger and hopelessness etched deeply into the faces of adult and child alike.

Sean had crossed wits with her, sometimes even

passionately, but there had always been a reserve to him. Perhaps this was why? Because when he talked of hunger and famine he was not seeing only words, but suffering faces? Had he wanted to spare her the knowledge? Did he think her too faint-hearted to bear the sorrow? Or too well cared-for to understand?

Could this be why he had never sent for her? Why his letters had been wonderful at holding out hope just short of true promises? She shook her head. No. That was just her way of trying to justify the horrible thing he had done—abandoning his wife and now daring to accuse her of infidelity. Could he believe it? Or was this just a convenient way to rid himself of an inconvenient wife? She wished she knew for certain why he had decided now, after five years, to sue for divorce.

She had tried to understand why. But there was no reason she could see—unless he had chosen to divorce her simply because he had run through her money and needed more.

If so, he would find no more English heiresses interested in him; no sensible young woman's parents would wish her to be married to a man who might divorce her in a few years. But perhaps he, like Betsey, had set his sights on America to fulfill his dreams? There were many wealthy heiresses there who seemed only to require a title from a husband, and little else.

It was dusk when she arrived. The fields, fallow now until spring, looked well enough tended and without an overgrowth of weeds, but the drive up to the abbey, which must at one time have been a pleasant journey shaded by overarching branches of the flanking trees, was now a nightmarish struggle up a tangled way.

"Sit in the middle of the seat, my lady," Sarah

prodded her, doing the same on the opposite bench. "Otherwise, I fear your hair might be torn off your very head." The gnarled and twisted branch tips were not merely content to scrape and twist along the sides of the carriage, but at times poked into the windows as well.

The rutted path emphasized with every jolt that she was neither expected nor welcome, but Kate pulled the tattered bits of her courage up around herself and determined to show Sean that she would not be bested. As they grew close, she could see the candles glowing in the windows of the hulking abbey. Did he really live there? It seemed more like a ruin than a home.

"Is that it?" Sarah leaned forward, squinting. The flickering glow of the candles, a sign of the season which usually made weary travelers' hearts lift with a sense of welcome, only made Kate's heart ache for the family she had left at home. No doubt they would be preparing for the Twelfth Night celebration tomorrow, laughing and teasing the excited children, the adults turning their thoughts toward spring and the warming of the days.

At last the carriage lurched to a halt, throwing her across the seat. As soon as her teeth stopped rattling, Kate reached for the handle, aching to be on solid, unbolting ground once more after her days aboard ship and a hard day's travel at a breakneck pace across Ireland in an unsprung carriage.

"See you aren't the worse for the wear today, mum—miss." The Irish driver was as genial as could be on the surface, but her days among the servants below stairs had taught her to recognize when resentment simmered under the surface of deference. It often heralded cold tea or slices of lemon without the seeds removed. Even Miranda's well-run household had had its secret rebellions.

Sarah was not so reticent, however. "Such cheek from the likes of you," she said with a stern *harrumph*. "Are you all in one piece, my lady?"

"I'm fine enough, now I'm here," she answered as if she didn't know the driver would sooner have dumped them at the gates than have his carriage all scratched up by the encroaching tree branches and unpruned bushes. "If you'll be so good as to get my bags, I'll instruct the butler to pay you."

His eyes bulged from his head. "Butler? Here? Do you think you can cheat me?" He approached, more than anger in his eyes, as if she had drawn her sword and demanded he empty his pockets.

Niall appeared then, just when she began to fear for her life. "She has not had the pleasure of a visit here yet, man. You'll be paid well enough."

He foraged about his person for a moment and came out with a gold coin—more than generous for the trip Kate and Sarah had just barely survived.

"Fair enough, then." The man was once again all smiles, but Kate felt a tremble of fear still alive deep within her.

The geniality of these people was hiding a depth of anger she had never seen before, but could still feel.

Even Niall, she noticed now, possessed a certain tension that had gone unremarked in England. For the first time she wondered if she would survive this trip. After all, being made a widower would make things much easier for Sean.

Niall took her hand and brought it to his lips for a kiss. "Has the fight been shaken out of you? Is my cousin safe from your wrath for the time being?"

She raised her chin and said nothing.

He laughed. "I should have guessed the answer. Too bad I did not think to wager on it before you arrived."

Since there was no sign of either butler or footman, she moved to her trunk, determined to carry it in herself. Sarah gamely came to her aid.

"Leave it," Niall ordered with a laugh. "I'll have someone take it up to your room for you—unless you'd rather I take you back to the coast to book passage on the nearest vessel heading back to civilization?"

Kate glanced around the small area where the lantern light kept back the shadows. There was no sign of Sean. Had he run away, knowing that she would be here? What had Niall told him?

She followed him up the crumbling steps of the abbey and through the doors that hung crookedly, as if they had been battered down sometime in the recent past and not been repaired by a man of skill. Behind her, Sarah followed more slowly, uttering low-voiced grumblings that were incomprehensible, but not favorable.

Kate was determined not to speak, but somehow a question made its way past her lips. "Is he here?"

Niall threw her a pitying look. "Waiting for you, my lady. Waiting for you." He addressed Sarah sympathetically. "You, my girl, had best get yourself to the kitchen to make a cup of tea for your mistress. I suspect she'll soon need it very badly."

Sarah eyed the great hall with disapproving eyes. "Looks as though I'll need to scrub the pot as well as make the tea," she said before she scurried away in the direction Niall pointed out to her.

The hall was dank and dark and Kate stopped for a moment to allow her eyes to adjust. The musty carpet, its pattern obscured by layers of dirt and mud, came clear in her vision as she glanced toward the floor and blinked to assure herself that she was, indeed, inside the abbey at last.

She saw his boots first and her heart seized with

an emotion she could not name, though it paralyzed her breath and sent sharp pain through her chest.

All her instincts cried out to turn and run away. Away from the inhospitable abbey. Away from the man who had married her and abandoned her without a single qualm.

She looked up to meet his eyes. "Happy Christmas, my lord. I have come to see which of us you meant to be the donkey."

Chapter 8

She had come. And she had sharpened her tongue for battle.

Sean stifled a sigh. To give her the edge now would be his undoing for more than this small skirmish, he had no doubt of it. Her timing couldn't have been worse. He had business tonight, and he wanted no strangers about to interfere.

She stood proudly to face him, the hood of her cloak dropped back to reveal the determined tilt of her chin. He wanted to push her back out the door and into the carriage that had brought her here. Wanted to pay the driver to carry her away as fast as the devil riders were said to go in the dark winter night.

But there was no place he could safely send her until tomorrow. He watched her standing there, waiting for him to make his move as patiently as she had when they played chess together in London, when he first began to court her. When she lightheartedly set him his first challenge—to prove his wits were a match for hers. He had forgotten how beautiful he found her. How small and delicate and fierce she was. She filled the great hall with her presence, slight as she was.

Niall said, "Well, Sean, have you no kiss for your wife, after she has come so far just to speak with you?"

He glared at his cousin. "Leave us, please, Niall."

Niall didn't look pleased, but he bowed and left the hall.

Kate did not glance at the departing man. She had, in fact, not taken her eyes from Sean's face since she had first looked up at him. Sharp eyes, that saw more than he wanted her to, even in this dim light. Should he postpone his business? No. He would just have to see she had no desire to wander. Which shouldn't pose that much of a problem.

He returned her even gaze, not hurrying to speak. After all, what did one say to an unwelcome wife who had landed on the doorstep at the worst time possible? She had changed little in appearance. Perhaps there was a sharpness to her jawline and a tighter press to her lips?

The trusting look was gone from her eyes, of course, but that was only to be expected. He'd seen the shadow of question that always lingered there during their courtship. Now it was no shadow, but a solid accusation. She had said nothing more after her initial volley, but her posture, her glare, all spoke loudly, asking him why he had professed to love her? Why had he lied? Perhaps he should have been honest with her from the first? Impossible.

She gazed around her, at the ruined state of the abbey's great hall, for a moment before turning her attention back to him. When he didn't speak, she did.

"Please don't tell me you would turn away even

a wretched stranger during the Christmas season? Your candles suggested otherwise. But perhaps I am mistaken. I have been so before, lamentably."

"You are welcome for the night, of course." He bowed stiffly, unused to the courtly gestures of the city any longer.

Restlessly, she took a half step toward him. "Have you nothing else to say?"

He paused a moment, as if contemplating the question. "I can think of nothing pressing."

Her anger gave resonance to her voice. "Well, I can, and I expect you to do me the courtesy of listening." Though her eyes were fixed on his, he did not think she saw him. Or perhaps he seemed like a ghost risen from a grave to her, the way her eyes were wide and her cheeks were drained of color.

"My ears are yours." But that was all of him she could have—and that not for long.

Just then, as she opened her mouth—to berate him or plead with him, he could not tell—the door opened again and Bridget entered the hallway, laughing. Her maid followed a few steps behind, breathless and apologetic. "I'm sorry, my lord, the time got away from us . . ."

The women stopped, staring at the tableau in the hallway in confusion. Sean stifled the impulse to pick up his sister and bundle her out the door. The damage was well enough done now.

He cast about for a way to halt the disaster that loomed on the horizon. He had not informed Bridget that his wife was coming to the abbey. He had hoped they'd never meet. He preferred to keep his sister safe among those who would love and protect her—and understand her nature. And now the two women stared at each other with frank curiosity. He could think of nothing worse than for the two of them to spend a moment longer together.

His stomach dropped when Bridget stared at Kate with that penetrating, faraway gaze she too often held. "You bring a whirlwind with you," she said to Kate, whose puzzled half smile of greeting froze on her face.

After a moment, Kate said stiffly, "No, I've only brought one trunk." Her confusion was plain, checked only by the strange situation she found herself in.

Bridget glanced at him and frowned. Damn. She sensed his desire to push Kate from the room, and panic flared in her eyes. "Sean? What trouble does she bring?"

He did not want to introduce her. Did not want to have to explain to Kate the oddities of his sister. They were none of her business and Bridget, like Sean, did not wish to be pitied by anyone.

He waved his hand to indicate she should leave them and, miraculously, after a fleetingly mutinous expression, she did.

Kate's eyes flickered away from the spot where Bridget had stood, as if she had broken some spell and regained control of herself. Her expression suggested his sister's laughter and her odd comment about bringing a whirlwind had wounded her somehow.

But he dismissed Bridget from his mind. Kate was here. And he must find a way to ensure that she left first thing tomorrow morning. And that she never wished to, or would dare, return.

What, he wondered, could he say that would convince her to go? He saw her dismay as she took in the surroundings. It was nothing like Anderlin, the home she'd grown up in. Even Bridget's laughter had not warmed the stone-cool walls, bright as it was.

No. The abbey was not like her home. Nor like any of the duke's fine residences. Stone. Damp. Dark.

Being Kate, of course she did not instantly turn on her heel and head back to home and safety, thanking the stars that he would soon not be her husband. No, that would have made matters much too simple for his Kate.

Instead she stared at him, her lips parted as if she meant to speak but couldn't find the words.

He decided a show of indifferent strength was called for, so that they didn't lapse into useless sentiment. "Come to thank me personally, have you? Wish you'd given me just a bit more notice. I'd have had someone sweep the mouse droppings away."

"I thought you were here making improvements, my lord. Or perhaps I misunderstood?" She vibrated with the anger and tension that came only from facing down something unpleasant after hard travel. But he would not allow himself to sympathize. He had not asked her to come.

"You should have seen the abbey five years ago. I have made many improvements." That was a lie; he had not wanted to waste money on making the abbey a showplace when his tenants and countrymen were dying of starvation. He had invested in seed for the future, not curtains for the windows.

"I would have, gladly, if you'd asked me." She glanced around, allowing her contempt for her surroundings to show. "You prefer this to me, and London?"

"Why, my lady? Do you think I waste my time here among the hungry and dying just because a king saw fit to grant my father a title? Perhaps I should approach the fine Squire Jeffreys and ask if he'll pay my passage to America, as he has done for so many of the people who used to tend this land for him—and for my ancestors, too, before Queen Elizabeth saw fit to throw my family from our land and send us into exile? Should I flee like my countrymen?"

She faced down his anger with scorn. "It is not fleeing your country to represent them in Parliament, Sean."

"Laws. Unfair laws that no Irishman can repeal with words alone." He thought of what he had to do tonight and let his own anger show. "How many have to die before you English stop thinking it's your God-given right to keep your boots on our necks?"

She had not expected him to be angry. She took a step back. One brow rose in challenge. "You English? You speak as if we sit around in parlors thinking up amusing new ways to torment your poor countrymen."

Had she forgotten he spent a year in England, listening to the condescending opinions of the Englishman upon the subject of the lazy Irish? "Don't you?"

She didn't seem to know whether to attack or placate, so she answered weakly, "We have better things to do."

He pressed his advantage. "Ah. Knitting sweaters for the poor starving Irish babies to be buried in." He wanted her angry and frightened and thoroughly disgusted with him. It was the best way to get her to leave quickly.

She waved her hands in the air, as if she wished to erase the angry words. "Sean—if only—"

"What? If only I worked harder? If only my people spent every day with their noses to the grind-

stone, they'd get their reward when? In their early
grave—in their flimsy coffins made from wood
your folk deign to leave in our forests?"

"Your fields . . ."

"My crops were promised to your avaricious
countrymen—who were going to send them away
from the starving people of this land anyway." That
was a lie. He had not done what so many other ab-
sentee landlords had done. He had not sent his
crops to feed the people of England or America,
filling his coffers while leaving his people's bellies
empty. But the lie made his point for him, and she
would not be here to uncover the truth.

She stared at him silently for a moment, and he
saw the moment that she realized his argument
was meant to distract her from the bigger question
that lay between them. Her eyes flickered away
from his face, but then returned in a steady gaze.
"Why did you never come for me?"

He closed his eyes, not wanting to see the naked
pain in her expression. He couldn't, however,
dredge up his anger again, so he settled for changing his tactics mid-battle and softening his voice
and attack. "I know I should have expected an affection might grow up between you and my cousin,
considering my long absence. I only wanted to see
you well looked after."

"You don't believe that I would betray you—or
that Niall would." Her voice was flat, accepting of
no argument.

"No? Are you not a beautiful woman?" He allowed his voice to soften as he spoke the truth. "Is
your heart immune to love when I have so shame-
fully neglected it?"

"Your cousin was a friend—nothing more. You
must believe me."

" 'Tis a tale as old as time. But I do not hold it

against you. You are a hot-blooded woman. Maeve would have been proud."

"I have never been unfaithful to you—though you've given me plenty of reasons with your abandonment. There is no reason for you to divorce me."

"Katie, I'm sorry to have been such a bad husband that I drove you into the arms of another man. But you must know I cannot let such an insult go."

"I have not—" But she cut off her protest and said, instead, "Why did you not ask me, directly, if such a thing was true?"

Not being an idiot, he knew the trap that lay in answering that simple question. Simple question, but no simple answer. "This is between Niall and me—you must not get in between us."

She sighed, as if she had heard the argument before. "Don't be absurd. It is about me, though the law doesn't see it that way."

He supposed the duke had explained the matter thoroughly to her, so he said only, "My legal quarrel is with Niall. You have no part in this. I understand that you were lonely and vulnerable without me. It was Niall who should be horsewhipped."

"You think me vulnerable to Niall because . . ." She trailed off, speechless. And then, sharply, she chastised him. "You are a fool, Sean McCarthy. The king was wise to name you Lord of Blarney. You argue with both sides of your tongue."

Aware that time was slipping away and he must complete his deeds tonight under cover of darkness, he decided to press his advantage now. "And you, my love, argue in the dulcet tones of a fishwife. No doubt because you are exhausted from your travels." She must know that he was no longer on her family's lands, but on his own. And that he would not be treated like an errant house servant. "I will show you to your room."

"I have come all this way—" she protested.

"And you are undoubtedly tired." He took her elbow, pretending that it was surprise that made her flinch, not distaste. "Come, we'll get nowhere stabbing at each other this way. Tomorrow you will be more rested and perhaps your sweeter nature will have re-emerged."

She refused to move. "We have to talk."

He put his hand on the small of her back and propelled her forward. "We will talk in the morning."

"Sean—" She was not willing to buy the goods he intended to sell her. But for tonight, he had run out of time to try to sell them to her.

"Katie, it is all my fault. I must beg your pardon for my foolishness. No man should leave a beautiful woman alone with any man who has a pulse, no matter how much he trusts him. Forgive me for my part in this situation. But do not ask me to swallow my pride and allow myself to be cuckolded. I cannot do it."

She said nothing, although her look was not forgiving in the least.

"You will be comfortable here." He stood at the door to the room he had decided would be hers. The smallest, and least comfortable. It was mean of him, but he did not want her to mistake his hospitality for anything but necessity. He wanted her gone tomorrow. A night in this room should see it done.

"My trunk . . ." She looked as if she were afraid it might disappear if she did not carry it up herself.

"I will have it brought up shortly." He had not yet taken his hand from the small of her back. The contact was more pleasant than was wise right now. "No doubt your maid should be up soon with a small meal. Nothing fancy, you understand. Tea. Some bread and perhaps a wedge of cheese if one can be found."

As if she had just now noticed that his hand rested in the small of her back, she pulled away and crossed her arms tightly. "I am not hungry."

He did not believe her stubborn declaration, but he had no time to argue. "As you wish." If she missed a meal, she would not be the worse for it. No, it took more than one missed meal to starve a body. He should know that well enough by now.

"I hope you know I have no intention of leaving before we discuss this matter."

"As you can see, the abbey is no place for a discussion, especially one which will be unproductive for us both."

She squared her shoulders and he realized that the five years he had hoped would soften her will had prepared her to fight this battle full out. "I do not sail back for a month, so do not hope you can delay so long that I will be forced to return with matters unresolved between us." She glanced at the room and set her jaw mulishly, no doubt to prevent the complaints that she wished to utter.

Stubborn woman. But he had no more time for her tonight. "Good night Kate. Sleep well."

"Good night, Sean. I'm certain I will."

Her words were sheer bravado. He admired them, but he did not want her braving a step outside her room tonight. "My heart warms to know you are comfortable here in my home. By the way, if you hear any moaning or groaning, just ignore it."

"Moaning?" Her eyes narrowed in suspicion.

"Moaning." He spoke with cheerful reassurance, trusting that his words would have the opposite effect. "Not too loud, I assure you. Lady Dilys was as refined in life as she is in death."

"Lady Dilys?"

"A visitor to the abbey centuries ago." He nodded. "She died in childbirth in this very room, with her first child. Legend has it that she enjoyed being a gracious hostess and continued the practice even after death."

Her eyes narrowed. "You're just trying to frighten me. I don't believe in ghosts. Or leprechauns either."

He held a finger to his lips. "Hush, Lady Dilys might hear you and take offense. She is said to have a very tender disposition when she is insulted."

Her temper flared again and the door shut on her sharp, "Indeed." Through the solid oak, he heard her continue in muffled tones. "Then she and I have something in common. I warn you, Sean McCarthy, I have not had any . . . congress . . . with your cousin."

"That is not what I have heard, my lady. But the matter is between my cousin and me, as you well know."

The door thumped in its frame. "It is not true. And I am willing to prove it." The door thumped yet again. "Good night, my lord."

A ghost. Trust him to try to convince her there was a ghost in this room. He was no doubt trying to scare her away. Did he not know her at all? Had he ever?

Kate tried to bolt the door when he left, but her hasp was rusted and bent so that it was impossible. This place was fit only for ghosts, who needed no corporeal comforts or securities. And ethereally beautiful young women who made a habit of dashing about outside, at night. At first she had thought the girl might be Sean's sister. But the fact that he had not introduced her and had sent her from the room with a guilty frown, gave Kate pause.

Was she the reason Sean suddenly wanted a divorce? Kate had been afraid to ask him. Perhaps tomorrow she would work up the courage. She stared out the window, into the darkness, wishing suddenly that she was back in the rackety coach riding for the coast again until Sarah came with tea and bread, as promised.

"The kitchen and the servants' quarters are clean enough," the maid allowed, with a glance of disapproval around Kate's quarters. "But I can stay here with you, if you'd feel safer, my lady."

"No, Sarah. I shall be fine here alone."

The maid's relief was palpable at Kate's answer. Had the girl already heard the rumor about Lady Dilys? Or was there a handsome young man serving Lord Blarney who had caught her eye?

She had her answer when she saw the young man who carried her bags up to her room. Definitely handsome, and with a winningly shy smile, as well. Sarah's poor heart was doomed. Kate could not think of a word of warning that would help the maid, though, so she said nothing.

As soon as the tray of food had been cleared by Sarah—with the help of a young girl who could easily have been the ghost of Lady Dilys, her skin was so pale—Kate ushered both women away for the night. The room seemed suddenly much more likely to appeal to a ghost once they had gone. She contented herself with placing a large chair in front of the door to do the job of the broken hasp.

Only then did she allow herself to ready for a night under this inhospitable roof. She was fortunate that she did not believe in ghosts, despite her sister's penchant for telling bedtime fairy tales during her childhood.

She was not certain what she had expected. Not this run-down abbey. Nor Sean so like himself and yet not. She did not want to admit to herself that he had never loved her, but she supposed she must at least begin to acknowledge that it might be true.

His eyes had kindled with warmth when he'd called her a beautiful woman. No doubt he meant it. But that meant nothing. Especially since there had been that laughing woman, who had come and gone so quickly she might have been just another ghost. Sean had looked at her with affection, and she had obviously returned that affection. Was she his mistress?

The thought was shocking, and yet not. Men had needs. She wasn't a fool, she had heard the gossip about men keeping mistresses, even married men with wives to warm their beds. How could she doubt that Sean had done the same with that laughing woman? Would it be worse to know that the girl was his mistress, or that she was the woman he wished to marry once he had succeeded in divorcing Kate?

She must ask him, no matter how much she feared his answer. Could he truly believe she had fallen in love with his cousin? Or was that just an excuse? She opened her trunk and took out the bundles of letters she had saved over the last five years.

He had written her faithfully every week and she had kept them all, from the shortest, a mere two paragraphs with his scrawled mark, to the longest— five pages. It was the first one he had written— right after he had decided he would not return to London as she expected.

She unfolded the stiff pages and reread his

words, looking for a clue as to whether he had known, even then, that he would not ever return to her. There was no answer to her question in the familiar lines, no matter how many times she read them.

Chapter 9

Prove it? Kate's threat still echoed in his mind as he sat in his office, waiting for the clock to strike midnight. He thought it an unlikely possibility.

He sighed. Perhaps in six months' time he'd be free to find a nice Irish lass who wouldn't look at the abbey as if it were infested with rats—or, at the least, would simply get a few good mousers to manage the problem. The thought was singularly unappealing.

But no matter that Kate had come to turn his world upside down, he had work to do tonight. The others would be gathering here soon. He could not be distracted. He would not let Kate distract him, at least not tonight, he decided as his uncle entered the room, earlier than usual though he was dressed for their mission tonight.

The man didn't even wait to take his seat before he asked, "Well? What does she say? Did she bring money from the duke?"

Money. With his uncle there was no more important subject. "Of course not."

His uncle leaned toward him, his strong fingers

biting into the wood of Sean's desk. "You should write him, convince him that you must have funds in order to keep the girl comfortable."

"And what would I want with making her comfortable, I ask you? I want her away from here, as should you."

"You are a fool, then." Connor scowled. "You could perhaps convince him to buy the castle for her—"

"The castle is a ruin and I don't think Jeffreys would sell it, even if the duke so lost his mind as to agree to such a bargain."

"You must make the most of what providence sends you, Sean. The girl is here, that's a sign for certain."

Sean tried to mask his impatience. He owed everything to his uncle, he could not bring himself to be disrespectful, but he would not agree. "No sign, just a mistake. She will be gone before nightfall tomorrow, and we will all sleep better, I promise you."

"And if she doesn't choose to leave? Will you take that as a sign, at last? You have yet to make a profit with these agricultural improvements you have implemented."

"Next year—"

Connor slapped his hands on the desk. "It is always next year with you. Next year we will be doing the same as this year—playing boy's tricks on the English and eking out a profitless living from the land. Ask the duke."

"I'll manage on my own—without taking advantage of my wife." Any more than he already had done.

"Why? Her fellow English haven't shown the same scruples against us."

"Exactly. And that is why."

"We need the money."

"And I will get it." He would. Or die trying. But not from Kate. Not again.

"How?"

"You'll see. You're too impatient. Give me some time." Even to himself, the words sounded thin.

"Five years is not long enough?"

Too long. But he would not say so. Sean shook his head wearily. "I'll consider your advice, Uncle."

A new threat occurred to him when his uncle beamed at him happily and said, "Do you want me to talk to her? Sometimes these things are better handled by someone other than the husband."

"No, Uncle." Kate would surely tell him of the divorce action. "I will speak to her if I decide it is right." He did not want his uncle to know about the divorce, he'd be against it and could perhaps ruin the plans Sean had made. "It is time to focus on our business tonight, and put the question of my wife aside."

Kate was a stubborn woman—stubborn with a smile and a laugh, that one. She wouldn't let him know how she felt, but she wouldn't give in to his blandishments, either.

He'd have to get her out of his life before she told his uncle about the divorce, found out what was going on and became a danger to his cause— or the danger threatened to sweep her up. He didn't want her hurt, Sassenach or not.

"You've got to show them you're a leader, lad. The duke's money would—"

"Tomorrow, Uncle." He didn't want to hear about being a leader again. The definition seemed to shift from minute to minute—whatever his uncle wished it to be at the time. "Tonight we need our wits on our task. I don't want any of our men swinging at the end of a rope. Do you?"

"Only one man I want to swing. Jeffreys. If you won't ask the duke for help, haven't I told you what you should do—burn him and his kind out once and for all? Stop playing these games. Take back what is ours."

"It hasn't been ours for nearly two hundred years."

"Thieving Sassenach. Deserves to die."

"He no more deserves to die for what his father did than I deserve to die for what my father did." For what had happened to Bridget, however, he would not wish the man well.

Connor was not to be appeased. "Your father was a saint."

"My father was an impractical dreamer who managed to save the king's life. You are the one who managed to catch the fickle ear of a fickle king once."

"His bravery got our position back. And it is up to you as his heir to get the castle back. Which you refuse to do."

"We don't need a ruin that will take millions to renovate; we need good healthy soil, and good healthy crops, to bring life back into the land. People are starving; I must feed them."

"Why not do as others do? As he does? Send them away in leaky boats to leave this beautiful land behind forever?"

"I am not him."

Bridget burst in, frowning at his loud and angry protestation. "Who are you not, brother?" She seemed fierce, though the black of the boy's garb threatened to swallow all but her pale, ghostly face. As he watched, she moved to the fireplace and rubbed her hands and face with ash. Ready for battle.

"No one." He would not say that name in front

of Bridget, and he dared his uncle to do so with a
fierce gaze that promised retribution should the
man be so foolish. She might think herself strong,
but he would not have her hurt again. Which was
one reason why he let her accompany them on
their raids—otherwise she would just find a way to
follow and he would not be able to protect her at
all.

His uncle smiled at her indulgently, overlooking
her unorthodox garb, as he had begun to do since
Jeffreys's men had nearly killed her. "Not for you
to worry about, lass. Just something your brother
and Uncle Connor will handle."

He wasn't sure if his sister would be stubborn
and insist on prying the name from him, but evi-
dently she had more important matters on her mind.
Bridget frowned at him. "Who is the woman?"

The woman. Kate. He briefly considered lying,
but Bridget would have the truth from the servants,
so there was little point. "She is my wife."

His sister's face rarely showed surprise or shock,
but her color did rise a little in her cheeks as she
asked, "When did you marry?"

"Five years ago." He tried to keep the tension
from his voice, knowing it would only increase her
desire to know about Kate. "She's a bit angry with
me, so stay away from her. She'll be gone soon.
She won't hurt you."

"She brings trouble, but she won't hurt me."
Bridget smiled up at Sean. "Perhaps I should bring
her to meet the fairies? They might like her. She is
pretty. The fairies like pretty things. Maybe they
could help with the trouble to come, too?"

Fairies. Sean suppressed a sigh. "She is no thing,
she is a person. You have no need to meet her, or
she to meet the fairies. She will be gone soon. Do
you understand me, Bridget?"

Bridget glanced at him with a meek nod that ensured she would be seeking Kate out if he didn't lock her in one of the abbey dungeons immediately. His sister was a law unto herself. But he supposed she could hold her own with his wife. Two viragos. Both his to take care of, for now.

He thought of Kate, tucked upstairs and away from their secrets. He knew he should be relieved that she was safely shut away. But the temptation to go up to her—abandoning all his other plans for the night like a self-indulgent fool—was difficult to crush for a moment.

The letters spread about her on the bed were more confusing than helpful. His words were of love and caring and understanding. Even in the dim light of the candle glow she could read them clearly. But these were words that she found hard to believe came from the man she had spoken to earlier today.

Kate had promised herself she would not cry. She would not. She stood up, determined to clear away the letters and sleep. Tomorrow she would face him. She would ask him what she needed to know, and she would not accept any less than the truth from him.

As she moved, she became aware of a noise from down below. She stopped to listen. The sound came again, and she realized that she had been aware of it for some time, but had not paid close attention until this moment. Perhaps because it had grown louder this time?

She went to the door and pressed her ear against the wood. She heard it more clearly: a bumping, scraping sound, like horse hooves on a stone floor. Did they keep their stables in the great hall? Surely not, or she would have noticed signs when she arrived.

Common sense told her to stay inside the room, behind the door with its broken hasp and bolstering chair. A ghost offered far fewer dangers than whatever might be making those sounds. But something had changed with Sean, she had seen it in his eyes. He was a different man and she wanted to know why. Perhaps discovering the source of those sounds would answer one question, at the least.

As quietly as possible, she moved the chair away from the door and opened it. The darkness loomed thickly, but the sounds were clearer. Bumps. Scrapes. Low, unintelligible voices.

She crept down the darkened stairs in bare feet, feeling the crumbling, treacherous steps carefully for a safe place to step.

At last she heard voices more clearly. She saw figures, shadowy, dressed in dark hues, their faces streaked with ash.

"Feels good to be doing something useful again. I've spent too much time of late playing caretaker to your wife." Niall's traitorous voice was cheerful, as always, despite the cloak of darkness and the late hour.

Kate almost spoke up, his words made her so angry. As if she had need of minding like a toddler. Fortunately, she realized that she would find out more—possibly infuriatingly more—if she remained silent than if she revealed her presence to a group of men obviously intent on concealing themselves from sight.

"I didn't think you minded so much, cousin. You should have told me. I'd have sent someone else." Sean sounded weary and impatient. Was that because of her arrival, or because of what he contemplated doing in the next few hours, under cover of darkness?

"You'd not have found many willing to lie to the girl. She's not a fool; I had to dance a quick jig to keep her believing you would come to her eventually." Niall didn't think her a fool, but that was little comfort to Kate. His words hurt. He'd not only known what Sean planned, he'd willingly participated in ruining her reputation.

Sean's philosophical answer did not lift the painful pressure around her heart, either. "She believed it because she wanted to. Women are like that, Cousin."

Niall laughed, but there was a bite of anger that sharpened the sound so that it echoed in the night. "You have a turn at dancing to her tune, then. She'll have you jigging until your feet wear down—at least until you drive her off." Kate was suddenly glad she had slapped him so hard when he kissed her under the mistletoe.

To her surprise, Sean's answer was mild. "It's not her fault things changed, Niall. You've no call to be angry at her."

"I'm not angry at her. I'm angry at you. You should have brought her here years ago. She'd never have been able to stick it out and we'd have all been happier if she wanted to see the last of you as eagerly as you wish to see the last of her. But no. You had to keep her hopes up with those damned letters."

"I did not want to hurt her." Kate wondered what he might have done if he *had* wanted to hurt her. She wasn't certain she wanted to know. But it seemed likely she might find out in the very near future.

As if he had read her thoughts, Niall said sharply, "Well, you have no choice now, do you?" One shadow—Niall, she supposed—put his fist down hard on a nearby table. "I should call you out for wasting my time these last five years."

A second shadow figure stood taller, and Sean's angry words filled the quiet night. "Perhaps you should."

A new voice chimed in to say, "She has brought a whirlwind of trouble with her. Will you let it sweep you up?" Kate felt a chill slip up her spine that had nothing to do with the damp stone that surrounded her. The girl. She was dressed as a man, and Kate had not realized she was part of this skulduggery. What did that mean?

"Listen to her, lads." Another voice—his uncle's? "We have more important things tonight than your petty quarrels. Spill each other's blood tomorrow."

Sean, the tension drained from his words, laughed softly. "Bridget, my love, you are ever wise."

One shadow figure embraced another, and Kate felt as though someone had taken her heart in his fist and squeezed with every ounce of strength possible. Bridget was his sister's name. The little sister he had claimed to have come home to protect—and yet here she was, as thick in whatever trouble Sean was up to as any of the men who surrounded her.

To her horror, the clock chimed midnight softly and the shadow figures, in unison, swarmed toward her hiding place. She shrank back, grateful that her dress was dark gray and not some bright color that would catch the eye as they rushed past her, close enough to touch.

A cold breeze slapped her cheeks as they opened the door and then it died as the door closed and she found herself alone. Again.

She made her way back up to her miserable room, almost hoping to see Lady Dilys serving a ghostly tea. But the room was empty. She moved the chair back in front of the door and vowed not to leave the room for any reason until daylight.

The bundle of letters were on the bed, still. His letters. His lies. She wanted to cling to his whispered words, "I didn't want to hurt her." She believed that he had meant them. That he had not meant to abandon her. So what had happened that had altered everything and stolen all her dreams away from right underneath her nose?

She had tied the letters into packets, by month, pretty colored ribbons to indicate the year. Now she untied the ribbons and scattered the letters on the lumpy bed. She would not sleep tonight. She began sorting through them, looking for a clue as to what had changed her husband into someone who would turn his back on a seat in Parliament and instead use the cover of darkness for undoubtedly illegal deeds.

The letters were as she remembered, full of promises. Promises, words that gave hope of being together soon. Soon. Soon. Five years of soon was much too long. She had been a fool. She would be a fool no longer.

Sean closed his eyes against the light of day. He was getting too old for these nighttime forays that left him no time for sleep. Perhaps, if he had had enough rest, he would not be so easily swayed by the emotions the woman across the breakfast table roused in him.

She nibbled at the toast on her plate, watching him with open curiosity. "You seem tired, my lord."

"I did not sleep well." Not much of a lie, considering he had not slept at all.

"I slept like a babe." She smiled. And then she launched her assault. "Who was that woman?"

Woman? His foggy brain grasped for meaning in her question. "Lady Dilys?"

She pressed her lips together and shook her head. "Not your make-believe ghost—who you will be happy to know left me in peace last night."

"Perhaps she took pity on you your first night as my guest." He would not mention the dark smudges under her eyes. Were they caused by fear of Lady Dilys, or had she lain awake last night to plot her campaign against him this morning? "She's said to have a soft heart for women whose husbands have abandoned them."

She stared at him unblinkingly. "Who was she?"

"I believe she was a lady who died in childbirth many centuries ago."

"Not Lady Dilys." She poked her fork into a bit of egg with repressed violence. "The woman yesterday. The one who appeared in the hall right after I arrived." Her voice and gaze were both sharp with curiosity and another emotion he could not identify. "The woman you gestured away before I could get her name."

"She is no one important," he lied, though Bridget would have spitted him to hear herself dismissed so blithely.

His wife took a sip of her tea as if she were as calm as a glassy sea. But he was not fool enough to be blind to the tension beneath the surface. "To you, or to me?" She challenged him, her eyebrow cocked arrogantly.

"To you, of course. Are you certain you slept well?" He could sense that his wife was in a new, more dangerous mood this morning. He wondered if Lady Dilys had plagued her sleep, despite what she had said. If so, he refused to feel guilty. He had not asked her to come. He had not wanted her to come.

"I confess I slept well enough, although I did awaken once or twice to some very odd noises. Have you another ghost besides the quiet Lady Dilys?"

Had she heard them last night? He thought he'd put her far enough away that she would hear nothing except the creaks and groans of an old run-down abbey. "Ghosts. Lady Dilys is just one of many, I assure you."

For a moment he thought she might challenge his statement. Instead, she shrugged and lifted a wrapped bundle to the table. "Perhaps so."

He tensed, wondering if she had brought her pistols and was about to challenge him to duel. "I should have assured you that none of our resident ghosts are dangerous. You should not have let the noises disturb your sleep."

"I did not. I had other things on my mind. I spent the night going over these." She bent to the floor and lifted an armful of papers with a small gasp of effort. Before he could rise to help her, she had dumped a handful of well-read letters onto the expanse of tabletop between them. His letters to her.

"I believe these are yours, my lady, not mine." He wondered, if he touched them, if they would burst into flame from the heat of his shame.

Her indignation broke through her attempt to remain cool and collected. A flush crept up her cheeks. "If you don't want me, then I certainly don't want these . . . these lies, pretty though they might have been."

"They weren't lies," he lied.

She wasn't listening to him. She stood, her stare worse than a pistol ball in the chest, as she leaned across the table until he could feel the warmth of the anger radiating from her.

"I have heard it said, though, that those with sins

on their conscience often see sin in others." There, now he had laid the matter on the table again.

She gasped in outrage so great she seemed unable to speak. But she would speak soon enough, he knew. She would protest her innocence, again. And he would refuse to believe her. How long would they have to dance this jig before she grew tired and accepted the divorce? He understood why Niall had been so angry with him last night.

"I have not had a lover. Not your cousin. Not any man." There was fierce challenge in her eyes. And hurt. Hurt he had caused. Hurt he wished he could soothe away by taking her in his arms. What was wrong with him? He knew a divorce was best. For both of them.

"Gossip says otherwise." Gossip he had been careful to have Niall spread, but he did not have to tell her that.

She paled. "Who would tell such lies? Don't they know it will ruin me? How can you believe them?" Her eyes gazed downward to the letters and she lifted one, smoothed it open. "Do you know that today is the fifth anniversary of our wedding?"

"I had not remembered," he lied. "But you are correct. We were married on Twelfth Night." Which was why he preferred to celebrate the occasion by getting well and truly drunk. He would have started already, if he did not have to deal with her.

"I have waited a long time for you, Sean." She spoke quickly, as if hoping that at least some of her words would strike him and change his course. "I do not deserve to be discarded like this."

"Could you not believe that I am giving you a chance to be with the man you love, rather than the useless husband you have?"

"The man I love? Niall? Have you spoken to

your cousin? The gossip is a vicious lie. I promise you that. Surely you can believe your own cousin if you choose not to believe me." Her gaze sharpened on him. "Unless you have some other cause to divorce me."

"I am not the one who must believe you, Kate. English society can be vicious; we both know that." He did not want to think of her at the mercy of those who had nothing better to do than gossip and find excuse to cut someone. "I have my already dubious reputation to guard. You would not expect me to accept the title of Lord Cuckold, now would you?"

Her lips twisted in a bitter parody of a smile. "And what about my reputation?"

He had an answer prepared for that question, thank goodness. "The duke will protect you, I am certain. Has he not done so for your sisters?"

"My sisters all have loving husbands." She laughed bitterly. "There is no protection for a woman who is divorced by her husband."

"You will find another husband soon enough. Perhaps Niall, if he is not too cowardly." He had once thought it an acceptable solution, but now that she was here, in his home, the scent of roses clinging to her, he would have called the words back if he could.

She laughed gutturally, as if she might choke on the suggestion itself. "I have no desire to marry another McCarthy man. Not after the first has proved so disappointing."

He knew she was trying to hurt him. Though he could not blame her, neither would he allow her to see that she had. "If my cousin is not to your taste, then you are free to choose another."

She paced to the window and looked out, though

there was nothing to see as the night's fog had not yet cleared. "I will not consent to this divorce."

"I do not need your consent." The words were harsh, but true.

She bent her head, leaning her forehead against the glass as if to cool her brow. "Your charges are false."

"So you say." He didn't know whether it was wiser to pretend to disbelieve her than to believe her.

She turned to face him, and there was not a shred of resignation in her stance. "I will fight you on this, I promise."

He thought briefly of Maeve, who had made her own laws for a time. Fortunately for him, the only laws he had to consider were the English ones. This time, they were on his side. "You have no standing."

"So Simon has told me." The lift of her chin suggested she still hoped to find some way to circumvent the law.

"Then you understand there is nothing you can do but accept the inevitable?" He was thankful, for a moment, that he had not been the first to explain to her that a wife had no party to her husband's suit to divorce her, that it was entirely between the husband and the lover.

She smiled, and the flash of triumph in that smile sent a chill up his spine. "I can be called to give evidence."

Give evidence? Parade herself in front of stern, unbending men to tearfully plead her innocence? Was she truly that foolishly stubborn? He tried not to show how her threat disturbed him. His voice was even as he replied, "That is not usually done."

She nodded and he dared to hope that she had put aside the idea. Until she said, "Because there is no evidence a wife can usually provide to prove beyond a shadow of a doubt she has not committed adultery. I, however, can."

He saw the conviction in her eyes and realized she meant what she said. "There is no proof—"

"But there is," she interrupted him with a sharp wave of her hand. "I can prove that I've been with no man at all."

He should not have been glad to hear it. Niall had not done the job properly if he had not bedded her. After all, she was as cunning and strong willed as Maeve, and he had told his cousin so. But he was fiercely glad that she had not fallen prey to Niall's charms. Despite the problems that caused him.

"How can anyone know such a thing for sure?"

She blushed, right down into the bodice of her gown, so that he didn't doubt her word for a moment when she said fiercely, "A doctor will know. I am a virgin. And I will prove it to the length and breadth of England—and Ireland—if you persist in this action of divorce."

Chapter 10

He had forgotten her temper. Had underestimated her desire to right the wrong he was doing to her. But he did not apologize. She would not dare put herself on public show in such a way. Even if her common sense had truly deserted her, the duke would not let her. "That would be humiliating for you."

"And for you, as well. What man does not bed his own wife for five years? It is well enough known that we married hastily because you were found in my bed—if I am proved a virgin, what will the gossips say about you? That you are a eunuch? Lord Eunuch. Isn't that much worse than Lord Cuckold?"

"Perhaps." Without doubt. He would be a laughingstock. And he would lose his suit for divorce. Still, there was no way the duke would allow her to expose herself in such a way. He laughed, as if her threat meant nothing. "But I am Irish, after all—what Englishman expects me to do the traditional?"

She gave an infuriated gasp of outrage and then collected herself and smiled, as if she understood he was only displaying bravado now to intimidate her into backing down. "It will be enough to stop your action."

"It will, unless you are lying."

"I am not." She dismissed his caution easily.

He stood. What could he say to end this between them here and now? To send her packing, glad to divorce him. "Then you should not have come here."

"What do you mean?" A dawning apprehension touched her eyes as he crossed the room to stand close enough to touch her. But he did not. He would not. It would be enough to threaten her. It had to be.

"You are my wife, Kate, whether I chose to make love to you or not."

"But you chose not to, and you must live with that."

"Nevertheless, you are my wife. Your body is mine. Nothing could stop me from taking you now. Here. And then what would your threats be but empty air?" He hadn't intended to, but her closeness made reason disappear and he pulled her to him, demonstrating the truth of his words. "Your evidence gone all too easily."

"You wouldn't dare." She did not back away from him, and he realized that she intended to challenge him to the limit.

He shook his head and touched her cheek lightly. "Katie, you are a foolish woman. I would not have guessed."

"I am indeed." Though she winced at his words, she did not flinch away from his touch. Instead she laid her face against his chest. "Who but a fool would have believed the lies in your letters?"

He sighed, resisting the urge to kiss her and make good his idle threat. "What do you want?"

"What?"

"I can see that I've wounded you with this action, but I am determined to divorce you. I made a mistake marrying you and it is time to correct it."

"Why are you so certain it was a mistake?" She pulled away from him and gazed up into his face as if she might divine the truth there.

"Trust me. I know it." He looked away, through the window and into the fog that had still not cleared off. He glanced back to see her bowed head "Tell me what I can offer you that might ease your pain and allow you to accept that I do not wish to be your husband any longer."

"Did you ever?"

"Would I have climbed through your window and risked life and limb if I did not?"

"Even then you did nothing more than kiss me." She would not be appeased. "Did you restrain yourself because you loved me? Or because you didn't?"

"Would it ease your pain for me to say yes or no?" Sensing her vulnerability, he leaned down and kissed her gently, though he knew his words would hurt. "Would it soothe your bruised pride for me to make up for what you missed on our wedding night? I will if you like. It is not necessary for a man to love a woman to bed her, as I'm certain you know."

She stared at him without answering for a moment, and his heart beat faster. He wasn't certain whether he wanted her to say yes or no. No, that was a lie. He wanted her to say yes, though he knew it wasn't at all wise.

Then, abruptly, she pulled away from him and gathered all the letters on the table into her arms. He thought she would toss them into the fire, but instead she threw them, so that they flew at him, pelting him lightly before they fell to the floor.

"You are not the man who wrote these letters. You cannot be."

He picked up one sheet and scanned it quickly. "It is my handwriting, there can be no doubt."

She glared at him coldly. "Then you obviously wrote them to the wrong person, my lord. Please allow me to return them to you so that you can save yourself the effort of thinking of new lies to tell your next wife."

"I take it, then, that you will no longer object to the divorce?"

She glared at him. "I cannot wait to be done with you."

He nodded, ignoring the pain her words caused him. It was what he had wanted; he deserved the pain. Deserved the hollow, unsatisfied feeling within his chest. "I'll call a carriage to take you back, then."

She seemed shocked for a moment that the decision had been made so quickly and her visit was truly at an end. And then she nodded and snapped, "Please see that it is better sprung than the one that brought me to this hellish place."

He didn't dare show his triumph for fear she would change her mind just to spite him. He tried not to sound eager when he called for the carriage. But the servant who answered his bellow shook his head. "The fog is thick as a good cream soup, my lord. No one will be going anywhere today."

"Fog?" They spoke in unison, equally appalled at the idea of Kate staying another night in the abbey. But a quick glance out the window proved the servant's words true. The fog was thick, and it did not show any promise of burning off quickly.

Sean sighed. "It seems you will celebrate Twelfth Night with us, my lady. I hope you will not look down upon our poor celebration, in comparison to the one your family must even now be holding."

He could see that she wished to refuse. For a moment, he was tempted to allow her to spend her Twelfth Night with Lady Dilys. "The parlor is much warmer, and brighter than your room. Do not let your fear of my ill manners drive you from the meager hospitality I have to offer."

"What will you do with your sister then? Lock her in her room, so that you don't need to explain your soon-to-be divorced wife to her?"

For a moment he wished he could take back his offer. But no, it was better that they met under his watchful eye than if either—out of sheer female curiosity—arranged to meet behind his back.

"I would like the chance to know your sister," she said defiantly.

"No doubt she wishes the same." He would have to tell Bridget to behave. But he had no true hope that she would. She was much too much like her older brother.

"I have but one favor to ask of you."

"A favor—"

He held up his hand to halt her protest. "My uncle and my sister do not know of the divorce. Could you please not mention it today?"

Her expression moved from outrage to mutinous denial in a flash. "I—"

He appealed to her reason—he knew she possessed a good portion, even if it was not readily visible at the moment. "Connor is an old man and Bridget a young girl. Don't they deserve to enjoy their last day of Christmas without dealing with our troubles?"

To his relief, her shoulders slumped briefly. "Very well. I shall mention nothing of it—as long as you behave yourself."

* * *

Despite her reluctant agreement, Kate thought of refusing to join their celebration. Of insisting on a tray in her room. But the scents of cider and cinnamon called to her, and she soon found herself down in the drafty sitting room with Sean, his sister, his cousin and his uncle.

"Sorry about the fog, my lady," Niall said. He smiled broadly, though, and she doubted he spoke the truth as he shot a glance at Sean. "It should clear off tomorrow—or next week."

"Next week?" The thought of staying here a week was intolerable. "Surely—"

"My cousin is teasing you," Sean reassured her, with a dark look at Niall. "The fog should be burned off tomorrow in time for you to make it to the coast."

"Fog or no, you'll not go." Bridget spoke softly, without looking at Kate, so for a moment she wasn't certain the girl even addressed her. And then the oddly piercing green-eyed gaze lifted and caught hers. "You're meant to be here. The fairies say so."

"Bridget—" Sean's voice carried a warning note, but the girl did not heed it.

"I asked them this morning, Sean. The fairies don't lie. They told me a beautiful woman would bring a whirlwind of troubles that will sweep our house clean." Bridget turned to Kate and smiled with sweet innocence. "It's not your fault you brought the trouble. You couldn't help it. The fairies don't blame you."

He glanced at Kate briefly, and she thought she saw defeat in his eyes as he smiled at his sister. "The fairies said our harvest would be good last fall, too."

Bridget frowned and repeated, "They don't lie.

But they were mad because you didn't remember to put out the corn for them as you promised."

Sean, for a moment, seemed to want to argue, and then his expression smoothed away and he said gently, "I know, Bridget. The fairies wouldn't lie to you."

"Of course they wouldn't."

He teased, "And I'm certain they'll see to it that you get the baby in your slice of cake this year, as you do every year."

Bridget, distracted as her brother had obviously meant to be, asked, "When shall we have the cake, Sean?"

Kate wanted to ask what was wrong with the girl, but she could not be rude and speak in front of Bridget as if she were not present. However, she did not want to be alone with Sean. Cowardly, she knew, but Niall and Bridget were safer companions than her husband right now.

She'd thought she finally understood why he had not returned to England. But now, thinking of how he had rushed away because Bridget was sick, she wondered if there was more to the story than he wanted her to know. If she drew him aside, she could ask him privately. But the thought frightened her. She could still feel the imprint of his lips on hers this morning. The heat of his breath on her cheek. The scent of his shaving soap. No. She didn't want to be alone with him if she could avoid it.

"Are you thinking of your own family?" Niall asked her quietly. "They are a much livelier bunch than we."

"They may be livelier, but we are strong," Sean answered sharply.

"Mama and Papa are here, Niall," Bridget chided softly. "We simply cannot see them." She turned to

Kate. "Our mama was blown away by the Big Wind and smashed against a chimney far away. But not before she tucked me safely in a fairy hole."

"My mother and father were lost in a snowstorm," Kate confided. "But they left my sisters and me safe in the care of my oldest brother and sister."

"How many sisters do you have?"

"Five. And one brother." Kate thought of her own large, loving family, no doubt gathered at a similar dinner. "And so many nieces and nephews that I can hardly count them." She felt an ache of longing that she was not there to celebrate with them. With family who loved her.

Bridget glanced at Sean. "I would like a niece or nephew to love. But Sean refuses." She glanced back at Kate with complete sincerity. "You are his wife—can you not get him to give you a child?"

Kate had no answer to give. A flush of shock suffused her, only made worse by Niall's choked splutter of laughter. He did, however, manage to offer a diversion. "It is time for a game of cards, I think."

Bridget leapt up for the cards, forgetting the conversation of a moment before, thankfully. "I shall beat you, Niall. I have grown skilled since we last played."

"Kate is no poor hand at cards, girl. Watch your predictions until we have tested our guest's mettle."

"What do you play?" Kate asked politely. Speaking of home had made her think of what she missed. The duke and duchess would even now preside over a houseful of relatives. No doubt Valentine and Emily and their sons would be there, as well as Helena, her husband Rand and their son.

"I think maw is the game for us," Niall said cheerfully. He had been equally cheerful when he

spent the Christmas in England, she realized. Had
he missed his own small family and simply hidden
it from her? Had Sean?

"As you like, then." She rose and went to join
them at the small inlaid card table by the fire.

Each year seemed to bring more empty places
to the duke's table, though. Juliet, with R.J. and little Will, had gone to Italy this year, to see a Christmas
performance by an opera student Juliet had spon-
sored. Betsey's seat would not be filled this year,
for the first time since Kate could remember. She
had left for America at the same time Kate left for
Ireland.

She wondered if Betsey's new husband would
allow Kate to visit. Perhaps she would do so, once
she was divorced. America had been good for her
wildest sister Ros; perhaps it was Kate's future, too.

Husbands had entirely too much power over
their wives. It was not fair. The laws should be
changed. She looked at her husband, remembering the feel of him pressed against her. He had
threatened to take away her evidence, but he had
not. Why not? She closed her eyes, wishing to be
home again and away from him.

She wished she'd never come. She wished she'd
just read his letters and believed his lies, no matter
the pitying glances from family and friends. No
matter that he would never visit her in the flesh,
only in pretty words and dreams.

She'd rather have the pretty words than this
awful truth. If she were home, she could read his
newest letter just as they read the letters from
Betsey and Ros that Miranda would put out on
dinner plates at the table.

If she were home, they would take turns reading
them aloud and reminiscing. That was what Twelfth
Night was for at home. What was it for here?

The celebration here was quiet, unlike the loud one, full of games and gifts, at home. She felt restless, as if she should offer to do something, but she did not know what.

"Would you care for a game of whist instead of maw?" Niall asked, as if he understood where her restlessness came from. After all, he'd spent the last few holidays at her home.

"No. I should prefer maw. I am in your home this year, not mine."

Bridget said softly, "If you are Sean's wife, this is your home."

"Of course, Bridget. You are right. How silly of me." She could see Sean frown, but she did not care.

So they played maw and Kate learned fast and played hard so that in the quiet hush their laughter stood out more than it might have amidst the hustle and bustle of her usual family holiday.

Bridget, for some reason, carried around the tiny carved figure of the Christ Child from the cake, which had indeed been in her slice. Somehow, though, Kate suspected that Sean, not the fairies, had arranged that piece of magic.

Up close, Kate realized how ridiculous it was that she had considered Bridget to be Sean's mistress. Though nearly a woman grown, she had the mind of a child. Fey might be the kindest word possible for a girl like her.

She had given the tiny figure a place of honor as they played, asking it questions and patting it when it answered in a voice only she could hear. Niall did not object, although he had refused to deal cards to the figure, no matter how Bridget pleaded.

Kate glanced at Sean, who seemed unconcerned by this bizarre behavior. His glance shifted away, and she realized hotly that he had been watching her.

She turned back to the game, embarrassed that he had caught her glancing at him. Humiliated that he had not wanted to catch her glance, even for a brief smile or a lifting of his eyebrows in acknowledgement of her presence. Was it possible that he could hate her so? And even if he didn't, why didn't she hate him?

"It is your turn," Bridget said impatiently.

Kate glanced down at the table, trying to recall where they were. What she was supposed to do.

"Do you want to hold it?" Bridget asked, thrusting the child into her palm without waiting for an answer. "It will give you good luck."

"How sweet," Kate murmured, unsure what to do that would not offend the fragile-looking girl.

"Why do you think that Sean will not give you a baby?" Bridget looked at her innocently. "Don't you want one?"

Kate was not prepared for the maelstrom of emotions that engulfed her. Children. She had watched her sisters give birth, held her nephews and her nieces, laughed and dreamed of motherhood. She had imagined children with their father's dimple and his green eyes.

But now. She glanced at Sean, remembering the feel of him against her. He had meant his threat to scare her away. And it had. But perhaps she should not have let it.

He had asked what she wanted to acquiesce to the inevitability of divorce and she had not known. But now she did.

She smiled at Bridget as she smoothed one finger down the carved wooden cheek of the infant Jesus. "Yes, Bridget. I do want a child. Very much." The ache was always there, but she tried to tamp it down, as she must. One needed a husband to have a child. And it appeared that, despite the marriage, she had not truly acquired a husband.

The girl lifted the figure from Kate's fingers and held it to her ear, listening intently before she smiled and nodded her head. "Good. Then I shall ask the fairies to give you one, since Sean will not."

Niall had been valiantly fighting his urge to laugh, but at that he sighed loudly. "Are we to play cards, ladies, or speak of foolish things?"

"It is not foolish to wish for Sean to have a baby. Especially now that I know he has a wife." Bridget smiled at her cousin indulgently before turning her gaze on Kate again. "He loves you."

"Enough prattle, Bridget," Sean said suddenly. The glass of whiskey that he had held tightly for much of the day lifted in the air. "These are not matters for your ears, or your tongue."

"But—"

"Shall I send you to your room?" Sean stood and gestured to Niall. "Come, let us bring in some wood. Perhaps a roaring fire will cease my sister's tongue from wagging." The men left, Connor following behind, although he did not seem hale enough to carry much firewood.

"Still, he loves you." Bridget whispered with a smile, her eyes far away. "I asked the fairies. They say he has been sighing for you since your wedding day."

The fairies could not have been in the room with them, then, when he had offered to bed her without love, if they could tell the child such lies. "I think he's been sighing over other things—but not me. He could have had me at any time. All he had to do was ask."

As if to belie Kate's conviction that Bridget thought like a child, the green eyes sharpened and the girl said, "Men aren't really very good at asking, you know. Sean is quite bad at it."

All at once, Kate remembered that this girl had been among the men last night. She shook away her preconceptions and asked bluntly, "What is he good at?"

Again, Bridget's answer was sensible and lucid. "Taking care of his people."

"Has he introduced his tenants to the most recent horticultural techniques, then? Found a way to make the land feed the people?"

"He's not good at that." Bridget fidgeted. "He is good at showing the English who is boss."

"You must be careful not to do anything dangerous, you do know that, don't you, Bridget? I wouldn't want to see you hurt." She'd have said the same of Sean, if she hadn't seen them together last night. He hadn't made one protest that his sister would accompany them to witness and perhaps participate in their crimes.

The girl's open expression shuttered closed. "He wouldn't do anything to hurt me. Or to hurt you."

He had already done all he could to hurt her, but Kate did not argue because just then Niall and Connor returned. She had a brother she adored and she knew she'd never believe anything bad about him without seeing it with her own eyes—and perhaps not even then.

Sean himself did not return, which seemed to lighten the mood of everyone else. She wondered if the discussion of children had bothered him as deeply as it had bothered her?

Kate played several more hands of maw and found herself telling one of her sister's fairy tales—Rapunzel, of all stories—to a rapt audience of Niall and Bridget. She had a smile on her face as she climbed the stairs to face her room—and the invisible Lady Dilys—once again.

Sean obviously cared for his sister, since he had a maid trailing her all day long. What an exhausting job that must be, Kate thought, after having spent the day with the girl. With compassion, he had dismissed the maid to the kitchen for her own celebration. The poor girl had looked pleased to leave her charge in the sitting room among family. Kate expected she didn't get much of an opportunity to rest if her job was to follow Bridget everywhere the girl wandered.

Which only made it worse that Sean would let such a creature out at night, exposed to danger she could not possibly understand. She decided to speak to him, though she didn't expect her words to do much good. He ought not risk his sister in his illegal activities.

What kind of father would he be to a child of his own if he were so careless of his sister? Still, Bridget's suggestion burned inside her. Would it matter if he had no desire to be a father, as long as she vowed to be a good mother?

One thing was certain, she wanted a child. And he wanted a divorce. He'd offered to bed her, without undue enthusiasm, but not with any particular distaste. Other men found her attractive enough— she'd even had opportunities to take lovers, but she had not. In this way, they could both have what they wanted.

Perhaps she should agree, despite his humiliating lack of enthusiasm for the idea. He'd said nothing about children, but since that was a natural result of such actions, he had to have been willing to accept such consequences. Hadn't he? Or had she had too much wine?

Kate considered fancifully whether she should

ask Lady Dilys's opinion? Hadn't that lady met her unhappy end in childbirth? The thought sent Kate into a plunge of doubt. Perhaps she should reconsider. At the very least sleep on the matter before she brought it to Sean tomorrow.

Tomorrow. She was to leave, unless the fog had still not cleared. She'd have to pray for fog. Or, better yet, a good howling storm that would trap them all inside, no one able to travel. No one able to risk his life in the dark of night.

Chapter 11

Dawn brought fog again. And a swift shower of icy rain that made the roads and pathways impassable. Sean could not in good conscience send Kate on her way today, though he was tempted to leave himself, despite the dangerous condition of the road.

He had not been comfortable in his own home yesterday, sharing a holiday with Kate. Or perhaps it was that he wished much too much that his life had taken a different turn five years ago. That he had been able to be a husband to Kate.

Perhaps even make a real family, as he had planned to so long ago. He sighed. Despite what he had said, he had not forgotten that Twelfth Night was the anniversary of their marriage. Bridget's comments about babies had cut through him.

Kate had no idea of Bridget's history. And he could not explain it to her without giving her more information than he wanted her to have.

And now they were trapped together in the abbey for, at best, this entire day. He glanced down at the estate books spread out in front of him on the desk. He wasn't certain he wanted to work all day on them. But perhaps it would save him from the betrayed glares of his wife, or the speculative glances of his cousin.

She had thrown everything off key with her presence. He had found it unbearable—and his cousin had enjoyed his discomfort. Niall had watched him with a half smirk of satisfaction all day.

He couldn't blame his cousin for enjoying his distress; after all, he'd brought it on himself. But he didn't have to stay there like a sacrificial goat shackled to a stake. He had taken his leave after Bridget began to talk of babies. Even the whiskey couldn't distance him from that pain. Niall had chided him for leaving.

He wondered if his cousin would ever forgive him for sending him away to look after Kate. Or for being the one whose father had saved the king and won a title.

Unfortunately, he had only an hour's respite before the knock came upon the door. He knew by the quiet rap that it was not Niall, Connor or even Bridget who dared to interrupt his work.

Knowing that he would regret it, he called, "Enter."

She had not dressed for traveling, so someone had told her about the weather. "Good morning." Her words were innocuous enough, but her expression was not friendly.

He might have thought she was merely annoyed at any further delay, but she seemed less annoyed than frightened. In fact, he suspected that her hands were folded together to stop them from trembling visibly. What could she want now? "I'm sorry for the delay. This time of year the weather can be unpredictable."

"I'm glad for it, actually. We need to speak."

"Not about the divorce. I hope I have made it plain to you I will not change my mind."

She shook her head, although there was a guilty flush on her cheek, which made him wonder if she had accepted the truth yet. "I must speak to you about your sister."

Here so short a time and already meddling. "She is not your concern," he said abruptly. No doubt she had the womanly urge to "fix" Bridget's oddities—without any notion of what had caused them in the first place. She was not the first woman he had dealt with on this subject. As he always had, he would let Kate know he was not pleased with her interference and he would not encourage it in any fashion whatsoever.

She did not take his hint, nor did she sit down, but faced him across his desk. "She doesn't seem to be your concern, either." She was furious, he realized. If she'd been a man he'd have expected her to pound a fist down and shake the floor. "Do you want her to hang?"

Hang? What was she talking about? They would not hang a child for talking to the fairies. Had she found out about what happened five years ago? "I would die first."

"You may indeed die first, but she will follow if you continue to allow her out with you as you did the night before last."

He relaxed. So. He should have guessed that even Lady Dilys would not keep her bolted safely in her room. He ought to have accommodated her down in the cellar, with the ghost of the Headless Knight to keep her company. "You don't understand—"

"Do you mean to say you had some legitimate reason to be out the night before last with ash streaked all over your face?"

"I mean to say you must have been dreaming."

"The way I dreamed you in my bed five years ago?" She widened her eyes mockingly to feign shock. "Oh, but no, you *were* in my bed, weren't you?"

Sean struggled to feign amused indifference by sitting back and crossing his arms behind his neck. "Confess to me, Katie. Are you more incensed that I was then, or that I'm not now?" He added a grin wide enough to show his dimple to full effect.

She let out a little exclamation of frustration. "Stop trying to distract me from the subject of your activities—and the risk to your sister, if you don't care about your own skin. You can't keep flouting the laws." She shook her finger at him like a scolding mother. "You will be arrested. You should learn from history. From your ancestor."

The man who had held Queen Elizabeth off with sweet words and the insubstantial promise of promises to come so that the term blarney had been immortalized? "He was arrogant. I am realistic."

"Is it realistic to drag your sister into your criminal activities? What do you do, anyway?"

She was leaving soon, and he sensed that he would rid himself of her more quickly if he was honest, so he told her the truth. "I have taken a leaf from the legendary Robin Hood. I merely help even out the distribution of wealth and food around here."

She saw through his pretty words and blunted them when she threw them back at him. "You mean you steal?"

He had had this conversation with himself more than once in the last five years. But he resented the arguments when they came from her lips, with her aristocratic English accent. "Some might call it enforcing a tax upon the rich who make their wealth on the backs of the poor."

She raised a brow and crossed her arms in front of her like a dissatisfied schoolmaster. "Does the law call it that, my lord?"

My lord. There were times he hated his title. Times he felt he had betrayed his country simply by using it. "Ask your countrymen. I take nothing that does not belong to me."

"I've read the papers, Sean. I know things are not perfect here." Her arms fell to her sides and she turned away, to the window, where the ice sheeted and blurred the view of the fog beyond. "Why are you not fighting within the law? You have a seat in the House of Lords where you can make all the difference, yet you choose to let it go empty year after year."

He supposed he owed her an explanation, though he did not think it would comfort her. "While I'm making 'a difference,' as you say, my people are starving and being driven off the land."

She didn't argue with him. He supposed she had seen the evidence plain enough as she traveled to the abbey. She'd never been one to flinch from the whole truth, when it appeared before her so starkly. Her question to him was as stark. "Nothing will ever change for the better this way. Hasn't history proved that over the centuries?"

"It has to change." Even as he said it, he realized that he had long ago lost faith that it ever would. He couldn't mark the day he'd lost the faith, and he'd not noticed it gone until just now, speaking with her.

"If it doesn't, what risk to your sister?" Kate persisted. "I understand why you feel the need to play the hero, hopeless as your cause is. But why would you be willing to sacrifice her?"

As if he had a choice. "You don't understand Bridget." The girl would follow them if they did not allow her to accompany them side by side. "She goes where she wills. Even her maid cannot stop her—only follow and keep her from the worst of her impulses."

"Did the illness do this to her?"

The illness? For a moment he cast about in his mind for her meaning.

She added, "I never thought your letters were entirely truthful about why you had not returned. Was it your guilt that the illness had left her a permanent child?"

"Yes." He had forgotten that he had used illness as his excuse to leave his bride on his wedding night, but it was better than the truth. "Although, to be honest, she was always—" he searched for a word.

"Wild?"

"Spirited. Before the . . . illness." He wouldn't tell her the truth. Wouldn't have her pity his sister. "She is not so touched as it might seem, on first glance."

"No?"

"No." He said it firmly, as if he could make his words the truth by uttering them without doubt. "But, as I said, that is not your concern."

She stared at him for longer than was comfortable, a blush slowly working up her neck and into her cheeks. Then she lifted her chin stubbornly and he braced himself for what she had to say next. "Perhaps it is my concern."

Women. Always trying to fix what could never be fixed. "She is my sister. You will not be my wife for much longer. She is my concern, not yours."

"If she is touched, due to some bad blood in your family, I may need to know."

"There is no bad blood. She is not touched." He

forced himself to calm. "Why would that matter to you? You will be done with us when you leave here."

Sean had the strongest urge to reach over and clap his hand on her mouth as she hesitated, and then plunged forward with her request. "Earlier you asked me what I wanted to allow you a divorce without protest."

"I did." He was wary. "But I thought you had no need of incentive after our last conversation."

"So I thought at the time." She could not meet his eyes and lowered her gaze to the accounting book spread out in front of him. "But I may have spoken too hastily, out of anger and hurt pride."

Spoken too hastily? That did not bode well. He closed his eyes, feeling as if she would next draw out a sword and run him through. What would she ask of him? What could she ask of him? He had nothing to give. "What would you like me to do for you to ease your pride?"

She did not answer him directly. "I have been thinking about that very thing. And I have an answer for you. Will you agree?"

Still she did not get to the heart of the matter. How awful was her request that she could not simply blurt it out and must torture him with wondering? "Am I bargaining with the devil, then? Do I not get to know what I'm agreeing to before I say yes?"

She sucked in a breath, whether to gain courage or because she had been holding her breath he could not guess. "No. I want you to agree first."

He opened his eyes to find that she had plucked up the courage to meet his gaze again. "I will not agree to remain married."

She sat back with a look of surprise. "Of course

not. I will ask nothing that will prevent you from obtaining your divorce. In fact, it may even make it easier."

"What is it?" She was tormenting him. Teasing him. Did she truly have a proposition, or was she trying to find out more of what he was up to so that she could go running to the authorities in revenge for the divorce?

"You doubt that I am capable of proving my innocence and preventing the divorce, do you not?"

"It has been five years." He smiled, although he definitely didn't like where she was heading with all her questions. "And you are an attractive woman."

She smiled a bit bleakly. "Forgive me if I choose not to believe those words from you. After all, you have had no trouble avoiding me—even when you were in my bed."

"Those in England—"

Interrupting, she said, "You may not care whether or not I have been faithful." She leaned forward and took a deep breath, as if she were about to dip her head under water. "But you can see for yourself if you agree to meet my terms."

He had a horrible feeling that he knew what she was about to propose but he did not know how to prevent her, only to delay. "Terms?"

Her cheeks colored slightly and he could sense her agitation, but her voice was firm and unhesitant. "I understand what has happened, whether you choose to tell me the truth or not. You enjoyed the chase, but had not considered the ramifications if you should win me."

"You don't understand—" he found his own face warming with a flush. He had forgotten how straight to the heart she aimed her words.

She waved a hand impatiently, dismissing his

protest. "Once having done so, you no longer wanted me. The game was all."

"Not so." He spoke honestly, but at her frank stare of disbelief he realized how absurd the protest sounded in the face of his actions. "I told you I never thought of you as the enemy." Just as someone who could never be an ally. But he did not want to explain that to her. He'd have to tell her too much, more than would be good for her to know—or for him either.

She paused a moment, in consideration of his words. He braced himself for the question he could see forming on her lips. It didn't help that she was calm when she asked, "Then why did you not send for me after a month—a year—five?" She sighed, almost inaudibly. "And why would you divorce me for a lie that can be easily proven to be a lie?"

He found himself asking her the question he should have asked her years ago. "Would you have wanted to live here?"

There was a momentary flicker of dismay in her eye, but she did not miss the obvious flaw in his argument. "You could have let me prove my fortitude—or lack of it."

"I did dream of inviting you here, once." It had been a particularly weak moment just six months after he had come back home. He had never told anyone that secret, but somehow it seemed right to tell her now. The vulnerability that flashed across her face made him wish to call the words back. "But then I'd wake to the news of another starving child dead in the night."

No longer looking vulnerable, she argued angrily, "I could have helped."

"Fair enough." He felt unutterably tired and

wished that he'd had the sense to have this conversation with her long ago. Or, perhaps, to foresee the insurmountable problem and refuse to consider an English bride, dowry or not. "But I didn't want your help. And I don't want it now."

A flush rose up her neck and he knew that he'd angered her. Bitterly, she said, "Although, of course, the money for marrying me was good enough for you to spend?"

He thought of the open way men in London ranked the unmarried young ladies by the size of their dowries, their appetites and their father's estates and could not muster a whiff of guilt at being yet another such. "Is that not the truth for all of us?"

He refused to feel guilt for his actions, though he would change them in a second if he had the power to turn back time. He hadn't beaten her, only abandoned her. And she'd done well enough on her own.

"I dare not say. But I will not argue that it is all for you. Which is why I have come to offer you terms."

Terms? She wanted to bargain? With what? "I will agree to no terms I have not heard beforehand. I'm not a fool, Katie, believe it or no." He was brusque, determined to get her to spill her request so that he could refuse it.

"I want . . ." She struggled to get the words out, and finally whispered, "I want you to come to my bed."

He felt as if she'd punched him squarely in the belly. The idea was absurd; he knew it even as he wished to agree.

She watched him, the panic in her expression dissipating into surety. He thought of delaying further by pretending to misunderstand what she meant, but could see no purpose. If she'd said it, no matter how timidly, she would repeat it. "Why would you want such a fool thing as to sleep with the man who has sued to put aside your marriage?"

"I want a child."

She wanted him to father a child? His mind buzzed with the implications. He thought she only wanted— He had not expected such a thing. Although a moment's thought told him he should have. Impossible. "Ask my cousin, then. No doubt he'll gladly oblige."

Her cheeks burned brightly with humiliation at his rejection. But still she persisted with stubborn insistence. "You are my husband."

He shook his head, a wealth of sadness for what might have been but could not be. "I will not be for much longer. I suggest you ask your next husband."

He'd touched a sore point with her, he could tell by the way she flinched at the word 'husband' and closed her eyes for a moment before she said without a shred of doubt, "I'll not be fool enough to marry again."

"The duke—"

"Will not force me to marry. There is no need." There was a bleak look in her eye that made him realize she had already been living the life of a spinster because of his abandonment.

"You don't know what you're asking . . ." He couldn't do it. "You'll find someone else. You're a loving woman."

"No." She shook her head. "It has to be you. If the thought of being in my bed is so distasteful to you, I will ask for only one night. Surely you could bring yourself to give me that little?"

One night. He found himself surprisingly tempted by the idea. He would not have to worry about

Kate publicly humiliating herself or him if he ensured that she was no longer a virgin. But the momentary urge was swamped by common sense as he thought of the inevitable consequences. "Once is only likely to break your heart, not get you with child."

She blinked twice, thinking about what he had said. She nodded. "Then I ask you to share my bed until I sail in a month—no more. If it does not happen, then providence wills that I not be a mother."

He had no intention of agreeing, but he could see she had no intention of accepting no for an answer. So he quickly offered a new deal—one which would give him time to find a way out completely. "First, you must prove your fortitude. If you can stay a fortnight, then I'll oblige your request every night for another—whether you will conceive or not."

"Prove my fortitude?" She turned away from him and he thought she might refuse his offer. But she turned back and met his eye as she said with complete certainty, "I accept."

"You should be certain of this, lass. No matter how you feel, you may find another man worthy to be your husband."

"I do not want one." She shook her head firmly.

"It is natural that you feel that way now, considering our situation. But—"

She frowned. "Do you intend to go back on your word yet again, my lord?"

"No." He wouldn't go back on his word. But he would see that she did not stay the two weeks they had agreed upon.

"Good." She met his gaze squarely. "I will stay here, for two weeks as your guest, then two weeks as your wife. In all ways. At the end of that time I will leave and you will divorce me."

"Agreed." He had to find a way to convince her to back out of the idea within the next two weeks. First, he would make her see the illogical emotion underlying her request. "I hope this satisfies your urge for revenge."

As he had suspected, she did not like the sound of that word. "Not revenge only. As I said, I have no intention of ever marrying again. This is my only opportunity to have a child."

"And if, as is likely, you find a man to change your mind, have you thought of the consequences of that? Another man might mind raising my child."

Her lips twisted in a grimace. "How could I trust another man when I have been so thoroughly fooled by you? No. I want one thing from you—a child. Two weeks should ensure that."

They both knew better than that. Two weeks was no better than flipping a coin into the River Liffey and hoping it ended up heads at the mouth of the river. "And if it does not?"

"Then I will consider that you have kept your bargain and I am not meant to be a mother."

Not meant to be a mother. He hoped she didn't mean it. He hoped she would marry again and have a family. It didn't matter that the image of her with another man, smiling children around them, curled his hands into fists. He'd forced himself to forget all the things he'd dreamed of having with her. And now she was asking him to live his dreams for a fortnight and then lose it all. Again. Impossible.

Kate woke late in the morning to the bleating of goats, which did not much improve her mood. She'd gotten what she wanted, so why did she wish she hadn't? Perhaps it was her poor night's sleep,

caused by the pelting of ice against the window
and moaning of the wind. Though it had sounded
very much like a woman laboring to give birth, she
would not be taken in by Sean's claim of a ghostly
Lady Dilys. She would not.

He'd agreed. He hadn't wanted to, and she didn't
trust that he wouldn't find some way to wiggle out
of the bargain in a fortnight. Still, he'd agreed,
and she intended to see that he kept his word.
This time.

She lifted the heavy curtains away from the window and glanced outside. The fog had cleared at
last, but she would not be traveling. She washed
quickly, dressed and moved the chair from in front
of the door. Two weeks to prove her fortitude. She
must find something useful to do. But what might
that be?

Outside, in the hallway, she found a hod full of
dense squares of peat moss that burned pungently
in most of the grates. Next to it was a linen-
wrapped bundle that proved to be a small loaf of
very good bread. Breakfast, no doubt. Sarah must
have found the door blocked by the chair and
gone away to let her sleep.

Ignoring the temptation to turn back to her
room, close and bar the door, and simply wish herself back to London, Kate stepped out into the
hallway, exploring as she munched on the dense,
sweet bread. Some of the Christmas greenery had
been removed, but not all.

The kitchen was empty—even Sarah seemed to
have disappeared. Where could they all be? She
wandered about the seemingly empty abbey, man-
aging to see a good portion before Sean suddenly
appeared before her.

To her amazement, he seemed chastened and
less sure of himself when he greeted her. "Good

morning, lass. I hope Lady Dilys didn't keep you tossing in your bed."

"Not at all. I slept well knowing the night was fit for neither man nor beast and so there would be no reason for anyone to venture out."

Kate had no intention of letting him know how nervous she was when she thought of what might happen between them in a fortnight. He'd surely try to use it to coerce her to change her mind. Some things were best not for a man to ever know.

No, she decided, she'd take her cue from Maeve and demand her due without quarter. "I heard nothing but the sighing of the wind and slept like a babe."

He laughed. "As I recall from Bridget's infancy, that often involves a great deal of fuss and interruption."

Surely he didn't expect to convince her a child was too much trouble? She knew well enough what was involved in being a mother. She decided not to respond. "I suppose you must be off about your business. Tell me, please, how I may make myself useful while I am here?"

"Useful?" His eyes grew wintry. "Do you mean toss your coins to the poor starving lot of useless Irishmen?"

So, he was not any more amenable than he had been last night. She decided to ignore his jibes. "As you took them all when you married me, that would be quite impossible. I meant something more practical—have you a greenhouse to start your plantings early? Linens I could mend? A dragon I could slay?"

He crossed his arms, obviously unhappy at the direction of their conversation. "Sadly, I am the only dragon around here and I don't think anyone would take kindly to you slaying me. Not to mention that if you slay me while I've yet to come to your bed, you'll have no chance at the child you want me to get upon you, now will you?"

There was no shame in the man. None at all. "Well? Have you work for me or not?"

"None."

Irritated beyond measure, she said sharply, "Fine, then I shall find one of the locals to lead me to the Blarney Stone. I've an urge to kiss it and see if I can sharpen this tongue of mine further so that it is a better match for yours."

He grumbled as he gazed at her unhappily. "It's not in need of sharpening, in my humble opinion."

He thought she had been too sharp with him? "Then perhaps it wants gilding." She didn't think she'd been nearly sharp enough.

"As you wish." He shrugged as if he were indifferent, but she saw the set of his jaw and knew he was not. "But I'll take you to kiss the stone myself. It's not a journey to be made by the fainthearted."

Was that the reason he had left her in London? "Do you think me fainthearted?"

"Your heart is as stout as they come, Katie. If I hadn't known that five years ago, I'd know it now, wouldn't I? Haven't you traveled all the way here, come toe to toe with me and convinced me to bow to your will?"

"Not yet." She felt herself blush and hoped he didn't realize how apprehensive she was about their bargain.

Without warning, he moved close and bent to whisper in her ear, "Are you so impatient that you can't wait?"

She stood, feeling the heat that came from his powerful body. He wasn't touching her, and yet she felt him so close that she knew if she swayed an inch, they would touch. She wanted to sway that inch. "Impatient, or simply practical?"

For a moment she thought that he would close the gap between them and take her in his arms.

Before he could do so, though, Bridget entered the room without knocking and Sean pushed Kate away so quickly it was a miracle that she did not stumble.

There was an observant quality to the girl's gaze that made Kate blush. She turned to her brother and asked bluntly, "Were you about to kiss her?" She did not seem to realize the question was unconscionably rude—nor did Sean seem in any hurry to correct her.

"I did not care for what she was saying." He shrugged. "It seemed the quickest way to stop her words."

Bridget glanced at Kate and then back at Sean. "You should kiss her. I'll go."

She turned to leave, but Sean moved forward and caught hold of her wrist. "Wait."

Bridget paled and grew still.

Sean dropped her wrist quickly. "I'm sorry, colleen. I did not mean—" He interrupted himself with a glance at Kate. "Kate wishes to see the castle. I thought you might show it to her."

Bridget smiled, as if her panic of a moment before had never happened. "The Stone must be hungry for the touch of her lips, as you are. Should I take her there?"

He shook his head. "Just show her the castle for today. It is too icy to kiss the Stone safely today."

Bridget laughed, and glanced back at Kate. "He doesn't trust me, I'm afraid. I'm touched in the head, you know."

"Indeed." Kate could believe it, given the uncanny stare from those huge green eyes. "Has your brother never told you it was rude to stare?"

"He has. But I can't help it." The girl laughed softly, an unbearably beautiful musical sound. "My eyes can suck the soul out of you, you know."

"They most certainly cannot." Kate felt like a governess faced with a wild child. Unconsciously she stiffened her spine and pressed her lips together.

The child only laughed again. "She's for you, Sean. I can see it in her eyes. You can't let her go away. It'll be her undoing—and all the McCarthys' as well."

"What?" Kate dredged up anger to replace the cold fear that seemed to flow like molasses through her and settle in her stomach. As she contemplated what to say, the maid assigned to follow Bridget arrived, out of breath, her cheeks red and her hair mussed—no doubt from running after her mistress.

Kate pulled her gaze away from the child's mesmerizing one with difficulty to stare at Sean. "Have you never considered that she needs a stern governess and not a little bit of a maid to follow her about?"

"I'm not made for walls to hold," Bridget said softly. "Nor for any man, either." Her mouth turned down, and her eyes closed, as if to hold back tears. In an instant, however, she smiled widely and Kate was left to wonder if she had imagined the sadness. "But you are meant for my brother to hold."

He did not grin. In fact, his expression was grim for a moment before he turned an indulgent smile on his sister. "You've spooked my wife, Bridget. Shame on you."

The child laughed again. "Listen to me, Sean. She is for you."

Kate saw the tension that gripped them all—the maid, the girl and Sean. Nothing was right here. She had a sudden suspicion that, if she found out more, she might finally understand why Sean had never returned to her. Why he was willing to divorce her.

Chapter 12

Sean stared at his sister in dismay. The men who had taken her five years ago had not bothered to return her with all her mind. The folk at the abbey were convinced that she had the second sight. He preferred they think that than what he thought—that his sister had had her mind stolen by her abductors and she would not be right ever again, no matter what he did.

Now that he had agreed to let her stay, he must explain to Kate, who looked as pale as if Lady Dilys had appeared to ask her to take tea in the closest fairy fort. But he would not do so in front of Bridget. He touched her arm fleetingly to get her attention. "My wife will not be here long, Bridget. She belongs in England."

"She belongs here—"

"After you have shown her the castle," he said, desperately intent upon distracting her from her foolish pronouncements. "She wishes to be of help. Have you anything she can do?"

"She can stave off the troubles." The impish smile didn't fool him. His sister was serious.

"Bridget."

"You never listen to the fairies anymore, Sean. Do you want to anger them?"

"Never mind." He'd changed his mind, seeing Kate's keen gaze focused on his sister. If he found enough unpleasant chores for her, no doubt he'd serve his purpose of running her off. "Something always needs doing around here."

"True enough," Bridget said, changing the subject to Sean's relief. She turned to Kate and smiled. "Can you build a castle?"

"Build a castle?" Kate laughed. "I've never tried, but I hardly think so."

Bridget studied her carefully for a second and then nodded decisively. "No. But you'll have a fine babe in ten months' time. It will be a bit of hardship getting the boy out, I'm afraid. But you'll do fine. As long as you stay here where we can protect you."

There was a momentary shocked silence. Sean opened his mouth to countermand his request for his sister to show Kate around—it was much too dangerous.

"I hope to have a daughter," Kate answered sharply, before he could speak. She glared at him as if she held him to blame for Bridget's foolish words.

"Don't be silly. The McCarthys run to boys. Why, I'm practically a boy myself. I hunt. I ride. I fight."

"Fight? Your brother lets you fight?" Kate said faintly, as she glanced at him as if she thought he had gone mad himself.

He defended his actions, although she had no business calling him to account. She and her sisters were well versed in pistols and swordplay. "It seemed wise at the time to teach her to fight with a sword. I would expect you to understand—don't you have a set of blades of your own?"

"I do," Kate admitted grudgingly.

"An opponent of worth?" Bridget clapped her hands in delight and came forward to grasp Kate's hands in her own. "Yes. Come. Let us explore the castle. And after you can come have a match with me. I've been forced to fight boys too afraid to hurt the sister of the McCarthy and men who wouldn't dare use the sword against me."

Kate looked less than willing for a moment, and he had some hope she would refuse and choose to spend her time in her own room, out of trouble. But then she smiled. "I've practiced with my sisters and I'm not afraid to strike hard and fast."

"Excellent." Bridget nodded, her eyes glowing with anticipation. "I need a good opponent. I want to be skilled enough to kill, if needed."

Kate's smile disappeared, and Sean wished he had not suggested they spend the afternoon together. "Kill? I don't think—"

"Bridget wouldn't hurt anyone. She's gentle as a lamb." He frowned at his sister.

She made a face at him, but then relented. "Not you, at least. Unless you hurt Sean."

"Very well, then." Kate glanced at him and he knew she'd have more to say about his sister's care later. "I have no intention of hurting your brother."

"Then we will get along well enough." Bridget smiled. "Come, I will take you to meet the fairies, if you beat me at swordplay."

Sean wished he knew what thoughts floated behind the green of his sister's eyes. Was he making a mistake, allowing them to go off together? He did not believe Bridget would hurt Kate. But she might tell her more than he wished his inconvenient wife to know about his business—especially about the business they got up to at night. She'd already seen a little of what they did. Would she question Bridget? Would the girl answer her questions?

The day was cool and breezy, the sun pale and offering little warmth, but still welcome after the days of fog and ice. The ruins of Castle Blarney seemed to be picked out by the sun for special favor as they rode up. The crumbling walls gleamed gold in places.

A dog raced out to greet Bridget, nipping at the heels of her mount in familiar play. Bridget dismounted with a swift grace that surprised Kate. Unafraid of the chocolate-brown beast, the girl crouched and hugged and patted the dog. "Teagan. Good girl. Did you miss me? I have been away overlong."

The dog whined and barked her welcome, then threw Kate a curious glance, almost as if she were waiting for an introduction. Bridget said softly, "Sean has taken a wife, girl. Meet Lady Blarney."

Kate winced at the unfamiliar name and dismounted as well. "Do you come here often, then?"

"I belong here. The fairies are here. You will see if you are lucky. Don't tell Sean, though."

"Why not?"

Bridget didn't answer. "I like it here. The fairies are fond of the Stone, you know. This is one of their favorite places."

"Is it?" Kate didn't know whether to encourage her fantasies, or point out that the fairies were only imaginary creatures. "When can I meet them?"

"Not in broad daylight." The girl giggled as if she'd asked a foolish question. "You must come at dawn, or at dusk if you want to meet the fairies."

Kate decided she would learn more if she pretended to believe than she would if she argued the existence of the little folk. "Has Sean met the fairies?"

"He doesn't believe in them anymore." Bridget frowned. "They're mad at him, too."

"Why are they mad at him?"

"Because he went away."

Kate suspected the fairies were not the only ones angry at Sean for going away. "Did he not explain he had a duty to go away? He has a title, with duties and responsibilities in London."

"Lord Blarney." Bridget nodded, unconvinced. "It is a title that means nothing to the fairies. They were unhappy when he was gone."

Kate prodded gently. "I expect you were unhappy as well."

"I'm glad he's home." Bridget turned on her, her gaze fierce. "I hope you stay. I would like a sister."

Kate wondered what it would have been like to have only had Valentine, instead of being surrounded by sisters. But it didn't matter what Bridget desired. "Your brother doesn't want me—"

Bridget cocked one eyebrow as if to ask why that should matter. "Stay anyway."

Kate shook her head and sighed. She would never understand this family, no matter how she tried. "I don't see how—"

Bridget tied up her horse with a swift movement. "If you go, he'll follow. The fairies say so." Without warning, she turned and began to run toward the ruins. Teagan followed eagerly at her heels.

"I'm quite sure the fairies are completely wrong on that account," Kate said sharply, unsure whether Bridget heard her or not, although the dog turned and barked once sharply back at Kate as if in answer.

They wandered the ruins, finally settling to a

cold lunch in the lee of a large tree. Bridget pointed
out the Blarney Stone, up above the trees. "It is no
longer in our family, but it is still in our hearts."

"My goodness." Kate shaded her eyes with her
hand and squinted up. "People actually lean out to
kiss that?" She reconsidered her own desire to do
so. "One could get killed."

Bridget tossed a piece of cheese to Teagan, and
the dog snapped it up with a greedy gulp. "And have.
But you won't. Sean will hold you fast. If you stay."

"That, I'm afraid," Kate said as she stood and
brushed off her skirts, "is entirely up to your
brother." She looked about her, at the crumbling
ruin of a castle that hadn't been occupied for
nearly two hundred years and yet still protected a
stone that commanded the love and respect of
people from far away.

Her own sister Hero had traveled here with her
husband and both of them had kissed the stone.
But then, they believed that the legendary King
Arthur was more than a myth, too. Kate herself was
entirely more practical than that. If Sean had another change of heart and asked her to stay here
with him, would she?

"Are you ready to return—" she began to ask
Bridget, but as she glanced at the child, she
stopped. The girl sat frozen, staring into the distance.

Kate turned to look in the direction of the girl's
gaze and saw a mounted figure stopped some distance away. "Who is that?"

"Jamie Jeffreys. The son of the owner of this castle." The girl scrambled up.

"Will he be unhappy that we are here?" It
seemed unlikely; the castle was a popular site for
tourist visits. But she sensed a tension in Bridget
that had not been there before she spied the man.

"Jamie knows I belong here. He'll never turn me off."

Kate wondered if she should point out that Bridget should not be using the Christian name of a man unrelated to her. "Should we greet him?"

"No." Bridget said. "The fairies are mad at him, just like they're mad at Sean."

There was an agitation that was personal, not fairy-caused, Kate suspected, and prodded cautiously, "Are you mad at Jamie, too?"

"No. I forgave him long ago."

Forgave him? For what? "Then why haven't the fairies forgiven him?"

"Because he hasn't asked them to."

"But he did ask you?" Kate wondered if Sean was aware of this relationship. It did not seem wise to encourage it, even though the two seemed to avoid getting close to each other.

"No. Jamie doesn't like me like this." Bridget patted her own face absently as she spoke. "He'd rather someone like you—who is not like this."

"Like this?"

"Fey." She said it bluntly, but softly, as if she were afraid to speak more loudly lest her gift be stolen from her. "He liked me the way I was before."

"Before your illness, you mean?"

Bridget blinked several times, staring at Kate as if she did not understand what she had said. Then she bent her head and turned away from the mounted figure in the distance to whisper quickly, "Before the bad thing happened and the fairies took me for their own to keep me safe."

Kate didn't know what to say, what to ask. But it didn't matter, because Bridget turned and began to run to where they had left their own mounts. Her hair streamed about her loose and free, and the mounted figure did not move, watching until Bridget leaped upon her horse and began to ride away.

Teagan did not follow Bridget this time. Her job was to guard the castle, Bridget had said, and obviously she took the job seriously. She accompanied Kate to her horse, the animals touched snouts and then Teagan loped back to the castle, leaving Kate to follow Bridget back to the abbey.

As it turned out, Bridget was a very good swordswoman. Kate found herself in a corner with a blade at her throat in short order. "I give. You're better than my sister Rosaline."

The girl moved back to salute her. "You're better than you seemed here. Your skirts got in the way, even though you tied them up."

Kate nodded, releasing them. "I have a pair of leather breeches at home, but I didn't think to bring them since I am to be here only a short time."

As if it would require a wave of her hand, the girl said simply, "Send for them."

She shook her head. "I've already booked passage home, Bridget."

The girl's gaze grew distant, and for a moment Kate thought she would faint. But then she shook herself, and said, "The *Daisy's Pride*. The ship will go under, but you won't be aboard."

"How did you—?" For a moment Kate almost believed her. The confidence with which the girl stated her nonsense was chilling. But then she remembered how the girl flitted above and below stairs at will. Undoubtedly she had heard Sarah mention the name of the ship. "Where will I be then? In your brother's welcoming arms?"

Perhaps she should not have let herself speak

such a cynical question aloud, but the girl's answer was shockingly brutal. "Lying cold and alone. But not here."

That was not the expected answer, considering the girl had asked her more than once to defy Sean and stay in Ireland. For a moment Kate felt the anger bubble up inside her, but the innocence shining from the green eyes was too much for her to disbelieve.

Bridget had not meant her words to hurt Kate. The girl was mad, and perhaps should be locked up, but that was for Sean to deal with. Not that it seemed he had done so. He'd claimed to have returned because Bridget was ill. Was her odd manner a result of her illness? And what had he done to help his sister in the five years since he'd left Kate?

Five years. The same length of time she and Sean had been married. Was this the reason his letters had been evasive and secretive? She supposed one way to find out would be to ask him. Would he tell her?

Perhaps it was time to find out what, exactly, they were up to.

She retired early from dinner, too nervous that Sean might see what she intended in one careless sweep of his eyes. How long would it take them? Would they even go? She didn't care. If they went, so would she. She settled down, prepared to wait all night if need be.

The scraping and bumping sound she had been listening for all night finally sounded, and Kate nearly leaped from the chair in which she was sitting. They were going out again tonight.

She stood up and pulled on her leather riding gloves. She'd already put ash on her face and dressed in dark clothing. Would her disguise work? Now, at the critical juncture, she wasn't certain she had taken enough precautions.

She took a deep breath to calm the knot in her stomach and quickly reassured herself she was doing the right thing. After all, she didn't recognize herself in the wavy-looking glass that hung on the wall.

Still, she bent and scraped more ash from the grate to streak her face. She did not want to be caught. And she did not want to be the reason that Sean or Bridget were caught, either.

She slipped into her black cloak, pulling up the hood to hide her hair and shadow her face even further before she slipped out the door and down the stairs.

His conversation with Kate roiling in his mind, Sean tried to dissuade his sister from accompanying them tonight. "Perhaps it would be best if you stayed home tonight, Bridget."

Dressed as a boy in dark clothes and with streaks of ash on her cheeks, she seemed even more vulnerable than usual to him. Judging by the fervent light in her eye, however, she did not feel vulnerable at all. "I'm your luck, Sean. I have to go."

"Just this one night," he cajoled her.

She shook her head stubbornly, as he had known she would. "The fairies are mad at you and I have to protect you from them."

Niall whispered, "Yes, Sean. You are not in favor with the fairies and we need all the luck we can get this night."

Sean frowned at his cousin, annoyed that he encouraged Bridget in this. "It is a simple task we have. We can do with one less. And we don't even need the fairies tonight."

"Hush, Sean. They'll hear you." Bridget gasped as if he had blasphemed.

"I'm sorry, colleen," he apologized, though he thought her fancy foolish. "I just want to see you safe."

"Can you not make up to the fairies then? I would trust them to watch over you without me if you only said you were sorry you ever doubted them."

"I'm sorry," he said. But they had had this argument before, and he knew that she wanted more than that from him. More than he could give.

Bridget said sadly, "If I can tell that you don't mean it, so can the fairies, Sean."

Niall whispered impatiently, "Dawn will be upon us if you don't stop arguing with the girl, Sean. She will come with us, as always." Niall hugged his cousin fleetingly. "She is our luck, after all."

Connor said gruffly, "This is not the time for argument, although I would not mind knowing that Bridget rested safely at home while we were out."

Sean turned his head toward an unexpected sound, but saw nothing out of the ordinary. He took a deep breath. "Perhaps we'd all be better staying home until my wife has gone home."

"As long as she stays in her room, all will be right."

Sean had told no one that Kate had seen them the first night. He suspected Connor would renew his arguments that they should keep Kate in Ireland and use her to leverage more ransom from the duke. Only this time his uncle wouldn't be willing to ever let Kate go home.

"Come. It is time." They moved out to the horses, whose hooves had been muffled with canvas, and took to the road as stealthily as possible.

Sean was not too concerned they would be discovered. They had been doing this for a long time, and they were all very good at it.

Within ten minutes they had reached the storage shed and they swiftly loaded each horse's panniers until they bulged. Once a horse's panniers were filled, the rider led the beast away. By morning the panniers would be empty and hearths around the area would boast the smell of roasting potatoes as hungry bellies were filled once again.

When they still had three horses to load, one of his men came to warn him. "We're being watched."

"Continue as if we're alone." Sean moved into position, listening and searching for signs of who might have stumbled upon them and what kind of trouble they were in. If it was one of the many Irish people he'd fed, he didn't expect trouble. If, however, it was the sheriff, or one of his men . . .

He came back to the man who had warned him of the watcher. "Good work. I'll take care of it."

"Friend or foe?" The man asked, as he prepared to lead his horse away. They were all ready to cut the panniers and fly if they were discovered. But to waste food was sin and that they preferred to avoid.

"Friend," Sean lied. Or was it a lie? He didn't know. But he'd find out as soon as everyone was safely gone.

It wasn't until his horse, the last to be filled, had been tied to a bush that he was ready to deal with the watcher. Kate. What had she intended, following them? Watching them? She was not much of a spy, and for that he found himself grateful.

She was not far into the brush, a tactical error, and one that might have gotten her killed on another night. Fortunately for her, he had heard the distinctive wheeze of a horse, and he knew it wasn't a mount one of his men had been using. It was, however, one of his horses.

He came up behind her, glad that she didn't have any suspicion that he knew she was here, until he realized that anyone could have sneaked up on her, just as he had. That unwelcome realization flooded through him in a heated fury, just as he reached for her arm.

He was angry enough to snatch her off the horse and pull her to the ground, holding her fiercely struggling form down without saying a word. He wanted her to remember the feeling of helplessness before she knew who had captured her. Knew she was safe. If she did. "Hold still."

Abruptly, she stopped struggling. "Sean?"

He didn't answer. Because he wanted to teach her a lesson. And because he didn't want to lose the feeling of her body pressed against his a moment sooner than need be.

"I know it's you, Sean," she said. The trembling breathlessness in her voice was sweet to his ears. "No one else smells like you."

Her body lay limp as if all the fight had gone out of her. But wouldn't he be a fool to believe that? He leaned down to whisper in her ear, "Are you saying I stink?"

"I'm saying I know your scent." She turned her mouth to his ear, miscalculating so that her lips brushed his neck, sending an unwelcome jolt of desire through him. "I think I would know it anywhere."

He knew he should move away, but he didn't. "You're lucky I am the one who found you or you might not like what happened next." He thought of Kate hurt the way Bridget had been. Would she have lost her wits, too?

She laughed, the movement of her chest vibrating pleasantly against him in all the right places. "Of anyone, you're the one I can most trust my virtue with. You need a fortnight to work up the courage to sleep with me."

He fought the urge to prove her wrong, here and now. "Courage is not what it takes, my lady."

"No?" Deliberately now, as if his body had transmitted his desire to her, she moved under him, her lips brushing his neck, his jaw, his chin.

"No. I would need to be in the throes of absolute recklessness to breach your maidenhead." And he wasn't. Yet.

"My—" She stilled beneath him. "Does that mean you no longer think that Niall and I—"

He didn't want to answer her questions. Didn't want to talk, here in the dark, when he still had work to do and every moment he lingered put his life—and hers—at risk. He kissed her.

She responded at first, and then fought against his kiss, rolling her head away from him. "What are you doing?"

"Feeling reckless." He kissed her again, more deeply, and then rolled away from her before the reckless urge overtook him completely. He had work yet to do. He stood up and reached down to pull her up as well.

"Has your courage deserted you?" He could hear her confusion. He could feel it in the tension vibrating through her. He supposed it wasn't all bad; perhaps instead of driving her back to London, he'd drive her mad instead.

"We can't linger here much longer. I do not relish being shot tonight, even if you are of two minds." He reached a finger out to rub a smudge of ash from her cheek. "Or should I leave you for the watch to find?"

Chapter 13

He had hoped his words would chasten her. But she was not the least bit apologetic. "I wanted to know what you were doing, so I followed you."

"And what did you find out?" Was she a spy? He didn't think so. Just curious—much too curious for her own good.

She glanced around the area. "That you have an unnatural fondness for potatoes."

He found himself justifying what they had done. Wanting her to understand, even if she didn't approve. "These were meant to go out of the country because they'll fetch a better price in another country than they will here, to be eaten by the folk who raised them. I am freeing them to feed the people who cultivated them."

She brushed leaves and twigs from her skirts. "So you stole them."

Steal. Was it that simple? He thought he had known the answer to that long ago. But he was not so certain now. "Not at all. I simply rescued them before the tragedy."

"What tragedy?"

"The fire." He took her by the hand and led her back to the nearly empty shed. She watched, puzzled, as he lit the oil-soaked rag lying by the door of the storage shed and tossed it in. Knowing how dry the timber was, he turned away, pulling her with him swiftly. The rush of the fire blazed up at his back.

She tried to stop. Tried to turn back. "It will burn down."

He pulled her away from the flames. "He'll build another. I'll even offer my shoulder to help, if necessary."

At the edge of the trees, he paused to watch his handiwork, the flames that danced in the night. In the light he could see her face. Somber. Staring at him as if she'd just realized that she'd never known him. "You could hang for this."

Knowing he shouldn't, he bent and kissed her lips, once, gently and without urgency. "But I won't." He felt, for a moment, as if he were saying farewell to all her illusions about him. It was past time, no matter how mournful.

She wasn't ready to accept what was, though. "If you won't see reason, perhaps I should speak to your uncle—"

No. That he could not have. He grasped her by the shoulders. "Don't."

"You cannot—"

Should he explain? Would it make her any more reasonable? "I will not be able to keep you safe if anyone else knows what you have found out."

The word itself caused her to still and glance at him warily. "Safe?"

He shrugged. She had chosen to follow him, to spy on him; she should understand the brutal reality of such a choice. She was not a girl having a lark. She was a woman interfering with desperate people. "As you say, a man could be hanged for the crime of feeding hungry bellies." He heard the harsh edge of his uncle's words ringing in his ears. What was he becoming?

But she could not see the truth of what he said; she saw only the lies she had read in English papers, heard from English lips. "Stealing? Arson?"

"So you see it." He was becoming a realist rather than the idealistic fool she had married. He had given up the dream of persuading English ears to hear reason. He would not waste breath on hers. "And there are some who'd cut your throat before they'd let you say a word of what you've seen."

"Don't be ridiculous." He saw the shine of uncertainty in her blue eyes. The longing that she would understand and accept his reasoning.

The certainty of his actions cut through him like a knife. It didn't matter if he wished to prolong her visit, keep her near him just a while longer for his own selfish pleasures. She had to go home. Now. It was much too dangerous to keep her close—for both of them. "I'm afraid our deal is off."

"What do you mean?"

"I can't promise you'll be alive in a month. I need to send you home to your family."

"Aren't you my family? Isn't this supposed to be home?"

"No."

"But—"

"You're the one who followed me. Do you fancy finding yourself lying in a pool of blood?" She winced and he wanted to comfort her. Comfort, however, would only get in the way of convincing her she must go home without delay.

*   *   *

He wanted to send her home? Now? She looked up into the darkness and shadow that was Sean. Had he been this man when she married him? What had changed him into a man without respect for laws? Without respect for others? "You can't keep flouting the laws. You will be arrested—your sister will have her future reduced to only the most unacceptable of options."

His jaw tightened and she saw her words had, at last, wounded him. "I will protect my sister with my life."

With his life. Though she knew he meant what he said, she also knew he was on the road to destruction, no matter how pure his intentions. "You may have to, if you continue this way. Do you know that she believes your fight with the English is a just one?"

He said stubbornly. "So do I."

He thought himself administering justice? "How can you think such nonsense when the laws are against you?"

"Your laws are against me." He was implacable. Her words did not penetrate his pride.

"They are your laws, too. You are an earl. The king himself awarded your title and gave you a voice that so many others might hear and listen to your wisdom." She pleaded with him in the dark night. The fire made a flickering glow that revealed his face to her and then concealed it before she could read his expression. "You have a seat in the House of Lords where you can make a permanent difference—one that will affect everyone in Ireland."

The flickering firelight revealed a bitter twist of his lips. "The king gave my father a title because he grew weary of my uncle continuously pleading with him. He cared only for his own peace, not peace for Ireland."

She had seen the devastation that poverty and disease had wrought and she understood his concerns. But how could he hope to fix the big problems with little fires and a small shifting of resources? "Nothing will ever get better this way."

"It has to." He was desperate. Need for her acceptance strained his voice. "I am committed."

Committed. He should be. "You will be dead within the year if you keep on this course."

"Do not underestimate me."

"You are a fool."

"And you are going home tomorrow."

She agreed. There was nothing she could do here. "Then you must make love to me tonight."

He drew in a breath and held it for a moment, before letting it go explosively. "You make a tempting offer, but I must regretfully decline."

"We made a bargain."

"Which you have broken by doing something so foolish as putting yourself in danger."

Damn the man. He would now claim *she* had broken their agreement? "Will you break your word to me yet again, then?"

Simon had not been certain whether or not Sean had known about the income from his roses. Though her husband had not touched those funds in the time since he'd left her, the divorce action would bring them to light. Even if he did not know now, he soon would. Perhaps she should take Simon's advice and use the funds to bargain. "Let me add to the pot, then. I will pay you for your services."

"Pay me to stud you? Have you hit your head?" His hands moved to her hand and gently began to probe. "I feel no knot, no swelling." He took her cheeks between his palms. "What, pray tell, do you think a fine stud like me would be worth to a lady like you?"

Hastily, she blurted, "A thousand pounds."

She had ten times that in the bank. She hoped he was not aware of that. She was encouraged when he dropped his hands from her face in shock. "The duke is a generous guardian."

She said, with half pride and half shame, for it was still a taint for someone of her class to earn money rather than simply have it dropped into her lap by a pair of doves, "My roses."

He frowned. "Your rose bushes grow money? Paper or coin, my lady?"

Was he teasing her? Now? She wished, briefly, that she could just take what she wanted. But she didn't know how. "The strains I cultivate are highly favored. People are willing to pay for them."

"And so you are willing to pay for me?" His face was in shadow, and she could not tell what he thought when he said, "I am overwhelmed with the honor. However, this is not the time for such a discussion."

He lifted her, easily, onto her horse's back. "I've hungry people left to feed tonight, my lady."

"I need your answer."

"You shall have it in the morning."

"Sean—"

"Go home, Kate. I have more work to do before I can contemplate playing the stud for you."

Kate rode toward home, grateful that he had been distracted enough not to insist on accompanying her back to the abbey. He wanted to send her home. He said it was dangerous for her here. She would be more content if she did not believe he was right. She was in a situation she did not understand, with a man she did not understand. But she wanted to. Even if doing so would not change his decision to divorce her.

The moon came out from behind the clouds, and she saw the silhouette of the ruins of the castle and stopped a moment. What more secrets did this family have? Would she understand if she uncovered them? Or would she be even more confused?

Her horse nickered and lowered its head to the ground, and Kate saw that the dog had come out to greet her. "Hello, Teagan girl, what are you doing out so late?"

The dog looked up at her and wagged its tail, as if to say, "The same as you, my lady, looking for intruders and satisfying my curiosity."

Kate hoped the dog's curious nature would not be as disappointed by what she found as Kate's had been tonight. Her own husband was so anxious to avoid her bed that he would break his word at the slightest provocation.

She dismounted, considering a midnight foray into the ruins. Perhaps she would climb up and kiss the Blarney Stone. Or perhaps not, considering that it was much too treacherous to do at night.

She patted the dog and found, as she wandered, that she had a companion for the evening. Somehow she found it comforting to have another friendly soul beside her in the darkness.

"So, girl—where are Bridget's fairies? Can you show me?"

The dog looked at her and wagged its tail again, but did not dash off in any particular direction, barking commands to follow to the fairy knoll. That, Kate supposed, would have been much too easy. Instead, the dog ambled at Kate's heels, content to see where Kate wished to go.

Teagan was a friendly dog—keeper of the castle, they called her. Short brown fur and warm brown eyes that expressed faith and confidence that Kate was no interloper. Where the dog would fiercely guard the walls from others, she allowed Kate passage for only the cost of a few kind words and a brisk pat on the head.

If only Sean was as trusting as this dog. Kate knew he was doing all he could to make her go home before his honor was on the line and he had to keep their bargain or break it. She hadn't considered herself unappealing, but these last six days had left her wondering if there was something wrong with her—or with him.

She'd done her best to show him she was sincere. To show him she was no condescending aristocratic fool who didn't see the devastation all around her. But he still wanted her gone.

To be truthful, she'd have gone home two days ago when the servants—if one could call them that—had decided to wash her linens with a few berries that had turned the white a pale, but decidedly blue hue.

Sarah had been white faced with shame that those she'd thought she'd befriended would do such a thing to her mistress, and she'd vowed never to let an Irish finger touch Kate's clothing again. But Kate had understood that she could not let Sarah take responsibility for this action. And that she could not let it stand without comment. So she had descended to the kitchens herself.

The servants had been shocked to see her, and even more shocked when she held up the clothing they had nearly ruined. They'd apologized, but the sincerely shining faces of regret hadn't con-

vinced her they hadn't meant to do exactly what
they did.

Without the smile that threatened to bloom on
her face, she asked them to supply several ingredients, a bowl and a spoon. They had done so, and
then stood open mouthed when she carefully
mixed together the ingredients to form a paste
that restored her clothing to its original color without harming the delicate fabric.

She knew they had been surprised when she
knew how to bleach them white again. And, as a
small measure of revenge, she had not revealed
how she had known such a thing—not even to
Sarah.

The advantage of the freedom she and Betsey
had had floating between the upstairs and the
downstairs worlds had taught her many skills the
sister of a duchess never had to learn. She knew
how to mend, get out stains, prepare a roast for
twenty guests and bite a wood sliver to keep her expression as impassive as that of a footman.

What those skills actually meant she couldn't
guess. But here, at least, she knew they had a purpose beyond her own small curiosity. And she enjoyed that status. All her life she'd been the youngest
sister, the one who was needed to be gotten out of
the way when important things were happening.

She could be useful here. And she would not let
Sean relegate her to youngest sister status again.
He might want to get rid of her, but there had to
be a way to change his mind. All she needed to do
was to get him to agree to have a wife. Easier said
than done.

The money she offered had not seemed to
tempt him. Perhaps, if she truly wished to stay, she
needed to find a way to impress Sean with her tal-

ents as easily as she'd impressed his servants. But what talents would a man like Sean admire most?

After a long night's work, Sean stumbled home tired to fall into his bed at dawn. But his sleep was fitful and fraught with unpleasant dreams.

He'd spent the night thinking of what she'd offered. To pay him for performing the duties of a husband. He didn't like the feeling. He never had, even when he'd been searching for a wife with a good-sized dowry and family connections.

He managed an hour's sleep before the door to his bedroom opened and she entered. "You're trying to force me to leave before you keep our bargain, but you won't."

He sat up in bed, trying to get his muddled mind to work right. Their bargain. Their devil's bargain. A child. Maybe. What was it she really wanted? Perhaps he should get her to admit it. "Why should I mind a roll with a pretty girl—unless you're expecting more from me?"

She shook her head, though there was a telltale blush on her cheeks that suggested she knew very well she wanted more from him. And knew very well that to say so would see that she had no hope, even of a child—not from him, anyway.

"Are you certain you don't want more? Perhaps for me to declare myself madly in love with you and carry you back to London, as I would have done five years ago?"

"I would not believe anything you said, Sean McCarthy, unless twelve others swore on their mothers' graves to the fact. I know better than that."

"Well, perhaps you are a bit wiser than you were

when I had to climb into your bed to get you to marry me." A flash of regret surged through him when his words sent her reeling, as if he'd struck her. "I'm sorry. I wish I hadn't been so foolish. I'd do anything to take it back and leave you unhurt. I promise I never meant to hurt you."

A cynical flash of disbelief narrowed her eyes. "Of course not, my lord. It was merely an accident."

"Exactly." He nodded. "Which is why I need to know if you expect more from me than just the hope of a child in nine months' time."

Stubborn to the end, she repeated firmly, "No more—I wouldn't want more from a man who would marry me and abandon me to my own devices for five years."

Her own devices. "I left you with your family—in comfort."

"How comfortable do you imagine it to have been to have to explain why my husband had yet to return year after year? To face those curious glances and sly smiles? To read your letters over and over and tell myself that you had not just married me for my money. That you would return as soon as you could. That you longed for me as I longed for you."

"More comfort than Kathleen Murphy, who lost her husband to the hangman for stealing a loaf of bread and left her penniless and on the streets with a child in her belly and nothing more than that loaf of bread in her hand." He had done nothing of the kind. She had had her family. Her roses, which had done very well for her. He felt the need to point that out to her in his own defense. "You were safe under the duke's roof."

"Very well, then. I'll accept that you had your reasons not to return to me. That your letters were not full of pretty lies." Her expression belied that she would accept any such thing easily. "But now you wish to divorce me and I ask only one small thing from you." She began to unfasten her gown, sitting on the bed beside him, turning her back to him. "Surely, you will not refuse me? Or send your cousin again, to perform your duties?"

Reluctantly, knowing he would likely regret this even more than he had expected, he moved to help her with the unfastening. Perhaps this would appease her. He knew it would not appease him, but he could live with his own hunger for her, forever if he had to.

She smelled, as always, of roses, and with her gown loose around her, the heat of her mingled with the rose scent until he no longer doubted he could satisfy her request. "I did not send him to seduce you, but to keep you safe since I could not."

She turned back to him, holding her gown so that it would not slip farther down her shoulders. "Why have you decided to divorce me now? I cannot have been a troublesome wife—unless you consider writing a letter every so often a bother?"

So. As he had suspected, she wanted more. "A letter every week can be considered a bother to a man as busy as I am."

She would not let go of her questions about his motives, though. "Do you want another, richer wife? Tell me the truth."

"I am not—" He bit off his words and shrugged. Perhaps that would be a reason she could accept. Certainly, he could not give her the truth. "The thought has occurred to me, I confess it."

She stood up abruptly and held her gown close to her. "The duke will see that you do not get one with a dowry."

"All this talk of another wife is fast reducing my ability to satisfy your request, Kate."

"Do you find me so unattractive that you wish I was some other woman—any other woman?"

He had hurt her. "I don't think it would be seemly to discuss my next wife's dowry with my present wife—especially considering what she is willing to pay for my stud service with the money she had made in her trade."

But he had stepped into a hornet's nest with his comment. She said furiously, "I did not want to be a burden upon the duke, seeing that my own husband was not willing to provide for me, so I decided to provide for myself. And I have done quite well at it."

How far would she take this absurdity? He decided to find out once and for all. "I'm relieved to hear that you will not be wholly dependent upon the duke's charity in the future when raising our—possible—son."

"I'd be better suited to raising a daughter—although I suppose I'll have to ask one of my sisters to deal with her presentation in society." Her voice dipped. "I don't suppose a divorced mother will do much for a young girl's reputation."

He sat up then, all temptation gone at the thought of Kate, trapped outside of society, raising a child and unable to marry again because of his foolish actions.

"I'm sorry, Kate. I just can't do it." He stood up, turning his back to her, and dressed quickly. He was tired, but his bed was not a safe place for him at this moment. He'd have to bed down in the stables later to get the rest he needed—he didn't think she'd venture out there.

He heard the rustle of clothing and hoped she was dressing, as well. But then her stubborn, proud voice said without a quiver, "Five thousand pounds."

He pretended to disbelieve her. He knew, to the

penny, how much her roses had added to her accounts. Or rather, to his accounts. "You have that?"

"I do, just barely."

He shook his head. She was a very good liar, surprisingly. Thank goodness he was well informed. "Ten thousand—five now and five when the child is born."

"You cannot be serious. That is an impossible sum." He waited for her to refuse; the sum would bankrupt her.

He smiled. "I am completely serious, I assure you, my lady."

"You prefer humiliation?"

"I don't believe you would do such a foolish thing—and if you did, I am certain the duke would take whatever measures necessary to protect you from ruining yourself."

"He is only a duke, not a god."

"Some in England would argue that as stridently as those here argue the *leith brogan* must be appeased." He paused for a moment to let that sink in, and then continued, "Will you make me write to him at once to tell him he must guard against letting you do anything so foolish as to present evidence of your virginity in public?"

She struggled with the fastenings of her gown. "He cannot prevent me."

He quickly helped her refasten her gown. "I believe that he not only can prevent you, he will do so—for your own good."

She shrugged away from the brush of his knuckles. "Are you concerned for my reputation—or yours?" She turned to face him, her expression bleak. "Either way, there is one remedy that makes this discussion unnecessary. But I suppose you find it beneath you to take your wife to bed."

There was a knock on the door and he prayed as

he called, "Enter," that the servant had not heard any last scrap of their conversation. Douglas was known in the kitchens for his love of gossip—and Sean knew the servants already whispered about the fact that he had put Kate in a bedroom so far from his.

His concerns about such trivial things flew away, however, when the man announced that the sheriff awaited him in the study. With a warning glance at Kate, he left her.

Chapter 14

Ten thousand pounds. He had somehow managed to ask for the sum that would leave her virtually penniless. Kate avoided Douglas's openly curious look to see her in Sean's bedroom. She fervently hoped that he had not heard the two of them arguing. Pretending that she did not wish to melt away in embarrassment, she asked, "What does the sheriff want, Douglas?"

"Same as always, my lady." Douglas winked at her. "But don't worry, he won't get it."

Kate was not so sure, and though she knew she would not be welcome, she hurried down to the study and stood at the door, not willing to enter and be told to leave. Not willing to trust that he would tell her truthfully what the sheriff wanted. She cautiously released the latch and pressed the door open an inch or two, grateful that his clandestine activities had made Sean oil the hinges on this door at least.

The sheriff was a large, florid man with a broad back. Fortunately, he stood at such an angle that she could see his profile well enough to see his expression. Not friendly. "Good day, my lord." He tugged at his forelock cursorily. "I have some questions for you."

"Sheriff." Sean did not look guilty of anything more heinous than having an extra dollop of cream on his scones this morning. Kate marveled at his ability to appear innocent even to her own eyes, even when she knew he was not.

"There's been another fire." The man seemed not to know whether to be deferential or belligerent and so chose to teeter back and forth between the two extremes. "Some folks say you might know something about it."

"Folks who work for Jeffreys, no doubt?" Sean stood up. He was taller than the sheriff, though not as broad. "Another fire, Sheriff? Were your men sleeping on watch again?"

The Sheriff turned crimson. "No, my lord. They were wide awake—but they had been distracted by a smaller fire set in an abandoned field and so were too late to apprehend the villains."

Sean pondered with a stern expression on his face, as if he were considering the implication of the sheriff's words. At last he looked up and said with the regal arrogance of the duke himself, "Still. That was closer than you have been, is it not? Things are looking up."

The sheriff nodded, apparently satisfied and even pleased by the not-quite compliment. "If you know anything, my lord—"

Sean shook his head. Kate would have thought the regret stamped on his features sincere—if she hadn't been there last night and seen him light the fire with his own hand. "I'm sorry to say I have no knowledge of the fire to offer you."

His initial belligerence evaporated, the sheriff became conciliatory. "I'm sure you understand, I needed to ask. Someone has been setting these fires and he must be caught."

"Indeed." Sean stood, as if to see the sheriff out personally. "Setting fire to full warehouses is an appalling waste of food. The cretins should be flogged."

"Hanged is more like it," the sheriff said irately, shifting his weight from foot to foot as though he were a child reciting a lesson.

"Well, it certainly can't be someone from around here, and I've seen no strangers—except perhaps my wife. But you could hardly suspect her. She has been here only one week, and she had been in England before that."

"Your wife?" The sheriff was openly curious.

Kate was about to back away from the door, when Sean said, without a trace of the anger she knew he must feel, "Come in, my dear. I'm certain the sheriff would be delighted to meet you."

Kate entered reluctantly, afraid the man would read the guilt on her face and arrest her and Sean on the spot.

He tugged his forelock again and mumbled, "My lady."

He seemed not to dare look directly at her. She bowed her head regally, sensing that would send the man scrambling from the room, and she was not disappointed.

He practically backed out of the room, waving away Sean's attempt to follow. "If you hear anything, my lord—"

Sean put his arm around her waist as if he were every bit the doting husband. "I'll let you know at once, Sheriff. It does no one any good to have food burned to cinders."

As soon as the door closed behind the sheriff, he dropped his arm from her and sat back down at his desk to stare at the books open in front of him. For a moment, with the room empty except for the two of them, she thought Sean had forgotten she existed. But then he looked up. "I would ask when you took up the habit of listening at doors, but as I recall, it began very young for you—and Betsey as well. I had thought you might have given it up by now."

She blushed, but fought the feeling that she was an errant child. "I merely wanted to remind you that, since you seem so bent on going to an early grave, you might want to take the chance to leave an heir."

"I thought you wanted a girl."

"What I want doesn't matter in such a thing. Or in anything concerning you, my lord, it seems. But I have thought about your proposal and I am willing to accept it. Ten thousand pounds."

The color drained from his face, and she was pleased to see that she had shocked him at last. For an instant she thought he would accept, but then he shook his head. "I'm afraid, as attractive as your offer is, Katie, I have to refuse."

Kate wanted to scream at his obtuse refusal. "But—"

He picked up a pen and began to scratch figures onto the page. He said wearily, "Kate, I don't need you to give me that ten thousand pounds. It is already mine, as your husband."

He had known. He had known and still let her make her offer. How galling that he could turn her world upside down and not feel the need to compensate her in the least. There was nothing she could do.

She felt herself begin to tremble with a rage such as she had never felt before. "Are you proud of that fact? That you have full command of a woman you don't want? Full command of the funds that resulted from her hard work? Full command of her body—to accept or reject as you will?"

"As long as I am your husband, I have that right, Katie. So will you not see reason and accept the divorce without making a fool of yourself?"

A fool of herself? No, he had made the fool of her five years ago when he had lied about returning to her. She opened her mouth to castigate him with the truth, then stopped. That would not give her what she wanted.

However, the sheriff's visit had given her an idea and it was all she needed. She knew how to get what she wanted from him. She stood up and snatched the pen from his hand. "If you do not grant my request, I will turn you in to the authorities."

He pushed away from his desk. Away from the blast of her fury. "Blackmail?"

"I prefer to think of it as justice. You are turning my life inside out. A child hardly seems too much to ask."

"You are not asking. You are threatening me." He pointed out, almost gently, "A baseless threat. A wife cannot testify against her husband."

Not again. She wanted to cry. Fury cut through her so sharp and clear that, in the ashes of her burnt hope, she realized, at last, what threat would work to bend him on this matter. "But she can testify against her husband's sister. His cousin. His uncle."

"You wouldn't—"

"What have I to lose? A fortune? A reputation? A name? You have taken them all from me. And now you would deny me any chance for a child. I have nothing but a few letters. Lies."

She could see that he was concerned that she would do as she threatened, at last. "Let me think on it, Katie."

"No. No more thinking. You come to me tonight, ready to be a husband for the rest of my visit, or I will tell the sheriff what I saw with my own eyes. Even you would not be so heartless as to let your own sister hang to avoid visiting your wife's bed for a few nights."

For a moment she thought he would protest, but instead he rubbed his eyes and said softly. "Very well, Katie. I hope you don't regret it, in the end."

"I am certain I won't." Fiercely she hoped she might have a daughter. But even if she had no child, she would be done with him. Her roses would not disappoint her. Not the way Sean had. Once he had divorced her, he would no longer have a right to her fortune, her body, or her heart. For the first time, she began to look forward to that day.

To her surprise, he bellowed Douglas's name, bringing the servant running. "Move Lady Blarney's things to my room, please."

"Where shall I put your things, my lord?"

"They shall remain where they are."

"Very good." Douglas was fighting to maintain an impassive expression, but there was no doubt he would be off to the kitchens to gossip as soon as he had completed his task.

"Is that necessary?" Sharing a room? With a man who had willingly stripped her of everything and soon would take her dignity as well?

"Now that you've given me no choice, Katie, I'd hate to disappoint you."

She did not know him. The man she had loved and married five years ago was an illusion and the man who would share her bed tonight was a stranger. She fought the temptation to order her things packed and a carriage readied for her departure. "This will not take the entire night—"

"Who can judge?" He shrugged. "Besides, the thought of Lady Dilys watching us is much too daunting to consider. No, if we share a room it will make matters more efficient all around, don't you see?"

"Efficient?"

"We want to make the best of our short time together, do we not?"

She had set the terms and she would not be the one to retreat from her position, even if her knees were jelly and her stomach knotted into a lump. "Of course we do," she answered stiffly before she left him to his books.

Douglas, no doubt wanting to impart his gossip, managed to move her things quickly and Lady Dilys's room was empty once again except for the little bed and dresser.

Sarah arrived shortly after Douglas's departure from Sean's now cluttered room. The third time the maid tsked over the awful condition of the room and its rackety old furniture, which had apparently been snatched from a fire barely in time some time in the very distant past, Kate sent her away.

She managed to find work putting each and every possession of hers away—although she had to request that a dressing table and mirror be brought from one of the other rooms in order to lay out her brush and comb.

At the bottom of her trunk she found the bundle and her heart skipped a beat. Sean's letters. He must have had one of the servants gather them up and give them to Sarah. Lifting one haphazardly from the pack she read: "My dearest Kate, the weather here is as fine as any day yet. But times are still too hard for me to send for you. Hold on to your patience, my love, and we will soon be together."

When had she begun to realize that the letters held empty promises? And why did she still keep them? At dark, coward that she was, she took supper in the room. She would give him no more chances to shake her courage and release him from his debt to her.

No. He must come to her. If he didn't . . . she could not carry through on her threat. The very thought of fey Bridget or laughing Niall hanging lifeless beneath the gallows made her ill. If he refused her again, she would have nothing left to use to coerce him. And what would she do then?

But even as she worried at the question, she heard his step on the stair and the door to his room—which had a working hasp, she had noted at once—creaked open.

He looked around at the changes she had made with some surprise, but made no comment. "Does the room suit you?"

"Well enough."

"I can always have the men leave off grubbing for food in order to build you a better one. Marble tile perhaps? With only the finest goosedown for your pillow, my lady?"

"There is no need to exercise your sharp tongue against my skin, my lord. I have asked you for nothing."

"Nothing? Is that what you value my stud service? I think not, or you would not have offered so much gold. Or threatened to see me hanged, either."

Ten thousand pounds. And even that had not been enough. "I ask only for what you owe me, as a husband. It does you no credit that I must hold a threat over your head for the privilege many wives receive as gifts of love from their husbands."

Her words were only the harsh truth, and she wondered whether he was as hurt by that fact as she was. But no matter, even if he didn't love her, she would hold him to his word this time.

If he couldn't give her his heart, he could at least take away the shame of being an untouched bride—and give her the hope of a child.

Gifts of love. The blasted woman had done everything short of holding a blade to his heart to get him into her bed. How dare she— Sean bit back his own tart reply.

He'd forgotten, in his thoughts of what the night would bring, how sharp his Kate's tongue could be. He'd known he'd have to be careful with her feelings tonight, but he had been thinking of her heart, not his.

Apparently she was ready to hurt him as badly as he had hurt her—it was a sad note when a man and woman could wound each other with only their words. He expected he would face her sharp tongue again tonight.

Not that he didn't deserve it; she had, after all, honed it on his injustice. But that wouldn't make things easier for him—or her—tonight. Foolishly, he'd expected her to be ready for bed in only her shift, tucked beneath the covers, waiting for him to join her and do what must be done. But here she sat by the window, still fully dressed.

Her gray wool bodice was fastened tight up to her collarbone. Her face was set and pale. She didn't look like a woman welcoming her husband, but more like a desperate woman facing the hangman's noose.

He closed the door behind him and moved to

slide the bolt home. She made a little sound of distress and he turned to see that her gaze was fixed on the bolt, as if she were a prisoner eyeing her last hope of freedom. He left the bolt unshot. If she chose to run, he'd not get in her way.

He removed his jacket and, as was his habit since he did not waste funds employing a valet, brushed it and hung it in his dressing room. He took off his boots with the ease of long practice and undid his collar and cuffs, reflecting that these were not in much better shape than the ones he had folded onto her dressing chair five years ago.

In the unnatural silence, every slide of cloth sounded loudly in his ears. When he returned to the room, she had not fled, however, but remained seated by the window, watching him as if she thought he were a highwayman about to steal all her jewels. Which, he supposed, he was in a way. Although she was the one insisting he commit the dastardly deed.

Unless she had changed her mind? "We do not need to do this, Kate, if you no longer wish to."

She stood up. "I not only wish it, I insist upon it." But that seemed the extent of her willingness to act. She turned to glance out the window briefly before she turned to face him as squarely as honest men faced the executioner and added softly, "I just don't know what is required of me."

He moved to kiss her, but she turned her head away, the muscles in her neck knotted under the touch of his fingers. He turned her away from him, so that he could massage her neck and shoulders gently. "You must relax, Kate, or things will not go well between us."

She leaned back against him, still tense. "They need not go well, they need only go quickly."

Quickly. Did she truly think he would just lift

her skirts and take her while she closed her eyes and bore the pain? What a disaster that would cause. No doubt she didn't realize, due to her inexperience. "I shall be as quick as I can be, without hurting you unnecessarily." He pressed his lips against the taut muscle in her neck, her shoulder, her tensed jaw. After a moment, she relaxed against him.

He turned her toward him again and bent to kiss her. This time his lips managed to brush against hers before she turned her head away again. "No."

That took him aback, but he could see that she was very serious about the matter. "You'll not find enjoyment in your first time this way, Kate," he protested. "Not if you don't let me kiss you properly. Warm you up, so to speak."

"I need no warming. Especially not from you," she said between stiff lips, almost as if she were afraid to move.

She needed more warming than an iceberg from the far north. So how was he to see to it? His memories from five years ago were warming him well enough—perhaps they'd do the same for her? He bent to whisper in her ear, "Surely you remember how pleasant it was to have me in your bed, my arms around you warming you up, no matter that it has been a few years."

"I remember that you refused to make love to me then."

So. Her memories were perhaps not as warm as his. "Kate, the act of love is not meant—"

"This is not an act of love."

"Technically—"

"This is business. Only business. A bargain struck between strangers who happen to be married for a while longer."

Her voice was so very cold, he found his own

blood chilled. He tried to cajole her into a better mood. "No woman's first time should be so cold-blooded."

"I think it fitting for a bride who must bludgeon her husband into her bed—and has waited five years in the bargain." She did not look at him.

"If you've changed your mind—" He wouldn't do anything while she was this frozen. She must be sure. He pulled back from her and crossed his arms. "There's no need to do this."

"I have not changed my mind." She gazed at him as though he were an insect to be crushed.

"I feel as though I'll need all the resources that Cromwell's men employed to breach the castle in order to honor your request this evening," he tried to joke with her. One little smile and he would not feel like a murderer of innocence and beauty.

"Consider it your revenge on my countrymen, then." She lay down on the bed, stiff, her eyes closed.

Perfect. Even though he hadn't been with a woman in some time, he didn't know if he could find a way to perform the required duties. One moment he would close his eyes and feel her skin under his lips, her shape under his fingertips and he had no doubts what he wanted to do. The next . . . He sighed and stood immobilized by his conflicting desires.

She opened her eyes and swept him with a distrustful glance. "Can't you bring yourself to do it, even now?"

He sighed. "You'll have to take your clothes off."

She responded by lifting her skirts to her waist. The sight of her white thighs exposed and vulnerable nearly took his breath away.

He could not turn away, but he could not join her on the bed yet, either. At last, with her unflinching gaze upon him, he moved to unfasten his shirt. "I hope you don't mind if I take mine off, then."

He proceeded to undress, despite the fact that she did not answer. A man had his standards. But he did wonder if the wool of her skirts would leave him with a rash once the deed was done.

He stretched out beside her, careful not to touch her, propped himself on an elbow and stared down at her unyielding face.

Memories that he had pushed away for so long flooded through him. Her lashes were long and dark against her cheek. He reached out a finger and brushed it against the tips of her lashes. She was so still that he knew she held her breath, but she didn't even twitch at his touch.

How could he get her to thaw? He knew it was too much to expect her to smile, or to welcome him. But it would unman him if she began to cry, and he had a suspicion she would if he could not reach her somehow, no matter how brave and strong she wanted to appear to his eyes.

Her breathing began again, rather unevenly, lifting her breasts in unison under the confines of wool, linen and corset. For a moment he fought the urge to unpeel her layers and reveal them. He didn't—not certain she would let him, or that he wouldn't feel he'd leave her vulnerable if she did.

He closed his eyes, remembering the feel of her curves from that brief stolen time in her bed, and was in no doubt that he could perform his duty with or without her cooperation. Of course, facing himself without absolute loathing the next morning if he hurt her was still in question.

He had to end this before one—or both—of them ended in the madhouse. He pressed his hand against her breast and felt the rapid beat of her heart against his palm. "I feel honored to have such a martyr for my bed. Perhaps you'd like to take an ice bath before we conclude our bargain—the better to freeze off that most offensive part of me after it has satisfied the honor of my word?"

She turned away from him, and her skirts slipped up to expose the curve of one hip. "Can you not get on with it in silence?"

Silence? She wanted him to approach the matter like a monk approaching penance and be silent as well? He thought not.

"I'm afraid I need a little help, my dear," he lied. "Since you will not provide it, I'll have to rely on my own tongue." He had a thought of how he'd like to use his tongue, but no doubt she'd break his neck between her thighs if he dared try such a thing.

If he'd had any doubts that she was still a virgin, he could not doubt it now. Why hadn't Niall done the job properly? And why was he so glad he hadn't? The woman was nothing but trouble. She'd threatened his own sister, though he very much doubted she could have brought herself to do what she threatened, no matter how angry she was.

"Did you know your skin is as white as a swan's breast here?" He used his fingertip to brush his signature onto the skin of her exposed buttock, eliciting a flinch and a cascade of wool to hide the sight from his eyes. He was tempted to move the material himself, but instead said only, "You know this can't be accomplished if you don't let me touch, don't you?"

She rolled onto her back and glared at him. Slowly, the woolen material retreated, exposing her thighs—pressed tightly together—once again.

He tickled the back of one tensed knee.

She jumped up without warning and he tumbled from the bed trying to avoid being struck senseless by the force of the top of her skull against his jaw.

Kate rubbed her forehead and stared daggers at the man lying somewhat dazed on the floor, holding his jaw. Between clenched teeth, she managed to grit out, "I did not ask you to make love to me, only to breed with me like a horse, or mule."

Like a daft child, he grinned at her, the reluctant and unhappy man of a few minutes before completely gone. "Mules don't have the equipment for stud work."

She felt the heat of a flush suffuse her entire body, even that exposed by the indecent disarrangement of her skirts. "Then a goat. Yes, I think goat is appropriate example for you, my lord. Always bleating away."

He propped himself up on his elbows, the muscles in his shoulders and chest flexing in such a way that she could no longer ignore the fact that he hadn't a stitch on, no matter how she tried. She refused to look away. No doubt he expected her to. She settled for meeting his eyes squarely with her own.

He examined her with a curious light in his eye. "I can hardly do the work of goat or a man with you all the way up there and me down here, now can I?"

Chapter 15

Though he spoke nothing but the truth, she was absurdly reluctant to invite him back onto the bed. His touch had been disquieting, to say the least, though she had managed to keep her eyes closed and avoid the sight of him looming above her, for the most part. "You are enjoying this, aren't you?"

"I don't think that can be helped, love. A man just tends to enjoy dipping his wick." As if he knew the leap her stomach would take at his words, he grinned more widely.

The idea that he could enjoy himself seemed grossly unfair. "Well, I wish you wouldn't this time." She'd rather he had all the pleasure of a thousand lashes.

He shrugged, a leisurely gesture, as if he didn't mind sitting cold and unclothed on the floor. "If I didn't enjoy it, I couldn't do it. It's the way a man is made, and that's a fact."

She knew well enough the truth of what he said, but her outrage at the injustice didn't ease. She glared at him. "It's fortunate for you that I didn't have control over such decisions—you would not be so happy then."

He had the nerve to laugh, as if she'd made a jest. "There's no reason to be angry at the way things are, Katie. You're best off to accept them. You could enjoy it too, if you'd let yourself."

Enjoy herself? With him? She hardly thought so. "I don't have to, though, do I?" She knew, from the gossip, that women did. But she didn't think it was necessary. Given her choice, she'd rather it hurt badly enough that she'd never miss being a wife again for as long as she lived.

"No. There is no requirement for a woman to enjoy herself." His gaze darkened for a moment. "She can be asleep or unconscious or unwilling if the man is a fiend and takes his pleasure from someone else's pain."

"I don't suppose, considering what it took for me to get you here at all, that I have to worry about such violence from you." A small part of her suddenly recognized that she was lucky he was not a man to lightly give her what she'd asked for. She couldn't quite understand how she was lucky, but she knew she was all the same.

"Never." As suddenly as it had come upon him, he shrugged away the anger. He put his hand over his heart. "You'll never have to worry about such things with me, Katie girl. If I have my way, you'll enjoy yourself every bit as much as I do."

She didn't like how much her heart leaped at the thought of having a night of pleasure with him—the night she might have had five years ago. "I don't want to enjoy it, I want to get it over with. Come up here and do it," she ordered. She fell back to the bed, prepared to feel the weight of him, the humiliation and pain of his invasion. It would all be worth it if she had a child, she told herself.

But he did not join her on the bed. His voice, annoyingly amused, came floating up from the floor. "Katie, I don't think you really want me to do this."

She sat up again, exasperated. "Haven't I offered you a fortune? Threatened to turn your sister in to the sheriff?" She didn't like the way her voice rose in an uncontrolled squeak of dismay. She paused a moment and then said, as firmly as she could, "Of course I want you to do this." She added for good measure, when he showed no sign of complying, "Quickly, too."

Still, he did not move from the floor. "Is that so?" He opened his arms wide and then lay down with them crossed under his head, so that he lay totally exposed to her. "Then come and have your way with me."

She tried not to look anywhere but at his face and didn't succeed. Nor did she move. "You are on the floor."

"Men and women can do this dance anywhere— in the stable on a bed of hay, on a tabletop, in a chair, even against the wall if space is limited and need is urgent. The floor will do for us well enough."

"You are a fool to expose yourself on the floor like that when it is still winter and cold enough to give you pleurisy." Kate looked at the wall, trying to imagine how the act could be done in that position.

"The wall is not for us, Katie." He sat up. "Not your first time, at least. Before you leave—" He reached out toward the bed, leaving his sentence unfinished. Not that she needed to hear the rest of the words when the picture of the two of them pressed against the wall, moving together some-how, became clear in her mind.

Worried that he was going to grab her, she fell back with a squeak of alarm. But all he did was pull one of the blankets folded at the end of the bed down around himself and command, "If you are certain that this is what you want, come down to me, Katie."

She stared at him mutely. This was not how she had planned things. She had wanted to close her eyes, pretend she was not there, as he did all the work that was necessary for the process to be suc-cessful. She had been prepared to hold her breath, grit her teeth, force back tears. Whatever was nec-essary. Except this. To be the one in charge.

He arranged the blanket under himself and pulled another to soften his makeshift bed. At last he pulled down a final blanket and covered him-self—at least the lower part of himself, though his long feet stuck out in the cold air. Propped on one elbow, looking as comfortable as could be, he lifted an eyebrow in query. "Do you need instruc-tions on what to do?"

Instructions. No, she needed a dagger to cut out his black heart. Sadly, that would not serve her current purpose. "No."

He laughed. "I assure you, I'm ready and will-ing, I only need you to—"

"I'm familiar with the process—theoretically, at least." She worried her lower lip between her teeth. Still she did not move.

He sat up and held out his hand to her. "If you can't manage it, my little virgin, you shall have to let me be the teacher for today—and you will have to follow my lead."

"I'd rather not." With a deep breath, she dropped

to the floor, stepped over him, lifted her skirts, and sat down to straddle his lap. She felt the bulge of his shaft and pressed against it with all her might. She looked up into his face, pleased to see she had shocked him yet again. "There. This should get the job done without all the prattle."

There was laughter in the crinkles around his eyes, but desire, too. This close there was no mistaking that he wanted her. "The blanket may cause a bit of a problem, though, don't you think?" She could feel the beat of his heart, the warm rush of his uneven breathing against her cheek.

She felt the thick wool against her most private parts and realized she had not gotten quite so far as she had hoped. With a moan of annoyance she closed her eyes, gritted her teeth and rose to her knees. "Move it out of the way, please."

"The blanket, or—"

Would he persist in humiliating her to the very end? "The blanket."

He steadied her with one hand on her bare hip and the other prodded down in between them, his warm fingers touching where they shouldn't, sending little shocks straight through her until she felt the part of him she needed to make use of touch against her, hot and hard. She pushed against him, pleased to note he wasn't laughing now. In fact, his breath had hitched when she moved and he had swallowed quite audibly.

She pushed against him, and his hands gripped her hips, forcing her into an unfamiliar rhythm. Was this all there was to it? "Why all the fuss? This is quite easily done." There were even pleasant little tingles of sensation that were quite nice. Not that she needed them. Or wanted them.

Sean didn't know whether to laugh or cry. She rubbed against him so warm and inviting and she thought the deed done. He moved against her, enjoying the sensation, wondering whether he should tell her she had not yet achieved her aim.

He held her hips and kissed her neck, her jaw, her ear. With his lips he unfastened the top of her gown, but she let go of her tight hold on his shoulders to ward him off. "No."

"You do like to tease a man, don't you, my lady."

She ground herself against him. Enjoyably, but not fruitfully. "Is this not what you want? What you enjoy?" For a moment, he thought she might inadvertently position herself correctly, but she moved too quickly and the moment was lost.

Shaking with need, but determined that it must be Kate and not he who determined the outcome of their evening, he said softly, "There is still a connection to be made. Or do you not need me to point out that the stud isn't engaged with the mare."

She laughed, rising up against him, with him, as if she thought he knew nothing. "How difficult can it be?" But the connection remained elusive and she gave an impatient gasp after a moment.

He kissed her neck and moved his hips against hers, but he didn't make any effort to bring them together, other than rubbing himself against her to point out the lack of fruitful contact.

She hissed at him, apparently at a loss for words, her color hectic.

"Do you want my advice?" He nuzzled her neck. "It will cost you a kiss."

"No, thank you, I shall manage to figure it out for myself. It is a puzzle, and I am good at puzzles."

"This is one most men and women figure out." He gasped a little when her fingers gripped him and tried to push him up into her as if she were stuffing a sausage into a goose. Which, perhaps, was as good an analogy as any.

"Have I hurt you?" She released him.

"No. In fact, if you move your fingers just so"—
he brought his hand to grasp hers between their
bodies, demonstrating his words as he spoke—"I
will soon present you with the seed you so desire—
only not in the most useful of receptacles."

She closed her eyes and for a moment he thought
she would give up control to him at last. Instead she
shifted her hips and positioned him correctly this
time. With a fierce push of her hips she seated him
as firmly as he might have liked to do himself. He
felt the stunning rush of pleasure as she twisted in
his lap and made a little cry of triumph or pain, or
both. "There."

For a moment all he could do was press her to
him and enjoy the sensation of being inside her at
last. He wanted to move, to push, to roll her beneath him and move until he gave her what she
wanted, all of him. Instead, he waited for her to set
the rhythm. After a time, he realized that she did
not realize what movement was still required.

He opened his eyes to see that she stared at him
in confusion. She whispered, "Well? Is that it?"

"Almost." He sighed as her brows knit and she
chewed her lower lip, but still didn't move. "A little
persuasion is necessary." He nudged her hips and
she moved infinitesimally. He nudged her again,
determined not to take over, despite his body's insistence that he do so immediately. "In my condition I don't need too much encouragement, but
you'll have to do better than that."

She moved once vigorously, nearly unseating
him. He followed to keep them joined and she
winced and stopped, staring at him in horror at
the position she found herself in. At last she let out
a little sob. "What a horrid business this is. You
could help, you insufferable oaf, instead of just sit-

ting there, smiling at me as if you didn't care one way or another."

The tear in the corner of her eye decided him. With a muffled oath he rolled over, taking her with him. He buried his face against the soft wool of her bodice and inhaled the scent of roses. "Hush, *mo mhuirnin*. The hardest part's over. I'll do the rest."

"Mauverneen." Her arms came around his neck. "I used to love it when you called me that."

He moved gently at first, but the sensation was too unbearably intoxicating. He had wanted her for so long. Now, with what had seemed an impossible dream in his arms, he could not hold himself back. He wanted to bury himself as deeply inside her as he could. So deep that she could never doubt she had been his wife, once. Soon he found himself gasping and thrusting like the goat she had named him until he lay spent on the woolen armor that protected the softness of her breasts from an incursion by his invading hands and lips.

He put his arms around her, to pull her close to him, to reassure her that next time he would see that she took her pleasure with him. She let out a soft exhalation and pushed him away before the last pleasurable pulsation had finished echoing through his body. "There, that wasn't so bad."

As he caught his breath, she rose from the floor, her skirts falling back into place. She looked hardly disarranged at all as she moved to the dressing room. He heard the splashing of water in the basin as he leaped up to throw on his shirt, suddenly feeling uncomfortably exposed, despite the fact that he was in his own bedroom.

"Not so bad?" he muttered, furious at her complete lack of appreciation for his consideration. He strode over to the dressing room door to tell her so and stopped, the words dying on his lips.

She leaned against the cold stone of the abbey wall, her neck bent like the broken stem of one of her roses, her head hanging down.

He turned away. Perhaps now was not the time to tell her she should be grateful he had made the process as painless as possible. Or that next time would be easier. It didn't look as though she would be as eager at the idea as he was. For a man who had been ungrudgingly celibate for years, he found the ability to ignore that part of him nearly impossible now that he'd indulged.

Would she change her mind, now that she knew what she asked? Considering her bravado scant minutes before, he doubted she would call a halt to their bargain. He slipped out the door. He'd let her prepare for bed . . . he stopped by the door for a moment. Was she planning to sleep in her woolen armor? She'd not be comfortable. He sighed.

"I'll be sleeping elsewhere tonight, love. You've the room to yourself," he called.

There was no answer from the dressing room.

He left the room, closing the door softly behind him. His hand remained on the latch as he debated if there was some salve he could provide to her wounds, or if that would be the stinging salt she didn't need right now. The quiet slide of the lock into place on the other side of the door was all the answer he needed to that one.

"Don't mind the ghost—it's only Lady Dilys's husband, the sad Englishman who starved himself to death here for longing of his homeland, because he would not leave his wife and son behind, dead or not. He'll not bother you . . ." He knew it would sound silly, but he might as well give her all the superstition now, or one of the servants would tomorrow. ". . . as long as you don't bounce upon the mattress like a . . . naughty child." There was little likelihood of that, he supposed, even though he found the idea much more appealing than was wise.

Again, there was no answer. No doubt she thought he was taunting her. He hoped poor Dilys's husband would sense her distress and leave off his moaning and sighs tonight. Come the morning, though, he wouldn't be surprised if she had decided to leave Ireland behind her forever.

The morning light brought more truth than Kate was willing to face immediately. She was no longer in Lady Dilys's gentle care; she was alone in her bed, and she was no longer a virgin.

He had left her alone again and the pain was so unbearable that she no longer had any illusion about why she had come to Ireland. She wanted to be a wife to the infuriating man, even if he never set foot out of Ireland again.

She rolled over and buried her head in her pillows, willing herself back to sleep, back to dreamless oblivion where she did not wish for impossible things. Instead, with her eyes closed, all she saw was Sean's face—smiling, serious, angry, and, most of all, twisted in the grip of desire as he moved inside her, kissed her, held her, murmured soothing words against her ear.

At last, she rose, acknowledging that the truth would be no different if she slept for a fortnight without waking once. She wanted him; she had wanted him from the first time he teased her that they were already engaged. All the tests she had put him through had been designed to protect her future, but her heart had already been given over to him.

This had been one last test. She had believed,

without acknowledging it, that once he had come to her bed he would not be able to turn his back on her again. But he had done it with ease. Not because he didn't desire her. After last night she had little doubt of that. But because he didn't love her.

And still, he had been kind and gentle with her. He had not lied to her. No matter that he had desired her, he had not taken advantage.

She would have to tell Sarah to pack their bags, ask Douglas to prepare the carriage. But first she would have to apologize to Sean. He had been right—she should never have insisted that he perform the duties of husband to a wife he did not want.

And she would also have to thank him. He had no doubt been as kind as possible—offering her the opportunity to change her mind by allowing her to control their coupling. She could not—would not—call it lovemaking.

Unsure if it was her own sense of the changes that the night had wrought in her, or unspoken compassion, she noted that the servants treated her more gently than usual. When she asked for Sean, she was told he was in the greenhouses with Paddy, the gardener.

She did not know if she would speak to him there, but she went, anyway, needing to walk, to avoid the quiet whispers and worried glances she imagined the servants were directing at her.

The greenhouses were small, rackety affairs, like the rest of the buildings on the abbey grounds. But the smell of earth and growing things was the same as in the greenhouses she had practically lived in at home. She took in a deep breath and wondered why she had let the shambling outside of the building keep her from stepping inside, where she felt instantly at home.

"What is the problem?" Sean's voice was a troubled rumble that carried clearly to her ears in the small building. For a moment she thought he was speaking to her, and then she saw that he had not yet noticed she had entered the building. His attention was all for the gardener.

After a brief urge to turn around and leave before he caught sight of her, she decided that pretending nothing was amiss would be easier with a third person, so she chose to approach him as he bent over a sheaf of papers with the gardener.

She slowed her step, listening to the discussion, unsure whether to interrupt or come back in a few minutes. The sight of him, fully dressed, still caused her insides to tighten. She allowed herself to examine him. He gestured as he spoke to Paddy, his arm sweeping through the air to encompass the entire greenhouse and all within it. The movement was so passionate and his face so full of dreams and hope that she almost expected the greenhouse to magically transform itself as he wished.

Every time she thought she'd dealt with last night, a surprising new reaction reminded her of what had passed between them. She wondered if it would be the same for him and stopped a moment, suddenly unsure she wanted to know. She was, however, utterly certain her feelings had not changed toward him. She loved the man still, despite his desire for a divorce.

She wondered why she loved him. She knew well enough why she'd fallen in love with him. He was handsome, charming, passionate, and he made her laugh. There had not been another man like him in all of London. She had been young enough to believe in true love.

But after five years, she knew better than to trust charm and beauty—or love itself. His sense of humor had rescued her last night—perhaps it had rescued both of them. He had reminded her of the young man who had wooed and won her. But since then he had become a solemn man, with anger bubbling just below the surface. She could see it now as Paddy shook his head, and Sean glared down at the papers as if they had betrayed him somehow.

She had wondered which was the true Sean, but now she thought she understood that both were. The famine and hardship in his country had changed him, as it would change anyone. How would it have changed her, if she'd come to join him? If he'd asked her to?

"I've done as your notes said, but they just aren't growing." Paddy waved his hand to indicate a neat row of pots with straggling plants, most just barely an inch above the soil.

"What is the soil mix?"

Paddy jabbed a finger toward the middle of the top paper. "Just as it says here—a third of each, with plenty of watering."

Sean squinted and shook his head with an exhalation of frustration. "Then why are we not getting the results that we should? These plants should be a foot high by now, easily."

Paddy seemed as frustrated as Sean. "There must be a mistake in there—maybe they gave you the wrong information since they knew you'd be taking it back to Ireland with you."

Kate approached quietly, unseen by either man and looked at the diagrams Sean had drawn for Paddy, who, like most of the servants she had met here, could not read the notebook of closely written pages Sean had brought home from England with him.

She suspected there was an error there, but she wouldn't dare to say so to either of them. Whenever she had found her results diverging from the expected, she usually discovered a transposition error, or a misrecorded direction.

Finding such a mistake, however, often proved an arduous task, involving research in the texts on the subject and conversations with others who worked with roses as she did. Paddy was obviously unable to read the texts, and cloistered here as he was, no doubt had no one to talk to but Sean.

As she listened to their worried conversation, she couldn't suppress her urge to help. She dared to offer an idea to the men, who still hadn't noticed her. "The solution is simple enough—send Paddy to England to train with Nautlick himself."

"Kate." Sean turned to her, his eyebrow lifted slightly in question. To her relief, he made no reference to last night, but only to her suggestion. "Nautlick?"

"I've had my hands in the soil since I was old enough to walk, my lady. I don't need training."

She hadn't meant to offend him with the term. Kate said quickly, "I simply thought if you saw different methods demonstrated, you'd have a clearer notion of which you wanted to try here."

Sean didn't like the idea any better than Paddy, but he did not say so directly. "Perhaps you have a good idea, Kate. We'll have to consider it."

"I'll not go on enemy soil," Paddy said, stubbornly.

Kate repressed a sigh. "Have you anything against growing a good crop?"

Paddy's dirt-encrusted thumb stabbed at the papers laid out before him. "These ideas don't work."

Inspired by the suggestion Paddy had made to Sean before he knew she was there, she said quickly, "I think they might have changed a thing or two—don't you see? That's why you must go—

to spy out the true way to make your crops successful."

"Me? A spy?" The idea appealed to him. He grinned and nodded. "To find out what they don't want me to know?"

"Exactly." Kate encouraged him. Sean had said nothing during the exchange, simply watched her as if he wondered if she was going to burst into tears or take out a pistol and shoot him through the heart. Was he considering her suggestion, or the events of last night?

Unaware of the current passing between Kate and Sean, Paddy said, "I guess I could do that. Seeing as how I want to do my best." The man pondered the point for a moment more and nodded his head. "I'd make a good spy."

"You would, at that." Sean seemed to break whatever spell had held his gaze on Kate and turned to look at his eager gardener for a moment before he added, "Thank you for the suggestion, Kate."

He took her arm and prodded her gently toward the door of the greenhouse. "Now that we have that settled, we'll leave you to your work, then, Paddy."

As they left the greenhouse, he said softly, "Thank you for your help." His hand slid to her elbow. "What brought you to the greenhouses? I wouldn't have thought they'd compare to those at home. And we don't grow roses here. We need food crops."

She didn't answer his question. "Paddy seems to be a good steward. The plants are well cared for. Have you considered growing something that you could export?"

His fingers tightened on her elbow in a quick spasm of frustration. "The restrictions on export are steep enough that the profit is too risky to try yet. I hope to be in a position to do so in a year or two."

She was relieved that he had realized he could not continue as he had been forever. "Will you give up your nefarious activities then?" All in favor, she wondered if there was a way she could help.

Chapter 16

Sean saw the eager desire to help spring into her eyes. But he was certain that was not why she had come in search of him. "Did you need something from me, Kate? I thought for certain you'd not want anything more—at least not until tonight. I thought I acquitted myself quite well last night, after all. You have no evidence at all to prevent the divorce now."

She didn't retreat, despite his reminder. "You have the patience of a saint, it cannot be denied."

As if she carried the same vivid memories he did, she blushed. "You needn't bait me, my lord. I have not come to lure you to my bed in the middle of the day."

"Good," he lied. The thought of taking her to bed was very tempting indeed. "Because after last night I decided that I have terms as well, if you expect me to meet yours in the future."

"Terms?" She glanced at him with only mild curiosity. What was she plotting now?

He touched her cheek with a soft brush of his

hand, and she turned her face into his palm and inhaled, no doubt the scent of the earth from the greenhouses he had buried his fingers in earlier while he spoke with Paddy.

He fought the urge to lean down and kiss her. "If you want me in your bed ever again, Katie, you'll have to take off your clothes. All of them."

She glanced up at him, and he was pleased to see true shock in her expression. Abruptly, she turned away from him and began to walk toward the abbey. He followed, matching her stride easily.

They had walked almost halfway back to the abbey before he spoke again. "Did you sleep well in my bed?" He wanted to judge whether he'd be in his own bed tonight. The lumpy mattress he'd bedded down on after leaving her last night left much to be desired and he'd rather not resort to it tonight, unless he must.

"Very well." She was lying, judging by the dark smudges of sleeplessness under her eyes, but he let it pass until he glanced at her and saw the tears shining unshed in her eyes.

As he spoke, so did she. "I'm sorry."

She laughed nervously. He stopped, and swung her toward him. For a moment he said nothing, worried that she would misinterpret kindness as some other emotion. "Kate—"

She grasped his forearms and squeezed to silence him, as she interrupted. "You were right, I shouldn't have insisted that you make love to me."

Surprised, he paused a moment and then said, "Still, I'm sorry. I knew it was not wise." Not wise at all. He didn't know if he could bear it again. He didn't know if he could bear it if he managed to send her away, as he wished.

"Perhaps it was not wise." She shook her head

and met his searching gaze squarely. "But I would never have believed you were right if—" She broke off a moment and then laughed softly. "It isn't as though you in any way forced me." She released her grip on his arms. "Anything but, Sean. I must thank you for that."

"Still—" He frowned down at her, puzzled by the change in her attitude. If he didn't know better, he'd swear she was hatching a scheme. She had the same mischievous look that she had gotten long ago when she planned some foolery with Betsey. But what could she have in mind? He had, after all, given her what she asked for.

She smiled at him, just as she had the first time he'd teased her that he intended to hold her to her promise to marry him, made when she was a child. "Do you know of another man who would have tried so hard to keep himself out of my bed?" She closed her eyes and her smile dimmed a bit. "I'm fairly certain you did so for my sake, not your own."

He suppressed the urge to reassure her that, were circumstances different, she'd have had a less reluctant lover last night. She didn't need to know that. Not, at least, until he knew what plot was hatching in her clever brain. "Does that mean you don't want my services any longer?"

"Would you object if I had changed my mind?" She didn't look at him, clearly afraid of the answer. He wished, fleetingly, that she had been slightly less courageous so that she wouldn't even have asked such a thing.

He took her hands in his and pulled her slowly toward him, until she leaned against him fully, the chilly wind diminished by the shelter of his arms. "I would agree now, if you wish it." He bent as if to kiss her, but merely whispered into her ear, "Just say the word and I am Sean McCarthy, Lord Blarney, silver-tongued stud goat at your beck and call."

Sean was surprised she didn't slap him. He could feel the desire to back away vibrate through her and, though he held her loosely, she didn't move as she said, "Considering your reluctance last night, once a night seems ample."

He remembered the way she had leaned against the dressing room wall for support less than twelve hours ago and marveled that this was the same woman. What had happened to bring about this change? "Then you didn't know what you asked for. Now you do. And once a night no longer seems like enough."

He hadn't meant to speak the truth, but he consoled himself that she wouldn't believe him. He brushed her cheeks with his lips, his breath warm against her cold cheek. "Not to a man starved for the feel of a woman as I have been."

She laughed, disbelieving, as he had known she would be. "Lord Blarney cannot find a willing woman nearby? Perhaps when we visit the Stone, you should kiss it as well. I fear your tongue has lost the gift."

"Perhaps it has, at that. My words didn't convince you that what you asked might break your heart, after all." He watched her, waiting to see the flash of vulnerability he knew was lurking beneath the surface.

"No." She buried her head against his shoulder for a brief moment. "You have convinced me about the divorce, though."

He knew he should be pleased. And he would be, as soon as the sharp pain knifing through his chest had gone away. "So perhaps I have not lost all the silver off my tongue, then."

She lifted her head to look up at him in surprise. He hoped she hadn't heard the disappointment in his voice. But Kate closed her eyes, "I'm going home. You were right. I won't make any protest about the divorce." Not that she could. He decided to be a gentleman and not point that fact out to her.

"That's sensible of you." He sighed. "After what you saw, you are best out of here as soon as possible."

A flash of compassion crossed her features. "I know you don't want to come back to London, but you are a fool to risk everything to break the law. Can you not find a way to see to your people without breaking the law?"

"One day I hope to, but I have not reached that time yet." He shook his head. "You do not know the frustration of knowing there is food stored within a few miles of starving people and it is destined to be shipped away to other countries to feed those willing to line the landlord's pockets. It isn't right. And I am determined to do something about it—even if it means I risk hanging."

Hanging. Kate shivered at the idea. "Have you spoken to the landlords?" The words of apology she had prepared shriveled to a lump in her throat at the thought of leaving him alone to face his battle. She knew it wasn't wise. She knew it. But still she wanted him. Why could she just not be sensible? Was it because his life was in danger and the foolish man refused to give up risking his neck?

"They are interested in coin and little more. You'd see that for yourself, if you stayed. But I'm glad you've decided to go. Though perhaps you'll want to come back to see me swing if I'm caught."

Kate didn't laugh at the horrible joke. It was Paddy's words that gave her the idea. If Paddy could be a horticultural spy, why couldn't Kate do a bit of spying on her own to bring peace to the area and convince her husband to give up his Robin Hood ways.

But first, she had to find a way to stay just a bit longer. She could think of only one. "I intend to go as soon as our bargain is met."

He glanced down at her unhappily. "I meant what I said, Kate. I'll not meet your terms unless you meet mine."

She thought of lying in the bed with him tonight without the armor of wool and corset. "That seems fair enough," she consented with a rush of light-headedness.

She walked more quickly into the abbey, leaving him to gape at her in consternation. Perhaps she would regret it. Perhaps. But she was certain, either way she would rest easier knowing that he was safe, even if he was no longer her husband.

Her first mission, she decided, would be a visit to the man who had trapped Sean in this unhappy stranglehold. Jeffreys. He was the biggest landlord in the area; surely if she could convince him, he could bring his influence to bear upon the other landlords in the vicinity? In case her efforts proved futile, she decided not to tell Sean what she was about unless she was successful. He had enough on his mind as it was.

She called upon Jeffreys, but he was out. The footman seemed almost reluctant to take her card, but she insisted with an unruffled smile, as any good spy should. She included an invitation to dinner for two days hence, hoping Sean would not mind when he found out what she had done.

* * *

He had been surprised that she did not flee at once. That she still wanted him in her bed, although she recognized that he had been right. It had been brave of her to acknowledge her own error in judgment.

He wondered if allowing her to stay was an error on his part. The thought that he would have the opportunity to show her that making love did not have to be a clumsy, embarrassing affair was little enough consolation.

He knew he shouldn't let himself enjoy the feeling of being a husband—it wouldn't last long. But he did anyway. And he looked forward to tonight, spending the night in his own bed, with his wife, for the first time since he had married her.

It would be a memory to warm him in the future. At least, he hoped it would be enough, because it would be all that he could have.

This time she wore only a shift when he came into the room. He reached to loosen his collar and paused. "Are you certain of this, Kate? There is no need to prove your courage—I already know it well."

She smiled. "I want this, Sean." She smiled again, a little wryly. "And this time I know what it is I want, and I won't expect more than you can give me."

He quickly shed his own clothing and put out the lamp, so that there would be darkness between them tonight. Later, if she stayed, there would be time for light, for him to enjoy the sight of her. She'd already seen him in all his glory—though she had seemed decidedly unimpressed, he remembered.

He climbed into the bed and settled himself beside her as if he weren't an eager lover, but a man well used to a woman in his bed. He may have joked about being a stud goat, but he did not want to behave as if he were one. Tonight, for her sake, he would concentrate on showing her the pleasure of warm skin touching warm skin.

"So, my lady." He turned toward her and she jolted away from him when his leg brushed hers. "Will you be in charge tonight? Or will you leave it to me?"

"Since I had charge of last night, it is only fair that you lead tonight."

"Fair enough." She was trembling when he moved to pull her into his lap. He whispered in her ear as he gathered the hem of her shift in his fists. "Katie, I said nothing at all." She did not make a sound of protest as he lifted the shift up and over her head, but when the cold night air hit her as he tossed the shift to the end of the bed, she gave a powerful shiver.

He took her into his arms and rubbed his hands along her back, her arms, her shoulders, trying to warm her, trying to learn the feel of her, so that he could conjure it up in his lonely bed once she was gone.

She was, as he had hoped, less shy in the dark. Though she moved tentatively at first, her hands skimmed along his arms and wrapped about his neck. He began to explore the soft warmth of her breasts with his hands and she sucked in a quick, harsh breath, but did not pull away. After a moment, she leaned in to his touch and it was his turn to struggle for breath when she brushed her lips against his neck and nipped at the lobe of his ear.

When her hands moved down to explore him,

he guided her, showing her what pleased him, and then he grasped her hands and pulled them up and away to rest by her head as he bore her down to the softness of the bed and stretched himself over her. "Tonight you gave me leave to be in charge, Katie."

"Do you not like my touch?"

He nuzzled at her neck. "I like it all too well. But tonight we will go slowly. And that means that I touch you." She did not bar his lips or his patient fingers access to any part of her, and he felt a jolt of triumph when his touch made her writhe and moan until she convulsed beneath him.

"Are you sure of this, Katie?"

She didn't answer with words, only pressed her lips to his neck, slid a kiss up to his jaw, and captured his mouth with hers.

He came into her smoothly, and she wrapped her legs around him instinctively, drawing him deeper, deepening the kiss between them at the same moment.

They moved together in a unison that made him feel as if they might have melted together into one soul. He felt the surge of orgasm overtake him and let himself be swept away; his thoughts tumbled about until he knew nothing, not even his name.

At last he rolled from her, pulling her with him so that they rested together like spoons. He brushed his lips against her hair. He was pleased with himself, until she said, very softly, as if she wasn't certain she wanted him to hear, "Would you want me as your wife if I agreed to stay? If you thought I could be a partner to you in your efforts here? Could be of use to your people?"

The idea jolted through him like a bolt of lightning, leaving an ache behind. It was impossible.

* * *

He had not answered her question directly, Kate reflected, as she lay beside him, listening to his even breathing. But when he rolled away from her, his arms had tightened to bring her with him and he had curled his body around hers, warmer than any brick or pan of coals could ever be.

That was answer in itself. He wanted her to stay with him. He wouldn't admit it because he was a stubborn man. She didn't understand all his reasoning, but she was beginning to. If he weren't engaged in illegal activities, no doubt he would have sent for her long ago.

Most likely it would do no good to ask him if she could stay. But she had been right to try to mend fences. Not that such a thing would solve all his problems. At least not at once. An alliance of landowners would be the best way to see to feeding the population, as well as to securing greater profits in the coming years without starving anyone.

She reached for his hand, warmly possessive against her breast, and lifted it to her mouth to press a kiss against the rough knuckles that had surprised her with a gift of pleasure so intense she blushed all over even now at the memory.

Thankfully, the room had been so dark he could have had no notion of how close she had come to losing control and crying out his name . . . or worse, that she loved him. He wouldn't want to know that. Not yet. Not until he had found a way to feed his people. Solving his problems would solve hers, too.

In the morning, he was still beside her and she turned to watch him sleep, until she noticed that his breathing was less even than it should be. Daringly, she reached her hand out to lay it flat against his hip, but he did not respond. She moved her fingers against the muscles of his stomach lightly, wondering if it tickled. If he even noticed her light touch. In a moment she could not doubt that he did.

"Do you not know it is dangerous to rouse a sleeping man that way, Katie?"

She noted there was no trace of sleepiness in the green eyes that watched her closely. She slid closer as she tightened her fingers around him. "I thought I might have a better chance of being in charge if you were asleep. Do you object?"

He didn't answer, just laughed raggedly and pulled her head down for a lingering kiss.

She received a note that Jeffreys and his son would come for dinner that night with scarcely an hour to notify the kitchens. The cook looked at her as if she'd said Lady Dilys and her ghostly husband would be down for dinner, but had not answered Kate's inquiries as to why the news was so shattering.

"We don't mix," was her only answer.

She glanced at the note of acceptance. The reply was terse and gave no indication whether they were pleased or displeased at the invitation. But she supposed an acceptance was proof enough that there could be the start of a truce between the families— no matter what the cook thought.

She had not dared tell Sean until she heard from Jeffreys. Now, holding the acceptance note, after the cook's reaction, she was suddenly afraid the fragile bond that had built between them would crush under the weight of his anger.

He was not pleased. In fact, he was incensed beyond comprehension. "You invited him? Into my home?"

"He is your neighbor."

He was infuriated enough to hit his fist against the wall, though the stone suffered less under the onslaught than his own hand. "He is my enemy."

She was determined to get him to see reason. "Then, for the good of everyone, it is time to make peace."

"You don't know what you're asking of me." He looked at her bleakly. "You don't know what you're asking of Bridget. If I had not sent Niall and my uncle to Dublin—"

Bridget? "What has Bridget to do with this?" She thought of Jamie Jeffreys watching them as they picnicked beside the castle. Of Bridget's hasty departure. What was it that he would not tell her? "Why did you do this?"

"I wanted to help. I want to find a way for you to do what you need to do without breaking the law—"

"You mean, you thought because I slept with you that I could be persuaded back to London with you, if you could just take care of the pesky business of making certain that all my people had enough to eat?"

"I didn't—"

"You were wrong. I've done without a woman in my bed for long enough before. No matter how pleasant you are between the sheets, I'll not let you be a distraction. And I'll not let you destroy my family." He strode out of his study and into the hallway, bellowing for Douglas.

She followed in time to see Douglas, face pale, come running. "I've just heard, my lord. Cook told me."

"He's not to step foot in this house. Do you understand me?"

"I do." Douglas nodded solemnly and Kate suddenly feared that rather than mere discord, she might see blood shed tonight.

Before she could think what to do, what to say, Bridget appeared, looking annoyed but not worried. "What is the commotion, Sean?"

"Nothing, Bridget."

At her skeptical look, he added, "Just a disgreement between Kate and me. It is already resolved."

He looked at his sister as if he were afraid she would collapse at the very name Jeffreys. And it was equally obvious she had not heard the cook's rumors. Kate realized that no one had told her, not even Cook, because they wanted to protect her. From what?

Bridget looked at her. "What did you do?"

Kate, remembering that she had said Jamie Jeffreys' name without bursting into tears, risked telling her the truth, though she could see that Sean did not want her to. "I invited the Jeffreys for dinner."

Bridget became still, expressionless. Her maid let out a little moan of dismay.

"She did not know, Bridget. I did not tell her. She was trying to bring peace between Jeffreys and me." He exchanged a glance with Douglas. "Do not fear; they will not step foot in this house as long as I draw breath."

Bridget shook her head. "It is time for you to forgive him."

Sean looked as though she'd asked him to personally forgive the wandering ghost of Cromwell for the atrocities he had visited upon Ireland. "I will never forgive him."

The girl went over to her brother and put her arms around him, resting her head lightly on his shoulder. "You must."

He put his arms around her as if he could protect her from the world. "After what he—"

She broke away from him and put her hands on

her hips. "Your wife is right. It is time to put the past behind us."

Kate was alarmed when she saw that Bridget was trembling, though her words were reasonable—surprisingly so. What did she not understand? What had they not explained to her? She felt she had made an unforgivable mistake. But what?

The sound of the guests arriving riveted them all to the spot. Douglas stood rooted to the floor, clearly torn as he looked to Sean for instructions.

"Welcome them, Douglas," Bridget said.

"Let me send them away without trouble," Kate pleaded, when Sean looked incapable of offering welcome to his enemy.

"Let them in, Douglas," Sean said, his eyes focused on his sister's face. "But if they offer her insult, they will pay."

Douglas still looked torn, but he hurried to do as he was bid.

Kate stood transfixed in the hallway, wishing that she could call back time itself as father and son appeared, and Bridget's trembling became more pronounced. Sean moved toward her, but she flinched away.

"McCarthy." Jeffreys nodded politely enough, even though he had not used Sean's title to address him. Though her husband preferred not to hear the title from his family, she doubted that he would have given permission for Jeffreys to dispense with it. Her hopes for the evening, already low, dropped further. Tonight would be a true miracle if it passed without bloodshed and mayhem. A miracle indeed.

"Jeffreys," Sean acknowledged with bare civility.

"Good evening, Jamie." Bridget's eyes caught Jamie Jeffreys and she clasped her hands together, but she did not move.

Jeffreys was no more pleased than Sean at the greeting. "He's a man now, girl. Call him Mister Jeffreys, as is proper."

Bridget glanced at him, challenge in her eyes. "A man is not made by his father, but by his deeds. What has he done to deserve that name?"

Jamie flushed deeply. Kate realized there was more to the feud than simple differences and jealousy over a title and possession of a run-down abbey. She had made a serious blunder, and she had no idea how to fix it. She glanced at Sean in silent apology, not surprised that he took no notice at all of her.

Sean did not know what to do. Bridget should not have said such a thing, true as it was, if she wanted peace tonight. Part of him knew that the desire to run the men through would not be wise. Part of him didn't care if he was hanged for the crime. At least Bridget would be revenged at last.

As if they knew his thoughts and entertained similar ones themselves, there was silence and, for a moment, it seemed that the evening would come to blows, or the Jeffreyses would turn on their boot heels and leave without taking off their cloaks.

He didn't like the way Jamie's gaze was fixed on Bridget. "I'm to serve Her Majesty in India. I go to London within the month. Is that deed enough to prove I'm a man?"

Bridget shrugged, as if she had no reason to hate these men at all, to Sean's amazement. "Man enough to break bread with us at the abbey."

They sat down to dinner. Sean was not happy, but he followed Bridget's lead.

Kate glanced at him hopefully, but he glared at

her. She would not be happy to hear what he had to say when they were private. If, as it seemed they might, they survived the ordeal of dinner without killing each other.

Chapter 17

Dinner, he supposed, could be termed a success. No food, wine, or blood had been spilled upon the snow-white linens. Cook had outdone herself, despite her lack of notice. His servants, not usually known for their impeccable skills, could not have been faulted for anything except the glares they threw Jeffreys behind his back.

Kate was the most at ease during the meal, though he knew it was a false front from the way her fingers twisted the napkin in her lap. He supposed she had learned how to pretend ease and graciousness, no matter how she felt.

A good trait for the wife of a politician, he realized bleakly. And one that would serve her well when she rusticated as a divorced woman while her sisters traveled the world with their husbands and raised their children.

Jeffreys, as if feeling the strain himself, took his leave before it was time for the gentlemen to retire. When he stood and offered his apologies, there was a collective sigh of relief from everyone.

Still, Bridget had seemed stronger and braver

than ever as she stood by the door, saying her good-byes as if she spoke to neighbors she barely knew, rather than men who had accused her of attempted murder.

As if she knew what he thought, she threw her arms around Sean quickly and pecked his cheek. "She is meant for you. Do not be angry with her."

"To—"

"He is to be far away from me now. What more can you ask?"

"That a bullet take him in some faraway battle so you never need fear him again."

Bridget looked at him in puzzlement. "I never feared him, Sean. He was the one who was afraid. And I believe I've forgiven him for that." She smiled at Kate. "So see, your wife did well by me, after all."

He expected her to take the stairs up to her room, but instead she slipped out the door of the abbey to the outside. Without a cloak. He was about to call her back when her maid, cloaked and with Bridget's cloak draped across her arm, ran hastily to catch up to her mistress.

"I'm sorry, Sean." Kate and he were alone in the hall, the servants having mysteriously melted away without a sound.

"Sorry?" How many ways had he lost his mind tonight? To allow Jeffreys into his home? At his table? To break bread with him? And now he was contemplating—no, eager to find a way to forgive her so that he could share her bed again tonight with an easy conscience.

Fool. He looked at her. He wanted her. But he could not throw away his plans simply to satisfy some primal urge. "I'm sending you home tomorrow."

"But I can help you."

"Do you know what would have happened if my

uncle had been here tonight?" Thank God for the business in Dublin."

"If you had told me—"

"It is not your concern, Kate. You were to be here only until your ship sailed. I think we'd all find ourselves more comfortable if you waited the remaining time at an inn on the coast—well away from here."

"You don't mean that."

He rubbed his eyes wearily, half hoping that she would be gone when he opened them again. But she was still there, a plea for forgiveness in her eyes. "I can't trust you."

"You can. This was a mistake. I did not mean to hurt Bridget."

"Not even when you threatened to turn her in if I did not come to your bed?"

"I would never have done so." Anger flashed through her. "And it is not I who made her vulnerable to such a threat—it was you. I only want to help you escape the trap you've set for yourself."

"So that you can trap me for yourself? Turn me into a foolish fop of a lord who thinks London better than here, where my people are?" Realizing this was a dangerous conversation to have out in the open, he turned toward the stairs. "Come to bed, Kate. I will decide what to do about you in the morning."

"You will decide what to do about me tomorrow? Then what does tonight hold?"

"Sleep," he lied.

She crossed her arms over her chest protectively as she gazed at him warily. "Perhaps I should sleep in Lady Dilys's room tonight."

"Perhaps you should." He crossed to where she stood, picked her up in his arms and ascended the stairs two at a time. "But you will not."

He made love to her, not gently, but thoroughly, afraid he might never get the chance again. Afraid he could not let her go, even though he knew he must.

She woke to find him gone. He had been angry with her last night and yet he had not hurt her. Had instead shown her that pleasure had more than one face. It could be shy and careful, as he had been before. Or fierce and passionate and demanding, as he had been last night.

She had met his demands and made a few of her own that had surprised them both. They had ended the night locked in each other's arms, but now he was gone. And she was alone.

She dressed and wandered the abbey, seeing not a soul. They were, she reflected, a bit like ghosts themselves. If they did not want her to find them, she would not. So she settled herself in the library and chose a book to read until someone—anyone—forgave her enough to speak to her.

"I crave a match."

Kate looked up from her book to see that Bridget had appeared in the library. The girl stood at the window, silhouetted by the sun, which had made a rare appearance. She closed her book. "As you wish."

"Excellent." There was a sharp look in the girl's eye, and Kate had a momentary doubt that she was wise to cross swords with her so soon after inviting her sworn enemy to dinner.

Despite her concerns, she considered agreeing. After all, she reflected, perhaps she could get more information out of Bridget than she had out of Sean.

She offered an apology, to see whether Bridget was angry with her or not. "I am sorry for last night."

Bridget shrugged. "You did not know."

The girl did not seem to be angry at all, so Kate continued with her questions. "What is the dispute between you? Did Jamie hurt you?"

Bridget sighed, as if she had been asked to recite a lesson long since learned and discarded. "He stole a book of mine."

"A book?" So much animosity over a book? The men had been willing to kill at the slightest insult. Kate doubted that could be the whole of it.

"I found it, at the castle. And he said it was his, because the castle was his father's," Bridget said softly, with a faraway look in her eye. "It was a beautiful book, just where the fairies said it would be."

The fairies. Kate should have known. "If the book was buried in the castle, then it would have been Jamie's by right of law."

"What is English law?" Bridget's tone exactly echoed Sean's on the subject. She looked squarely at Kate. "The fairies said it should have been mine. Jamie shouldn't have taken it." And then she shrugged. "But he was only a boy, so I forgive him."

"All this fuss was over a book?" Kate had difficulty believing that Sean would be so foolish.

Bridget didn't meet her eyes. "It was a beautiful book. A work of art."

Art? All of a sudden, Kate realized that Bridget was speaking of an illustrated manuscript. Those, she knew, had been discovered in Ireland often enough in the last century and they were worth a great deal—both historically and in coin. Perhaps that was why Sean had cared so much about an old book?

"I have an idea, Kate." Bridget leaned toward her like an imp and whispered in her ear, as if she were afraid someone would overhear and forbid her. Which Kate was tempted to do.

Bridget's suggestion on a December day that

looked more like May was to take their swords and practice at the castle.

Kate wasn't certain that was wise, considering what she now knew about the animosity with the Jeffreys. "What if Jamie is there?"

"He won't be." There was a reckless glint in the girl's eyes. "Although if he was, maybe I'd challenge him to see how much of a man he's become."

That sounded like trouble. Rather than risk Bridget doing something so foolish as challenging Jamie to a match, perhaps it would be best if Kate accompanied her and saw to it that the two did not meet, even accidentally.

"Well? Do we go? The sun does not shine here often, you know, Kate. It is a gift from the fairies, and we should not waste it."

Reluctantly, Kate agreed.

Cook muttered an unintelligible warning as she packed a quick lunch for them. But Bridget only laughed and twirled her around the kitchen, promising her the fairies would clean her kitchen for her tonight when she was in bed asleep.

The day was unseasonably warm, and Kate couldn't argue with Bridget's idea. They tethered their horses and found a patch of ground that was suitable for combat, mock or not.

"We will have firm footing here," Kate decided, as she ground her boot against the matted grass.

"The fairies were good to us," Bridget answered with a smile.

The battle was hard and heated, as always. Kate was too busy concentrating on keeping her footing as the frozen ground melted and offered patches of slickly treacherous mud to harry her. It was all she could do to keep her eye on Bridget's flashing strokes, which was why she didn't notice that they were no longer alone.

"Hold." It wasn't until the shout pierced through her focus that she realized, dimly, that something was wrong.

She put up her sword at the same moment Bridget did, and suddenly they were surrounded by men on horseback.

"What—" Kate began to ask, when chaos broke out. One of the mounted men grabbed her and lifted her up in front of him as her sword clattered to the ground.

"Let her go!" Bridget screamed and Kate, panicked, saw that she had dropped her sword, too, and was grappling with a horseman who looked suspiciously like Jamie Jeffreys.

"Go!" Jamie ordered the man who held Kate, and a third man who sat up, alert for more trouble.

The man who wasn't holding Kate pointed at Bridget, who struggled against her captor. "What about her?" She didn't like the look on his face.

Jamie frowned at him forbiddingly. "I will see to the girl," he said in sharp command that was only a bit breathless from his struggle with the unwilling Bridget.

"She's a mad one, sir. Your father will not like that we didn't offer you help."

He looked down at Bridget, who had ceased to struggle, but now glared up at him. "I need no help with her. I'm not twelve years old anymore."

He tightened his grip around Bridget's waist. "She'll not hurt anyone now." He met Kate's eyes for a long moment and then glanced away. "Take her ladyship to my father. He'll know what to do with her."

"We'll wait for you." It was an insult to countermand his order, and Kate could feel the tension that drew tight between the men.

At last, Jamie shook his head. "Go. I will catch up with you in a moment."

"Sir—"

"I have business to finish with the girl."

Both men barked out laughter that chilled Kate's heart as they turned to ride away. What business did Jamie have with Bridget? She wished she hadn't dropped her sword so easily. What a warrior she turned out to be. Her sister Rosaline would disown her in disgust if she knew.

What would Sean do, knowing that she had not protected his sister?

Before they had reached the Jeffreyses' estate, Jamie rode up beside them. Alone. "I let her go."

He held himself oddly, so oddly that one of the men asked, "Did she hurt you, my lord?" There was a grin on his face.

He frowned and shook his head, though his words were at odds with his gesture. "She kicked me."

"If you have hurt her—" Kate didn't know why she offered the fruitless threat.

"Bridget suffered no ill treatment from me, I assure you." He rode up beside her, his expression and his words apologetic. "And my father will see that you are safe, my lady."

As he spoke, his hand slipped from his thigh where it had been pressed and she glimpsed a bloodied gash.

Before she could gasp out a question, he stared at her, cold and dark. His gaze was a clear warning that she should not speak.

She turned her head away. She would not feel sympathy for her captor; she would not.

Sean had hoped to avoid Kate. Avoid dealing with her again until nightfall. He trusted himself with her only in the dark of their bedroom. And he knew that must end soon enough, no matter how he wished to keep her here with him.

He thought he had succeeded in his plan until late afternoon, when Bridget burst into his office, her hair wild about her face. "They've taken her."

"The fairies?"

"No. Jeffreys's men."

At that, his blood ran cold. His first thought was that she spoke of her maid. But the poor breathless creature came hurrying in behind Bridget, dashing his fleeting hope. "Who have they taken?"

He knew an instant before she spoke. "Kate. Just like they took me."

He saw the rip in her skirt. "Are you hurt?"

She shook her head. "I sank my dagger into Jamie's thigh and he let me go quick enough." There was a bloodthirsty glint in her eye that might have troubled him, if he'd had time to reflect on it. Instead, he could only note that it matched the urge in his heart.

"I couldn't save her, Sean." She was breathless and nearly hysterical. He saw that she held her sword drawn at her side, useless now, a gesture of her helpless urge to rescue Kate. "But you can. I know you can."

He didn't need any more information than that. He left her to her frantic maid and went for the stables. Jeffreys would not escape justice this time. He would see to it himself, even if he ended up hanging for it.

He tried not to think of Kate, hurt and helpless.

"I did not mean for Jamie and my men to deal with you so roughly," Jeffreys assured her. "I just wanted to make certain that you were properly thanked for your dinner invitation."

"How?" Kate glanced at Jamie, who stared into the cup of tea he held as if he wished to escape into it. "By snatching me bodily away?"

Jeffreys held his palms out to her in helpless apology. "When they saw the girl attacking you, they naturally thought . . ." He trailed off and shrugged again.

Kate sat sipping tea and listening to the apologies of Sean's sworn enemy. She wished to slap the man, but she couldn't in good conscience. After all, his men had thought they were rescuing her from an attack by Sean's mad sister. "We were taking advantage of the beautiful day to practice in the open. What harm in that?"

"As you say. But I have reason to believe the girl could willingly do harm. And, forgive me for being blunt, I don't think your husband and his sister entirely approved of your inviting my family to dinner. I worried that you might suffer at their hands for your kindness. I told my son so."

"They were skeptical that the dinner would have any positive result." Kate tempered her words carefully. She did not want to insult the man when he found it so easy to offer his protection. If she were not careful, she might end up imprisoned here because he thought it was for her own good. "But neither of them offered me any threat of harm."

"Forgive me, but I have heard the rumors from London, my lady."

"Do you not know that listening to rumors is a waste of good ears?"

"Then he is not seeking a divorce and you have not come to throw yourself on his mercy?"

Kate didn't want to lie. "I did not come to throw myself on his mercy."

He frowned. "Barbarians. The king should never have given a McCarthy a title. But he had a soft heart for the man who saved his life."

"My husband is no barbarian, and I will not have you call him one in my presence." Kate rose, hoping that he would allow her to leave. She would prefer that Sean heard what had transpired from her lips alone.

"I don't know what the duke was thinking, to allow you to be married to an Irishman, even if his father did manage to charm a title out of the king. I suspect he'll lose it soon enough through his criminal actions, just as his ancestors did before him. But he'll not get Blarney. My family bought it and we've cared for it honorably and well."

So it was the castle he cared about. Kate sighed. When would men learn to care more about flesh-and-blood people than about crumbling stone and the ghosts of warriors dead for one cause or another? She said sharply, to halt his train of lament, "If you can call selling visits to tourists to kiss the Blarney Stone honorable."

He colored. "The stone is still there, is it not? Do you know how large a fortune we have been offered for just a piece of that stone through the ages? Cared for it, despite the McCarthys, we have. After what that girl did . . ." He stopped, realizing he had said too much.

"What did she do?"

"I heard the hounds baying for a moment." He closed his eyes.

Jamie, who had been silent by the fire, said softly, "She nearly pushed me off the castle wall."

"She?" Why she asked, she couldn't say. There was no one else who could have done it.

"Bridget McCarthy." Jamie's tongue lingered over the name almost mournfully, and Kate watched him more closely.

His father said angrily, "Sent by him."

Jamie shook his head wearily. "It was only an accident, Father. I have told you so many times."

"The girl bewitched you."

"She was my friend."

"Perhaps it was an accident caused by a misunderstanding over some object?"

Jamie glanced at her in surprise. He stood, and if she had not been watching closely, she would not have noticed the discomfort the movement cost him. "She slipped, nothing more." He moved his hand nervously, revealing the deep and now widening red stain where Bridget had cut him.

Jeffreys had his back to his son, as if he could not bear to look at him at the moment. "Nonsense. She was jealous of you and she tried to kill you. You're just too soft-headed to admit it."

Kate moved to block the sight of the spreading bloodstain from Jamie's father, just as an agitated footman came into the room. "You are required on urgent business," he said to Jeffreys.

"Excuse me." The man hurried from the room without a backward glance at Kate or Jamie.

Kate said softly, "You wound is bleeding. Do you need assistance?"

He shook his head. "It is shallow, though it requires slight enough movement to reopen it. I suppose I should be grateful that I still have my leg."

"She was afraid. I hope you do not mean to bring this matter to your father's attention."

"It is not her ability with a knife that worries me about Bridget McCarthy. It is her fey tongue."

"What did she say to you?"

"That she would cut off my—" He stopped and

reddened, as if realizing he should not repeat the words to a lady, despite the fact that they were spoken to him by a lady, albeit a mad one. "That she would cheerfully unman me if she thought I was a man. And that I might yet distinguish myself, so she would not pass judgment on me until I had the chance to prove myself."

"Do you believe she can see the future?"

"She thinks that she can. And sometimes—" He broke off and then sighed. "No. I do not believe she can see the future. Do you?"

"She has told me that the ship I am to take back to London will go down."

"She must want you to stay."

"Most likely that is the reason she says what she says." Kate laughed. "Although I may ask the captain of the *Daisy's Pride* how many years he has been sailing."

He looked surprised. "You are not to sail on the *Daisy's Pride*, are you?"

"I am."

He paled. "I am to sail to London on her, too."

"Then we can talk to the captain together." Kate smiled at him, though she did not like his sudden nervousness. He said he didn't believe Bridget could see into the future, so why did he care what she predicted about a ship she knew nothing of?

"Did you know Bridget before her illness?"

"Her illness?" He looked genuinely puzzled.

"Sean said that she was not like she is now before her illness."

His color deepened. "Oh. Yes. She was different then, although my father is right to say that she was wild. I didn't realize it then, of course. We were just children. But she had all her wits about her before . . ." He did not continue.

"I'm glad you didn't hurt her. We were merely practicing, you know. I'm not trying to protect her."

"I'm sorry I overreacted." He shifted the weight off his wounded leg, uncomfortably. "I suppose I just let my father's suspicions carry me away."

"Does Bridget know what you thought? Why you interrupted us so forcefully?"

"I tried to tell her." He glanced down at the spreading bloodstain, and his lips pressed tight. "But I don't believe she was listening well."

Kate realized, with sudden horror, that Bridget, once freed, would have gone directly to Sean for help. What might she have told him, if she did not understand why Jamie and the men had taken her off? She put down her teacup. "I have to get home at once. Can you help me? I'm quite certain your father—"

Just then, Jeffreys returned, a grim expression on his face. "Your husband wishes to speak to you. I have made it clear that I will not tolerate violence on his part, any more than I will tolerate it from his sister."

"He will not hurt me." Kate glanced at the man, seeing that he was slightly disheveled. Had they fought? "Where is he?"

"George will show you." He gestured toward the footman who had followed him into the room.

As Kate hurried out of the room, he grasped her elbow to stop her for a moment. "Remember, my lady. I will not let him hurt you. Not while you are in my home. But I cannot protect you if you go with him."

Chapter 18

For a moment, he was afraid that Kate would appear as bruised and battered as Bridget had been. Jeffreys had claimed she was unharmed. Had explained the "misunderstanding" that had caused his men to take Kate away. But he needed to see her. Needed to know she was unharmed.

When she entered the room, she moved right into his arms. "Sean, I'm sorry you had to worry. I am fine, I assure you. There was just a silly mistake."

Sean was not in the mood to hear any justification for the treatment of his sister or his wife. He crushed her to his chest even as he castigated her. "How dare you defend the enemy?"

"He did me no harm. I'm not defending him, I'm telling you not to do anything foolish on my account."

"What about my sister? They have terrorized her again."

"I don't think so. She gave the young man a bit more than a rap on the ribs—she stuck him." She paused, comprehension dawning in her eyes. "What do you mean, terrorized her again?"

He cursed his own careless tongue. "You don't understand."

She stood away from him, her arms crossed and her expression forbidding. "Then make me. Tell me what it is about Bridget's madness that you—and Jamie Jeffreys—have not yet told me. She wasn't ill, was she?"

He didn't want to tell her. "My sister is none of your concern."

"No?" For a moment he thought she would accept the truth, and then she said softly, "She is if the child I might conceive could be tainted with madness."

Tainted? His sister? He wouldn't let her believe that. "Bridget was as sane as any woman until she was twelve."

She waited for a moment, as if she thought he might go on, and then she prompted him. "So at twelve she just went mad? Overnight? I know it wasn't an illness."

"No." He ground his teeth. "Something happened."

She would not relent for a moment, although she seemed to realize that she was dragging up old, painful things. "What?"

"Jeffreys, that upstart Sassenach, had his men kidnap her."

Appalled, she asked, "Kidnap her? As they did to me today?"

"Bridget was not so lucky as you, to be offered tea and protection." He closed his eyes. She would have it all out of him, and then what?

"What do you mean?" She knew. He could hear it in her voice. Why would she make him say it?

"They did not treat her kindly—they thought her a threat to the boy. Fools."

"What did they do?"

"She wouldn't say." He opened his eyes to glare at her. If she wanted the whole truth, she would have it. He hoped she choked on it, as he did. "She didn't say anything the first few weeks she was back. But I can guess—can't you? She came back bloodied and bruised and with the light out of her eyes like it would never come back. But at least she wasn't hanged."

"Surely he didn't mean to hang her, a child of twelve? For what?"

"For trying to murder his boy. He would have, but the magistrate refused when the boy testified they'd only been playing and she'd not meant to hurt him. But Jeffreys didn't believe the boy."

"No." She shook her head. "He doesn't believe it now. But to hurt a child?"

"He claimed not to have known it was happening until too late. He claimed to have punished the men responsible, even though they had just been trying to defend his son from the wild Irish lass."

"Perhaps he spoke truthfully."

"A man doesn't defend himself with the part of himself they used on her, Kate. He uses it to love a woman, or to hurt her. But never for his own defense."

She didn't argue with him about that, though her eyes were full of pain. "If you had brought the matter to the authorities . . ."

"So the world would know why my sister went mad? Isn't it enough that I didn't kill him?"

"You'd have hung."

"I don't mind a rope at my own throat." There were days, in the beginning, when he wished he had. But what would have happened to Bridget then? "The first words she spoke were to ask me not to tell anyone."

"How did she come to be there at the castle with the boy? Shouldn't she have been in lessons with a governess at the very least?"

"Her governess had gone the week before. I hadn't been able to pay her for six months."

"And you?"

He knew he shouldn't blame her. He'd made his choices and he'd thought them wise at the time. But still he said, "I was busy meeting the whims of a well-dowered lady."

The whims of a well-dowered lady. Her. He had been courting her. No wonder he'd climbed into her bed that night. She felt guilt wash over her that she had put him through the ridiculous trials she had. She had made him play games when he had people to protect. "I'm sorry. How is she?"

"Angry that she could not protect you."

"She said the fairies had meant her to have the book they argued over." Kate knew it would be painful, but she had to ask one more question. "Did she push him?"

He looked at her a moment before answering, but she could see that he had grappled with the question himself. "He says no. She says no. But no one asked them before they kidnapped her, beat her—and worse."

"Was she—fey—before that?"

"She was a little wild, as any girl might be without a mother's gentle hand." He rejected her suggestion. "But she was gentle and never harmed a soul."

"Do you think he only threatened her life because he was afraid of what you would say about him?"

"Yes."

"I didn't know."

"It wasn't your concern." He turned away from

her, as if he couldn't bear the sight of her. "Let's go home."

Kate wanted to hit him. To scream at him. It wasn't her concern? If he had told her, she would never have invited the Jeffreys to dinner. Would never have allowed Bridget to take her to the castle, not even for a peaceful picnic. "You should have told me."

He turned back. "Why, would you have spit his fine English tea in his face then?"

"I didn't know, Sean. He did not hurt me. He thought she meant to kill me, and he just wanted to see me safely away from you while you were in such a foul temper. He was merely being over-protective."

"Of my wife."

She felt the fury sweep through her. How dare he speak of her as if he wanted her? "Why should you care? You've already decided you don't want me. Haven't you?"

"Come home, Kate." He didn't answer that question. "You're more fortunate than Bridget—this time. But I don't know if that will be true if you stay here any longer. Or don't you trust me anymore? Don't you trust my mad sister?"

It was a terrible thing to admit her own breach of faith. She could not bring herself to land the blow, so she said instead, "He knows that you have initiated the divorce. The news did not take long to travel. I'm certain they know in Boston—perhaps even Ros has heard in California."

"None of their business."

"Not even of mine, so the law says."

"Doesn't go down well, to have no say in your own life, does it?"

"No."

"You're my wife."

"For how much longer? Perhaps I'm tired of being a wife only when you find it convenient."

"Perhaps I should keep you."

"You wouldn't dare."

"I would if I thought it would save my people. Since I don't, I think I'd rather turn you free and let you bedevil your own countrymen."

The truth of his words was shining from his eyes, and she could not doubt it any longer. Feeling a blow to her chest, she struggled not to let him see she couldn't breathe.

She stood and stalked out without a word. She almost slammed a door, but stopped, suddenly filled with a clear, deep relief. It was over. She turned and made herself look at him. "Bridget says I'm to have a son—if I do, you'll stay away from him."

"He'll be—" he started to protest.

She shook her head fiercely. "If you don't stay away, I'll swear he's Niall's."

He shrugged. "The odds are slim that we would have created any child in this short time."

"Nevertheless, since you don't want me, you can't have me. Ever. Nor any child I might have. If you are seen to set foot anywhere on our property, I will convince my brother and the duke to order you shot."

For several days he expected Kate to return. He didn't know why he would expect her to do such a thing. He himself wouldn't have forgiven himself for what he'd said to her. But all he'd received was a terse note, telling him that she would be gone from Ireland as planned, would not put any obstacle to the divorce in his way, thanking him for his hospitality. He supposed it was irony, but he burned the note in the fireplace as soon as he'd read it, so he had no way to reread the words and reassure himself of that.

Bridget had been furious with him when he told her what he'd done. At first he thought she worried that he had left her vulnerable at the Jeffreyses. But she had soon made clear that she accepted the explanation of why Jamie had interfered. She'd even seemed to think he'd had justification for his beliefs, but he didn't ask her why. He didn't want to know.

Just as he didn't want to know that his sister believed she could see into the future. Believed that his wife's ship would go down and that she must not be on it. He had turned back to his books, spent his days at the greenhouse, taken a quick, cold supper in his rooms. Anything to avoid listening to the nonsense.

At least Niall and Connor were not back from Dublin yet, and he did not have to deal with their angry reproaches, or his cousin's jealous jibes. Would Niall have handled things differently? Would Kate have listened to him? Trusted him? After all, she certainly knew him better than she knew her own husband.

He'd have to speak to Bridget, he resolved. Explain that he and Kate were not meant to be. She'd understand if he explained it that way. But such explanations would be difficult to deliver until she had decided to forgive him. He hadn't seen Bridget for two days. He expected she was mad at him for sending Kate away.

He realized he had not seen her maid either.

"Douglas."

The man appeared magically and quietly as always. "Fetch my sister, please. I need to speak with her."

He knew it was an easier order to give than to carry out. His sister could be anywhere. But he did not suspect that she had left the abbey grounds. Until her maid was found bound in her room.

Douglas brought him the news—and the maid, still rubbing her wrists in relief at being untied. "Where is my sister?" He had wanted to tell her that with Kate gone, she was safe from ever having to see Jeffreys or hear his name again. But now he wondered if she was as mad as Jeffreys had said. Why else would she tie up a poor defenseless girl?

"She followed your lady, my lord."

Followed Kate? His blood ran cold. "Followed her where?" To Jeffreys? Had she decided to wreak revenge upon the family? Why now? Did she truly believe that strongly he and Kate belonged together? Did she blame Jamie for separating them? He shook his head, realizing he had not understood his sister for a very long time.

The maid's freckles grew prominent on her pale face as she grew even more pale. "We was riding by the castle and just talking and then she got a look in her eyes clear in the middle of a sentence of mine and took off for home. I found her packing a bag and tried to stop her. So she tied me up so I couldn't call for help right away." She looked at him somewhat reproachfully. "She didn't think it would take you two days to find me."

Bridget had reacted to something the maid had said. "What did you tell her?"

"That your lady had gone with the Jeffreyses, that they were all to sail on the same ship together to London, so your lady wouldn't be lonely on her trip home."

Sean's heart sank even as he made preparations to follow. Bridget was certain the ship was to go down. She'd told him so more than once, but he'd ignored her. What did she think she could do to stop it sailing? Or did she have some more nefarious plan in mind?

He looked up, meaning to order Douglas to get a bag packed for him, and a horse readied. But the man was gone, no doubt not wanting to waste any time waiting for Sean to realize what he needed done.

He looked at the trembling maid. "You must be hungry. Go get something to eat."

"I didn't mean to let her get away—"

"I'm not sure anyone can save Bridget from herself. I'm sure you did your best." And now he would do his. It had never been good enough in the past, but he hoped that this time would be different.

He wondered what Kate would have advised him to do? Perhaps he'd ask her, if he ever saw her again.

Jeffreys had been kind to her. Kinder than he need be, but she thought he took some pleasure in the realization that he was hurting Sean by taking her back to London.

She watched the familiar countryside roll away through the windows of the Jeffreyses' well-sprung carriage and reflected that she had learned a lot about marriage in her fortnight as a truly married woman. Most of all was that a man who didn't want to be a husband made the whole thing impossible.

She thought, once or twice, about renting a carriage to take her back, just so that she could make absolutely certain that this was what he wanted. Foolish thought.

If he'd wanted something else, he'd known well enough where she was. He could have come and told her. Besides, she owed Sarah a swift journey home. The maid had been plain in her joy when Kate had told her they were indeed sailing home as originally planned.

The port city was bustling, but Kate could not wait to board the ship. She had spoken to the captain, who had assured her that the ship was sound and he had been sailing for thirty years without a mishap.

She had been afraid he might be offended at her inquiry, but he reassured her that she was not the first passenger to seek a little extra reassurance. She wondered if she were the first who sought the reassurance because of a prediction from the fairies. But this was Ireland, so she thought not.

"So, are you satisfied that we will make it to London in one piece?" Jamie Jeffreys walked her back to the carriage with a smile on his lips.

"Completely." At first she thought it was thoughts of fairies and predictions that made the woman who caught her eye remind her of Bridget. But then the woman turned, and her heart nearly stopped. It *was* Bridget. She glanced full at them, then turned and disappeared.

Kate detached herself from Jamie Jeffreys and Sarah with a quick wave of her hand. "Excuse me, I just thought of an errand that needs to be run." She made her way through the crowd, ignoring the startled questions of both Sarah and Jamie, which quickly faded away in the noise of the docks.

She followed the cloaked woman, fear churning in her gut. What was Bridget doing here? She had a dreadful feeling she knew. The girl didn't want them to get on the ship. And she was used to playing "tricks" on the English. What trick would she play now?

At last she caught sight of the girl entering a

rackety building, one very much like the shed Sean had put fire to. Her heart beating hard in her chest, she came up behind the girl and asked sharply, "Bridget, what are you doing?"

Bridget turned quickly, but did not appear to be startled to see Kate. "Delaying you and poking the English in the eye all at once."

"Don't." Kate eyed the neat bundle of faggots and hay that would be easily ignited by the tinderbox and oil-soaked rags in Bridget's hands.

"I couldn't stop Jamie's men from taking you, but I'm not going to let you die on the *Daisy's Pride.*" She glanced away for a moment. "And I'm not going to let him die, either."

"I'm not going to die. Jamie's not going to die. We've spoken to the captain. The ship is sound, the weather is fine." Kate wondered how to reason with a madwoman. "You can't see the future. No one can."

"Jamie says that, too." Bridget frowned, but she appeared more sad than angry. "No one believes— but I know."

"How will this stop the ship?" Kate again tried reasoning. Perhaps if they spoke long enough—

"This cargo is meant for the ship. If it burns, they'll have to delay a week or so, and you'll take another ship and be safe."

"How do you know?" Kate expected her to credit the fairies, but instead Bridget said quite lucidly, "I asked one of the deckhands what could happen to delay the ship."

"Come with me. I'll send a note to Sean and stay with you until he comes to take you safely home."

For a moment Bridget seemed ready to accept. Then she shook her head. "Jamie will still go on the ship."

"I'll convince him to take passage on another ship."

"He won't listen. He's stubborn, just like Sean."

Stubborn. Just like Bridget. "He will. He doesn't want you to get hurt."

A flash of pain spasmed across Bridget's face. "He doesn't know how to protect me, any more than Sean does."

"No. We have to protect ourselves. And them as well." Kate was struck by the truth of what she said, although she had spoken out of desperation.

"How can we, when they're so stubborn?"

"I can refuse to let Sean drive me away." Kate said.

"You can." Bridget smiled. "And I can kidnap Jamie."

Kate didn't think the kidnapping idea was any more sound than the fire, but she wasn't going to say so now. "Good. Give me those, then, and let's go protect ourselves for a change."

Bridget relented then, with a little exhalation of relief.

Kate took the fags and oil-soaked rags, glad that she had averted a disaster. But just then they heard the sound of boots outside the doorway. Bridget slipped away like a wraith. Kate was not so fortunate.

Chapter 19

Kate tried to slip by the burly man at the door, but he put his arm out to bar her way. "Halt, lass. What have you there?"

She stopped. She'd had the presence of mind to drop the rags, but she still held the tinderbox under her cloak. "Bread."

He lifted his lantern and the light picked out the pile of faggots and rags. "Bread?" He didn't believe her. "Show me."

She tried to dash by him, but had no luck. The big man called out for help, and in moments she found herself in the street, surrounded by curious passersby and suspicious police.

The guard said, "Looks like I stopped her just before she got to light the fire. Pile would have sent everything up."

The policeman looked sharply at her. "Who are you?"

Kate opened her mouth to speak and then stopped. If she said her real name, they might look with suspicion on Sean. Or trace it back to Bridget. So she lied. "Mary Duffy."

She caught sight of Bridget in the crowd. The girl was pale and silent. Kate tried to signal her silently to slip away. There was no use both of them being caught up in the mess.

"What were you doing here?"

She decided the truth might serve her best here—if she omitted Bridget's name and description. "I saw someone acting suspiciously and I followed . . . him."

"No sign of anyone else, that I saw," the burly man said with a shake of his head. "Just her."

"He ran away when he saw me," she improvised.

"And handed you the tinderbox?"

"Yes." It sounded foolish to her ears. As the men glared at her and moved closer to close off any hope she had to escape, she wished she'd thought to come up with a complete—and believable—lie.

The guard took her hands roughly in his and held them up to his nose to sniff. "Oil. Just like on the rags in there. She's the one I saw. The only one." He shook his head and sneered at her. "Out to cause mischief, were you? Well you have—for yourself."

"This is a mistake."

"Surely it is." He grinned, a bloodhound who'd managed to tree his quarry. "Yours."

He seemed to recognize the terror that weakened her knees and revel in it. "Thought you were going to warm yourself by a fire tonight and instead you'll be shivering in a cell."

She knew she should be afraid for herself, but somehow she felt she would be fine. The duke would straighten everything out if she couldn't do so herself when she faced the magistrate. He'd be furious with her, of course. But he would set her free. She had no doubt.

So, even though the unfriendly crowd jeered at

her, she couldn't find room in her heart to worry for her future; she was too worried about Bridget. As they carted her away, Kate swept the crowd for signs of the girl. There was no sight of her. She didn't know whether to be glad the girl had gotten away, or worried about what she would do next. Hadn't she threatened to kidnap Jamie?

The cell they tossed her in was filthy, and as cold as promised. But she had barely time to let the reality sink in before the door squeaked open and the guard said gruffly. "Visitor."

She expected Bridget, but smiled when she saw who had come instead. She was surprised at the temptation to throw her arms around him. She barely knew him, after all. "I take it she didn't manage to kidnap you, then?"

Jamie Jeffreys looked around the cell grimly and then at her. "She tried, but when she told me what happened, I pointed out that getting you out of here would require that I have some freedom."

Kate felt a sweep of relief to know that there was someone who would help, even if he were a boy of eighteen. And then she panicked. "Does your father know?"

He looked at her as if she'd asked him a foolish question. "My father believes I sailed on the *Daisy's Pride.*"

"I'm sorry. I'm grateful you'd even be willing to help me, considering—"

"Why did you give a false name? I can't believe they'd hold the wife of an earl in conditions like this."

She had no intention of confessing that she was afraid the authorities would find out about Sean's illegal activities. After all, Jamie's father was one of the authorities, and she would not test his loyalties to such an extent. "I didn't want my husband to know."

"I thought it might be something like that. Bridget seems quite upset at his decision to divorce you." He shifted his feet in the dank straw. "You must tell them now."

"I can't."

"You—"

"I know it seems unwise to you, but I would rather that no one ever know my true identity. If you could get word to my brother-in-law, the Duke of Kerstone, he will help me, and no one will be the wiser."

"I can send a message, of course, but it will take some time." He glanced around the cell, not hiding his distaste. "You will not be comfortable."

"I cannot help that." She remembered how Sean had accused her of betraying him. To have his wife arrested for arson would, without doubt, be a betrayal of him.

"If I spoke to my father—"

"Absolutely not." Though she suspected Jeffreys would help her, she wasn't certain he wouldn't use her situation against Sean somehow. "There must be some other way."

"Bridget will not be pleased. She told me not to come back without you." He looked unhappy. "I can't promise that she won't tell her brother—"

She grasped his arm tightly. "You must not let her. Tell her that she risks her brother's reputation."

"Surely—"

"Tell her that." Bridget would understand the whole of it, she trusted, despite the cryptic nature of her words. "Tell her exactly that. She will not go to her brother."

The guard came to the door. "Time's up."

Jamie glanced at her regretfully. "I cannot bear to think of leaving you here."

"I can do this." She wasn't certain she could, but she would not show weakness to him. He might tell the truth himself to help her if he thought she was not strong enough to survive this trial.

"If only—"

She said, as forcefully as she could while whispering to keep her words from the guard's ear, "You must find a way to release Mary Duffy without revealing that I am the wife of the Earl of Blarney." Especially to the earl himself.

"It will make freeing you more difficult."

"They cannot believe I would do such a thing."

His young face held only disbelief that she could be so naïve. "They can, and they very well might." He patted her hand. "We will get you out, my lady."

The guard approached and put his hand on Jamie's shoulder. In a moment, he was gone, leaving her alone to hope she was as strong as she had said she was.

"Have you seen this woman?" Sean showed the miniature of Bridget to the men loading cargo on the dock. He had missed the *Daisy's Pride*. It had sailed the day before, with a full complement of passengers and cargo.

The man didn't glance long before shaking his head.

Damn. Where was she? He glanced around the teaming dockside. She hadn't wanted the ship to sail, he knew. But more importantly, she hadn't wanted Kate or Jamie to sail with it. Had she found them? What might she have done to prevent them from sailing?

He cursed his foolishness. He should have seen Kate to the coast himself. Should have put her on the ship. Should have locked his sister in a tower and thrown away the key years ago—for her own good. For all he knew she could have been taken up by white slavers and be long gone.

He started toward the closest inn. He'd check them all if he had to. He'd show them Bridget's miniature—and the one of Kate that her sister Helena had given him. Someone had to have seen one of them.

Kate found herself brought into the court with very little ceremony. She had hoped to present a dignified presence, but it was difficult when she hadn't even been able to wash the dirt of her cell from her face or clothing.

At first it seemed that the magistrate would simply listen to the testimony of the man who had found her in the shed.

Frightened, she dared to ask, "May I speak?"

The magistrate, his eyes cold and unfriendly, frowned at her. "What lies would you like to pour into our ears like vicious poison?"

"I frightened away the person who meant to start the fire. I meant only to prevent a fire, not cause one." She tried to meet his eyes, unfriendly as they were, and to speak in a steady, calm voice that bespoke complete honesty.

"Lies, my lord." The man who had caught her cried out in outrage. "I saw the wicked shift of her eyes when she was caught. There was naught but guilt in them."

"What reason had you to be there?"

"I thought the man suspicious." Her voice faltered, revealing that she realized the weakness of her own excuse.

"Your hands smelled of oil—and probably still do," the man grumbled.

The magistrate ruled in a thunderous voice, "Mary Duffy, you are found guilty of mischief and intent to do murder."

"Murder!" Kate was astonished. She had heard them read the charges when she entered, but she had not been able to make out the words for the buzzing in her ears—she had not managed to eat the gruel they had served to her and had only forced herself to drink the brackish water because she knew she must.

The man who'd caught her called out angrily, "There were two lads set to guard the merchandise. If you'd been successful in setting your fire, they would surely have perished."

Kate protested faintly, "I was trying to stop the fire."

The magistrate, his limited patience exhausted, banged down his gavel. "The court will hear no more from the criminal."

"But—" Kate felt as if she were floating above herself.

The horror of what he said made her vision darken until she could not see the man, but only hear his terrifying voice. "Silence! You are sentenced to hang by the neck until dead."

Kate felt her knees buckle and gripped the worn wood of the rail in front of her, not caring that the splinters dug deeply into her fingers.

When the judge said calmly, " Sentence to be carried out at dawn tomorrow," her vision suddenly cleared from the shock. She saw, in the sea of condemning faces, the horrified stares of Jamie and Bridget.

Tomorrow. The sentence passed through her like a shock, leaving her incapable of feeling anything, though her vision was acutely focused on Bridget and Jamie. The boy's face was white and his lips mere half open, as if to reveal her identity then and there.

She shook her head and cried out, "No!"

Everyone else in the courtroom no doubt thought she was reacting to the harshness of her sentence. But he knew what she really meant and pressed his lips tightly together.

They rushed her back to her cell roughly, and she tried not to wish that Sean had been there to save her. No doubt he would be glad to discover she had spared him the expense and scandal of a divorce. A man was received so much more sympathetically in society if he was a widower.

Sean found someone who had seen them both at an inn not far from the dock. They had not seen Kate recently, but expected Bridget and her husband to return in the evening, as was their usual habit.

"Husband?"

The serving maid looked at him sympathetically. "Young runaways, are they?"

He thought that the best cover for him. "I had hoped to get to them before—"

She shook her head. "They don't act like lovers, I'll tell you that. But they share a room and what red-blooded man, young or not, wouldn't take advantage of that?" She made clear her own willingness to take advantage of a room with him, but he paid her for her information and declined to take a room. "I won't be staying that long," he declared. Just long enough to collect Bridget and kill Jamie Jeffreys.

He sat in a dark corner of the inn's tavern, waiting and watching. When they entered, he stood too soon. Bridget saw him, and her eyes widened in alarm. Without a word to Jamie, she disappeared back out the door.

Jeffreys, without a glance at Sean, followed her. By the time Sean made his way through the crowded room, they were nowhere to be seen.

Damn. He'd have to search all over again. But they were fools if they thought they would elude him.

Kate didn't want to die.

She paced the cell they had placed her in after the trial—careful not to come too near any of the other inhabitants, who in the gloom were somewhat difficult to see. Despair and dirt had grayed their features and clothing until they faded into the walls and dirty straw.

She might have been afraid of them in other circumstances. But her mind could not focus on anything but the dilemma. She might get a new trial, if she divulged her identity. Or she might not. Most likely, either way, she would implicate Sean and ruin him.

One of the women in her new cell moved away from the wall where she had been a mere shadow and smiled at her—a horrifying vision of diseased gums and rotting teeth. "What a pretty neck to be stretched."

She grimaced. "I still have hope that my friends shall intervene before then."

"Before tomorrow?" The woman cackled. "Are

the fairies your friends then? Because you'd need fairy magic to escape here."

Kate felt an unpleasant jolting reminder of Bridget. Would the girl have become like this woman if she'd been charged with trying to murder Jamie? Or would she, like Kate, have had her sentence so efficiently scheduled?

"I know they will do their best," she whispered, more to herself than to her curious cellmate.

"It's a shame you're not breeding. They wouldn't hang you until the babe was born. That would give your friends a few months." The woman cackled. "Not that it's likely to do you any good."

Could she be? "I suppose that is a possibility." The thought wasn't particularly pleasant.

"You've been with a man?"

Kate blushed, unexpectedly embarrassed by the salacious glint in the woman's eyes. "My husband. We were hoping to have a child soon."

There was a gleeful liveliness to the woman's crooked gait as she shuffled to the small window in the door. "Guards! This one's to be a mother. You'll have to wait to stretch her neck."

Kate was surprised at the quick response. A guard came in and pushed the old woman away. "Get back, Annie, and stop your cackling. You don't know anything."

"She's been with a man—her husband at that. And she's not had her courses since."

The guard looked at Kate. "That the truth?"

She nodded. If telling such painfully personal information would give her more time to decide what to do, she would do so gladly.

He sighed, and the old woman cackled yet again. "Too bad, too bad. One less neck to stretch tomorrow."

"If you're lying, it will go ill with you." The guard gestured her out of the cell.

Go ill with her? Was there a worse situation than being hanged until dead tomorrow? She shuddered. And then she realized that there was. What if she was to have a child, and then have it ripped from her arms so that she could be hanged? No, she calmed herself. There would be ample time for the duke to intervene in such a case.

She was interviewed several times before they brought her to yet another cell with a warning that she would be examined for signs of her condition frequently, and if it was determined that she did not carry a child, her sentence would be carried out forthwith.

Jamie came to see her that evening. "Bridget has a plan to save you tomorrow."

"I am not to be hanged tomorrow, it seems."

He seemed surprised. "What has happened? Have you told them—"

Aware of the guard close to the door, she interrupted him. "There is a possibility that I am to be a mother. They'll not hang me until I have the child." Or until there was proof she was not pregnant. But she would not think of that.

He flushed darkly. "I see." And then he frowned as he looked around him. "Is that not even more reason to tell them—"

"No. The duke will receive your message and send help soon."

"You hope for miracles, still." He rose, looking grim. "As does Bridget. I will not tell you her plan, then, as it will not work until you are on the scaffold . . . if it works then." He shook his head. "I've promised her I would not give up on you, but think of your child if you are not willing to consider yourself. Tell them who you are and you could be out of here within the day."

"I will not." No child would benefit from having his mother hanged, she knew that well enough. But having his father's title attainted and his father hanged too would, she realized, be infinitely worse.

"Very well then. We must hope for word from the duke very soon." His parting glance held more desperation than reassurance.

Three days later, she found out for certain that she would not have a child.

Chapter 20

" 'Course I know who she is. She's the arsonist who's due to be hanged today." The man seemed pleased and held out his hand for the coin Sean had promised him.

Sean stared at him in disbelief. The words cut through him like a knife. He had seen her only days before—was it possible?

The man wiggled his fingers. "I told you what you wanted to know, my lord."

Bridget was wild, but was she that wild? He knew, instinctively, that she was, but still he asked, "Are you certain it was she? Look again." He held out the miniature to the innkeeper.

"Won't forget that one. Mary Duffy. She seemed like a lady, but she wasn't any better than the lowest ruffian. She even lied to say she was with child, just to postpone her jig with the reaper a day or two."

Sean, confused by the false name, glanced down at the miniature of his sister and felt the shock run through him. He had shown the man the portrait of Kate in his haste. "Mary Duffy? Are you certain that is the name she gave?"

"Saw her took up myself. Heard her say it. Even went to the trial to give witness, but they didn't need me."

Kate. Why had she given a false name? "Where is the hanging to occur?"

The man wiggled his fingers again, and Sean dropped the coin into his waiting hand. After a moment of waiting, he dropped another. The man grinned as he gave him explicit directions. "But you'd best hurry if you want to see her fall, since it's nearly time."

Kate? She was supposed to be safely on her way back to London. He raced through the narrow, crowded streets, cursing himself. He should have escorted her to the coast himself. Should have guarded the ship until it sailed. Should have— He stopped, recriminations would not help him rescue her.

How had she come to be facing a hangman's noose? The man had called her an arsonist. He clearly recalled her horror when he set fire to the shed. What had she done? More importantly, how could he stop the proceedings?

"Pretty hair."

Kate was horrified to hear herself extend an automatic "Thank you" to the man who stood at her side with a large pair of shears. He was preparing her for the hanging, shearing her hair short. She closed her eyes at the tug and pull at her scalp. She had put her faith in Bridget's plan, since things had turned so quickly, before the duke could possibly respond.

Jamie had pleaded with her one last time to reveal her identity. Though he had conveyed Bridget's scheme, he obviously had no belief that it was wise. "This plan is madness. It may not even work."

He had not even been willing to share the plan until he was satisfied that Kate would not reveal her true identity. His doubts had come through with every detail he revealed to her in a low voice, so that the guard would not overhear. "Bridget has arranged for the rope used to hang you to be altered."

"Will it break?" Kate imagined falling to the ground, suddenly free of the feel of the rope around her neck, and swallowed reflexively. But then what?

"No." He shook his head, a scowl etched into his still delicate features. "That would not serve any purpose; they would merely collect you from the ground and hang you again with a new rope."

"Then what will happen?" She couldn't imagine that the sudden green pallor of his complexion was an indication that she would find the answer heartening.

He paused a moment and then said swiftly, "If it works, it will choke you, but not kill you."

If it works. "And if it doesn't?"

"Then you will die." He looked away for a moment, as if he couldn't bear to see her absorb the truth. "Bridget says it has been done before, if that is of any comfort to you."

Since it seemed to be of no comfort to him, Kate could not stop herself from asking, "Always successfully?"

He paused before answering yet again, the greenish cast to his complexion more pronounced. "No. But when one has no other choice . . ." He glanced at her doubtfully. "Bridget says it will work. She says she had a vision."

"She said she had a vision I would have a son, as well." That had certainly not been true.

He blushed. "She was puzzled about that. Her visions still show you with a child in your arms."

"And she saw the *Daisy's Pride* lost at sea." That was the whole reason for this mess in the first place.

He looked away. "Word is that the ship is missing."

Missing. And now Bridget had seen her surviving this scheme without betraying Sean. For some reason, Kate believed her. This would work. "If she says it will work, then it will. I will be as fortunate as the others whose necks were saved."

"Other criminals," he said sharply. "I don't know if it is wise—"

Kate thought of her own helpless condition and wondered at those who had gone before her in similar circumstances. "I suppose if your people are being hanged for no good reason, one must find a way to circumvent false justice. I know I am willing to try."

He met her eyes and grasped her hands as he leaned forward for one last plea. "Are you certain you will not change your mind? I can tell them myself. My father sailed on the *Daisy's Pride.*" He faltered for a moment, letting his grief that his father might be lost at sea hang between them, and then continued bravely, "But his reputation is well known here. I shall be believed."

Kate was tempted, for just a moment. "I cannot." She would trust to Bridget. Would trust to the ingenuity of a desperate populace that had faced oppression for centuries and found ways to circumvent some of the worst of the uneven justice.

"Very well. Then we shall have to give Bridget's plan a try."

"It will work." She spoke to console him more than herself. She believed her words, but they offered no comfort. What did she have to live for? She had no child, no hope of a child, and her husband did not want her.

"I will tell Bridget that you agree to this method of escape."

She laughed at the idea. "What does my agreement matter? I will be dangling unconscious from the rope until I strangle to death, or I am rescued. I have no part to play in this."

He looked toward the door where the guard stood. "Still, there is a risk for those who will attempt to help you. They need to know you will not betray them."

Kate glanced around her cell and said with absolute certainty. "I will not say or do anything that would put anyone else in this place."

She watched him leave with a sense of unreality. Would she ever see him again? Would Bridget's mad plan work for her, as it had for others? And if it did, what would she do once she had her life back in her own hands?

She closed her eyes, refusing to cry, not even when they came to lead her away to her own hanging.

She saw Jamie again when she stood on the scaffold in the sunshine. At first, the jeering crowd below her was a sea of unfriendly faces, but then she saw him, white-faced, clutching tightly to Bridget, who seemed serenely confident that things would go well.

Kate tried not to flinch when the rope was fitted around her head to lie heavy and limp around her neck. She could see no difference between this rope and any other she had ever seen. Had they chosen the right rope?

She said a quick prayer of hope that all would go well. At least, she told herself, if she did hang, it would be as Mary Duffy. No one would connect her to Sean. And he would never know. She had made Jamie promise not to tell him. He assured her Bridget had made a similar promise.

A disturbance in the crowd distracted her from the last movements of the hangman, and she welcomed it. Until she saw the man who was bearing through the crowd like a maddened bull. It was Sean.

"Don't—" she tried to tell him as she fell, all words choked from her as she slowly began to strangle in front of his eyes. *Don't tell anyone who I am!* she screamed soundlessly until darkness closed around her.

Sean beat his way through the crowd, his eyes fixed on Kate's slender figure. Surely he could reach her in time.

She saw him, he thought. There was a spark of awareness in her eyes, and he swore she had been about to speak to him—just as she fell.

With a roar, he tried to reach her dangling body, but the crowd held him back as they cheered and danced and tossed him aside.

As the next prisoner was led up to the scaffold, and Kate's body was unceremoniously cut down and carted away, he turned in the crowd to follow the cart to the place where it dumped its precious burden on the ground as if she were a sack of potatoes. Perhaps not even with that much care.

He was too late. He could see that from a distance, but he refused to accept what his eyes told him. She lay cold and blue on the ground. "Kate. Katie. Oh, my Kate. What have I done to you?"

"Sean, do you want to get her killed with your foolishness?" Bridget appeared beside him, cloaked, her face hidden from his sight. "Let me do this."

He stood back, astounded, as she moved forward, wailing. A guard came to question her suspiciously, but she claimed to be Mary Duffy's sister, and within moments she had laid claim to the body.

"You there!" Bridget turned, her cloak falling back to reveal the glow in her green eyes. "Come help me carry my sister's body away from here."

Sean came, numbly, lifting Kate's slight weight in his arms. She rested limply against him, a dead weight. Dead. She was still warm, though. If he had been just a little earlier, he castigated himself . . . and then stopped. No. If he hadn't tried so hard to push her out of his life, she'd still be alive.

An urgent whisper sounded behind him. "Take her away now, my lord, unless you truly wish to see her hanged."

He turned to see Jamie Jeffreys. Sean looked into the blue eyes of his enemy's son and saw no arrogant malice or trickery, only grave concern and jittery tension. "Did you do this?"

"Tell Bridget I have paid my debt and owe her nothing—not even children." With that, the boy turned and strode away, as stiff-backed as any proud Sassenach.

Sean wondered if the two had married. But he didn't have the desire to know. Not now. He followed Bridget away from the scene, ignoring the cheers of the crowd as another man swung.

Bridget stopped at a neat blue door and knocked three times, then once. The door opened just wide enough for Sean to pass with Kate in his arms and then shut quickly. The sound of a bolt being shot home was loud in the darkness. And then a candle was lit.

"Quickly, there is no time," the strange woman said. "Put her down here." She used the candle to indicate a pallet on the floor.

"I will not," Sean protested. He would not let her go. Not yet. The rituals would have to be performed, he knew that. But not yet. Not here.

"Sean—you will ruin everything," Bridget said. "Give Kate to this woman if you want her to live."

Live? A sudden suspicion gave him hope, and he did as the woman bid. But once Kate lay on the pallet, he pushed aside the stranger and tried to rouse Kate himself. He rubbed at her cheeks, startled when her bluish color gave way to a pinker hue.

For long moments, nothing happened, and he began to believe that the pink color was an illusion of hope. But then she began to cough and struggle for breath. In a moment her eyes opened, blue and clear.

Chapter 21

Kate felt the panic subside as she realized she could breathe again. Realized that the shadowy figure kneeing above her was her husband. Sean had come. But how? She sat up, pushing his hands away while she rubbed at her aching neck. "What are you doing here?"

He blinked, as if he could not quite believe she would dare chastise him mere seconds after her near death. "Rescuing you."

"I didn't call him." Bridget stepped forward into the circle of candlelight. "I promise you. Maybe Jamie—"

"Neither of you had the good sense to call me," Sean said angrily. "I found out from an innkeeper who witnessed your arrest. Why did you not send for me?"

"Why should I have called upon you?" She wouldn't let him treat her as if she were the one at fault. He was the one who had discarded her.

"So that I could rescue you, of course." The vibration she felt from his tense body warned her that he was on the edge of losing his temper, but she could not bring herself to care. Nearly dying was an exhausting business.

"I thought you might be grateful to be a widower, rather than have to go through the inconvenience of a divorce." She didn't bother to strain the bitterness from her tone.

He answered her bitterness with his own. "I assure you, I had no desire to be a widower—and I was never surer of it than when I saw you dangling there at the end of the rope."

"I'm sorry, Sean. I know I've been nothing but trouble to you." She wanted him to gather her up in his arms, to profess his mistake in sending her away, but he showed no signs of doing so. She tried to stand, but her limbs were too shaky to support her.

He reached out to steady her with a warm, strong arm. "Trouble. You have been that."

Bridget said sharply, "She was willing to keep your secrets, Sean. And to protect me."

Before Kate could protest, Bridget had poured out the whole story to her brother.

Sean turned to her. "You lied about who you were so that I wouldn't be at risk?" He didn't seem at all touched or pleased by her sacrifice.

"I promised I wouldn't betray you. I keep my promises."

She thought there would have been less pain in his eyes if she'd run him through with her sword six times over. "And I don't, do I?"

She wouldn't give him any quarter. She thought she deserved a little thanks for what she had been willing to do for him. "Not to me you don't." She couldn't help the temper that flared inside. "You didn't even manage to father a child—which would have given the duke time to come and rescue me."

"So I heard from the innkeeper. Please forgive me for—" His sharp tone cut off mid-sentence and she found herself suddenly crushed against his chest.

"Forgive me." His voice was soft and hushed against her ear, and he cradled her gently, as though she were a child. "I've been a stubborn fool. I should have been the one swinging this morning for what I've done to you."

"I hardly think your crimes were worthy of hanging," Kate argued, thinking of the horrible sensation of choking misery she had endured. "Fifty years of marriage and ten children would have been just enough punishment."

"Is that the sentence you think I deserve for treating you as I have?"

She didn't want to answer that question. Especially not now, with him so close to her. "No one deserves to be hanged for any crime short of murder." She pushed him away with a sigh and swallowed hard, rubbing at her neck. "I suppose I'm lucky the rope didn't break."

"Not luck," Bridget interjected. "Someone made certain that there would be just enough give to keep you alive, but not enough that you would fail to lose consciousness and appear dead. Apparently, it's a time-worn trick, practiced since Cromwell's time and possibly even before."

Sean gathered her into his arms again. "Trick or not, I'm grateful. I didn't think I'd ever see you again. But I wanted to imagine you in London, not food for the worms."

She grimaced. "I'm afraid that humor does not sit well with me, seeing how close to truth your joke nearly was. All I want to do is go back home."

She felt his muscles tense briefly as he held her. "Will you be wanting to go back to London then?"

"As soon as I've seen to Bridget. I don't care if you're divorcing me, I want you to let Bridget come to live with me so that I can get her the help she needs."

"I don't need any help," Bridget protested in surprise at being dragged into their conversation.

He ignored his sister and nodded to Kate. "I knew she had done something, but I never guessed she'd be so reckless."

He loved her, she knew that. But he had not been able to heal her. She didn't know if she could, but she was determined to try. The girl had saved her life, after all. "It's time to do something about her, Sean."

His grip tightened on her arms. "I'll not put her in a madhouse."

She shook her head fiercely. "Of course not. I want to take her to London with me."

"London! Absolutely not. She'd go completely mad surrounded by men like the ones who hurt her."

"My sisters are hardly burly men." Kate wondered what he thought her life had been like for the last five years. Niall, the duke, and her brothers-in-law were the only men she associated with in any fashion at all.

"She is not suited for such a life."

"How can you know that? She had never had a chance for such a life." She put all her conviction into her words. He might not want her for his wife, but surely he wanted the best for his sister? "I want to bring her where she can have the society of ladies. Those who will allow her to be herself while she faces what must be faced."

"I cannot allow that." She could see him struggling with the idea of his sister far away from him.

Though she sympathized, she knew he could not give his sister the care she needed.

"So you will allow her to accompany you in your illegal activities then? She is quite good at setting fires, you know." She didn't bother to hide her contempt, although her voice rasped rather than cut.

"I will not allow—"

"She cannot go on this way. If you do not trust me to take her with me, come with us." Her heart stopped at the unexpected invitation. She had not meant to issue it. Had not wanted to see him back away from her as if she were diseased.

"I cannot leave here—"

She interrupted, not wanting to hear the litany of excuses. "Why not? Two weeks will not change things here. Even two months is not unreasonable. That way you can see for yourself if she takes to the change well or not." Painfully, she reminded him, "You will not have to rely on letters from me that might only be sweet lies meant to placate you and make you think things are not horrible."

He had the grace to flush. "My words were not lies—"

"They were not the truth, either. I deserved the truth and so do you. Come with us to London."

"I am needed here."

"True enough. Let me take Bridget and begin to work with her. You may come when you are able, more than once if you like. I have paid you enough that you can afford several passages back and forth without denting the sum."

His eyes darkened. "I—"

"It does not matter what either of you say. I will not go." There was no doubt in Bridget's voice.

"Do it for Jamie if you will not do it for yourself,"

Kate said quietly. She was not blind to Jamie's love for Bridget, but she did not know if the girl cared for him as much.

"What has he to do with it?" Sean spoke quickly, hotly.

"He helped her rescue me. And his conscience would at last be at ease if he knew she had a future once again, as she did five years ago."

Bridget seemed angry at the suggestion that Jamie would care for her. "He's off to distant lands to gain his own glory—why does he need to worry for me? I have a future here. I will not go. I cannot leave the fairies."

There was a long moment of silence. "You will go." Sean's voice was implacable. For a moment Kate could believe the idea had been his in the first place.

Kate sighed, not willing to sit by as a battle brewed between brother and sister. "I wish to introduce you to my family, Bridget. You are not going forever. Just for a trip. I thought you said you wished to travel."

"To France, to Rome. Not to England." There could have been no more contempt in her voice if she had been speaking of the most vile, snake-infested swamp ever seen by human eyes.

Kate said softly, "If you do well in London, we can cross to France for pleasure."

"What do you mean by 'do well'?"

"Listen to my rules, wear ladylike clothing—and a complete moratorium on setting fire to anything or anyone." There would be more, of course. Doctors and examinations to see if her madness was curable. But no madhouses. Not ever.

"Pity. I know the Tower of London is full of evil spirits who'd like release."

"It is also full of living people quite content to wait until a ripe old age for their release."

Sean felt as if he might be a prisoner of the Tower himself. But he could not deny that his imprisonment was of his own making. He was sending his sister away with Kate and, though it hurt, he knew it was the right thing to do.

She struggled to her feet. "We must go, before we are discovered, or all our plans will go for naught."

"One moment, Kate." He helped her to her feet but did not release her arm once she stood on her own. "I must make something clear to you before we leave this room."

Bridget opened the door, and light flooded in so that he could see his wife. See her brave expression as she faced him, expecting, no doubt, that he would reassure her that he was proceeding with the divorce.

"You are never to do something so foolish to protect my worthless hide again."

"I—"

He bent to kiss her, feeling the rightness of it in the brief contact, but breaking off so that he could finish his sentence. He did not want her to doubt that he meant what he said. "You'll not get a divorce out of me if you, like Maeve, take a thousand lovers."

"So you want to be my husband, do you? After all this time?" She was not as pleased as he had expected.

"I do." He stepped back, though, when she frowned. "That is, of course, if you'll have me after all I've put you through."

She smiled, as if a great burden had been taken from her shoulders. "I am relieved to hear you say so, my lord."

"Relieved?" He had expected more joy, somehow. Perhaps she did not believe him yet. He could hardly fault her for caution. He had been a stubborn soul.

"I haven't spent all this time trying to convince you I'm a worthy wife to send you off now that you've finally come to your senses. Will you come to London, or should I send for my things?"

"You would stay here with me?" He was humbled by the offer. He knew well enough he didn't deserve it. "I couldn't ask you to do such a thing."

"You certainly could—and I shouldn't have waited so long to ask." She shook her head. "I knew it long ago, but I let my stubborn pride—and yours—get in the way. Sean, I belong where you are. I adore every inch of your stubborn, proud Irish self and I want to help with your fight."

"I can't let you do that."

She moved past him, out the door. Bridget reached in a panic to fling Kate's hood up, covering his wife's expression, but not before he saw her exasperated lift of brow. "I'm not giving you a choice. It's your abbey, or I'll build my own hut to raise your daughter."

"Son," Bridget said, following on her heels and leaving Sean to scramble behind them to keep up. "You're to have a son."

"What about Bridget's treatment in London? What about your business? Your roses?"

"Surely we can find someone to help Bridget here—and I can tend roses here as well as anywhere, can I not?"

He supposed he could spend a little on the greenhouses. Paddy could use them, too. He followed the women, checking right and left to make certain that no one noticed that Mary Duffy, the arsonist, was alive and walking among them.

Fortunately, no one gave them a second look, because neither woman waited for him to catch up before plunging into the busy streets in their hurry to get home.

Home. He began to smile. He finally had what he had always wanted. Despite himself.

Chapter 22

One year later

Sean faced his audience, knowing that his words would not be welcomed by many and would need to be repeated many times before the stubborn practices of centuries were completely erased. But he could not control the ending if he did not begin. So he cleared his throat and began. "My esteemed and honored lords . . ."

There was a rustle at the lilt of Eire in his speech, but he had deliberately emphasized it. He was proud of his Irish heritage and he would not have a man doubt it by the end of this day. "You know that the problem of the Irish has been a plague upon this land for some time, most especially since the most recent years of famine and disease.

"I propose an act of atonement." Groans.

"Restitution for the years of harsh justice." She was amazed to see that his lips did not twist bitterly at the word justice.

"Many claim that the fault lies with the Irish

themselves—that an ill-educated people cannot make sound decisions. I can agree." Murmurs of surprise. "So my proposal is a simple one: that England return the education they stole from the Irish."

A few of the neutral expressions moved into frowns, and there was a low hiss for a moment, but he paused until it died, staring down the listeners, making it clear he would wait until they quieted so that he could speak his mind. "Offer the people of Ireland education, and both nations will reap the reward."

There was a murmur at his reference to two nations, but he spoke over it. "My own steward has recently enjoyed a month in Kent studying with a practitioner of the new scientific agricultural methods."

He felt them shift with him—not all, but many more than he had expected. "He returned to Ireland to make tremendous strides in productivity for my lands—and I hope he spreads his newfound knowledge far and wide among my neighbors, and that they, in turn spread the knowledge."

Confidence flooded through him. He was not foolish enough to believe it would be easy. Just that he would not give up as long as one man still listened. As long as there was hope for the future. "Paddy is, in fact, a shining example of what a sound education can do for a man—for all of us."

He looked to the gallery, where Kate sat. He could not see her face well, but he knew she knew the difficult battle he had taken on. Knew that it would take him a lifetime. She lifted her hands and he saw that she held a bouquet of roses. Sean's Pride, she had called the variety—the deepest red petals with a heart of gold.

* * *

"I cannot thank you enough for your thoughtful Christmas gift."

"As gifted as you are, wife, I thought you might like a bit more silver to your tongue."

"Is it our guests you wish to impress, or are your motives more selfish than that?" Kate laughed, teasing him with her tongue as she kissed him breathless.

"It is that boy of yours that I worry for. Even at his tender age, he dares to doubt his mother's wisdom."

"He gets that from his father, no doubt."

"Never." He wrapped his arms around her, blocking the nip of the wind. It was a mild day, but December in Ireland was never without the need for warmth.

He helped her up the stairs, a mischievous smile on his face. At last she was to kiss the Blarney Stone, with a McCarthy to hold her safe so that she would not slip and fall in the attempt.

"Are you certain you trust me?" he teased as he removed her bonnet.

"After your performance in London? How could I not?"

"There are many who still don't."

She answered confidently, "You did well, my lord."

He kissed her. "We shall see. Education is a tricky proposition—it requires those to be educated to both listen to and accept what they are learning."

She didn't think he'd appreciate her pointing out that she knew that fact all too well. "Your people are eager—just see how Paddy did. And Bridget has become an absolute bluestocking. She is a touted speaker on the subject of illustrated manuscripts." And, after some harrowing months, the bouts of madness had dissipated. The girl would always be fey. Fortunately, the London gentlemen seemed to find that a charming attribute.

"I was not referring to the education of the Irish, my love, but the education of that loutish rabble that inhabits the House of Lords."

"If any can manage it, it would, of course, be Lord Blarney."

"I think Lady Blarney will be a great asset to me—as soon as she has kissed the Stone."

He held her legs firmly, and she was supremely confident of her safety as she leaned out into the opening, hovering above the trees far below, and planted her lips on the rough stone.

He hauled her back, into his arms and kissed her.

She tried out her new silver tongue and was quite pleased with the results. It was several moments before she broke the kiss to inquire laughingly, "Trying to steal some of the magic for yourself?"

He bent his head toward her again. "I don't need to steal it. As your husband, all you possess is mine by right."